E.R. PUNSHON

CROSSWORD MYSTERY

Ernest Robertson Punshon was born in London in 1872.

At the age of fourteen he started life in an office. His employers soon informed him that he would never make a really satisfactory clerk, and he, agreeing, spent the next few years wandering about Canada and the United States, endeavouring without great success to earn a living in any occupation that offered. Returning home by way of working a passage on a cattle boat, he began to write. He contributed to many magazines and periodicals, wrote plays, and published nearly fifty novels, among which his detective stories proved the most popular and enduring.

He died in 1956.

Also by E.R. Punshon

Information Received
Death Among The Sunbathers
Mystery Villa
Death of A Beauty Queen
Death Comes To Cambers
The Bath Mysteries
Mystery of Mr. Jessop
The Dusky Hour
Dictator's Way

E.R. PUNSHON

CROSSWORD MYSTERY

With an introduction
by Curtis Evans

DEAN STREET PRESS

Published by Dean Street Press 2015

First published in 1934 by Victor Gollancz

Cover by DSP

ISBN 978 1 911095 33 0

www.deanstreetpress.co.uk

INTRODUCTION

In 1933 Britain's Detection Club, a social organization founded three years earlier by some of the most renowned detective novelists in the country, including Agatha Christie, Dorothy L. Sayers, Anthony Berkeley, G.K. Chesterton, Freeman Wills Crofts and R. Austin Freeman, inducted, for the first time, several new members. These initiates were Gladys Mitchell, Anthony Gilbert (Lucy Beatrice Malleson) and E.R. Punshon, all of whom pledged to honor in their detective fiction both the King's English and the principle of fair play in clue presentation. Punshon's induction into the Detection Club in 1933 surely would have come as no surprise to anyone who earlier that year had seen in the *Sunday Times* Dorothy L. Sayers' glowing commendation for him as a "writer first and foremost." *Crossword Mystery* (1934), Punshon's third Bobby Owen detective novel, not only abides by the Detection Club's aesthetic precepts, it also validates the accolade that the admiring Sayers had bestowed upon him.

More than any detective novel Punshon had yet published *Crossword Mystery* beautifully balances puzzle appeal and character interest, the detection of crime and the probing of criminal personality, leading to a remarkable conclusion that readers are unlikely to forget. In the novel, which pleasingly includes both a "sketch map of Suffby Cove and village" and a crossword puzzle with clues and a solution, Punshon for the first time tasks his series sleuth, Constable Bobby Owen, B.A. (Oxon. pass degree only), with investigating nefarious goings-on at a country house, that holy of holies in British mystery fiction. "A little beyond the bridge, a turning from the main road led to Suffby village on the left, and beyond that to the low Georgian house Bobby had seen from the high ground beyond the creek," writes Punshon, surely suffusing the typical devoted Golden Age mystery reader in a warm glow of pleasurable anticipation of murder in stately surroundings. Yet Punshon never forgets (and neither should his readers) that, even in cases of putatively cozy English country house crime, darkness may come.

At the behest of Major Markham, "formerly of the Indian cavalry, and now Chief Constable of Deneshire," Bobby's mentor, Superintendent Mitchell, has deputed the young man to serve as a sort of bodyguard for wealthy George Winterton at his domicile Fairview, a Georgian house overlooking Suffby Cove. "He's a retired business man; former stockbroker, I believe; quite well off, interested in crosswords and economics," chattily explains Major Markham as he offers Bobby a "cheroot of almost unimaginable strength." Winterton insists that the recent drowning death of his twin brother, Archibald (like Winterton a stockbroker who had retired to Deneshire, residing at a house across the Cove at Suffby Point), was not an accident, but murder; and he declares that he too is in grave peril. Having a friend who is an MP, representing a London constituency, Winterton is able to obtain from Scotland Yard the promise of police protection, in the genial form of Constable Owen. Yet who, Bobby soon is asking himself, "would want to murder two quiet, inoffensive, retired business men, ending their days peacefully by the seaside?"

At Fairview Bobby encounters a classic rich man's mystery ménage. There are the Coopers, the couple who serve as Fairview's butler and housekeeper; Miss Raby, George

Winterton's winsome lady secretary; Colin Ross, an impecunious nephew addicted to racing forms; and a pet Airedale that, in a nod to Arthur Conan Doyle's classic Sherlock Holmes tale "Silver Blaze," failed to bark when expected. Although not residents of Fairview, a couple of other nephews are in the picture too, namely Miles Winterton, an out-of-work engineer, and James Matthews, an artist living in Paris who is, naturally enough, "the black sheep of the family." Also of note is the aggressive land developer Mr. Shorter, whom Bobby, upon his arrival at Fairview, finds George Winterton angrily ejecting from his house.

Was Archibald Winterton murdered? Is the close-lipped George Winterton truly in danger and, if so, from just what source does the menace arise? Can Bobby, for the first time in his recorded cases relying to a considerable extent upon his own resources, prevent a second murder (assuming there was a first one)? Readers will surely want to find out for themselves.

Crossword Mystery is a novel with an intricate, fairly-clued puzzle, incisive social observation (among English mystery novelists Punshon was as far as I know the earliest and most persistent decrier of the Nazi scourge in Europe) and an astonishing climax that surely is unique within the literature of crime fiction. So impressed with *Crossword Mystery* was the distinguished writer and Oxford University Press editor Charles Williams—like Dorothy L. Sayers an astute Thirties mystery fiction critic—that he declared he discerned in the novel hope for the revivification of detective fiction as an art form:

> It has for some time been clear that detective tales must either change or cease. A few good craftsmen may go on

> exquisitely reproducing the most austere and ancient plots, but murders must become greater or perish. There are signs that they are becoming greater, and that they will enter on a new career of real imagination.
>
> A few of these signs have been noticed here recently. Separately they might be accidents; together they suggest promise. There was Father Knox's *Still Dead*, with its casuistry; there was, superbly alone, Miss Sayers's *Nine Tailors*. And Mr. Punshon's *Crossword Mystery* is now added to them.

Williams particularly praised *Crossword Mystery* for "the vigour of the last chapter" and "the steady sweep of energy that moves it…" Later that year, his sentiment was echoed in the United States, where *Crossword Mystery* had been picked up by the prominent publisher Alfred A. Knopf, who issued it under a rather more direct title, *The Crossword Murder*. (The most celebrated Knopf mystery from 1934 was Dashiell Hammett's hard-boiled crime novel *The Thin Man*, one of the most conspicuous Thirties publishing successes.) In *The Saturday Review* William C. Weber deemed the plot of *Crossword Mystery* "engrossing" and its denouement a "knockout," while in the *New York Times Book Review* Isaac Anderson applauded the novel for "bafflement of a high order and a truly startling finish." I concur with the high praise afforded *Crossword Mystery* on both sides of the Atlantic. Today, over eighty years after it was originally published, it is indeed a pleasure to see the novel back in print, for such glittering examples of Golden Age detective fiction will never truly tarnish.

Curtis Evans

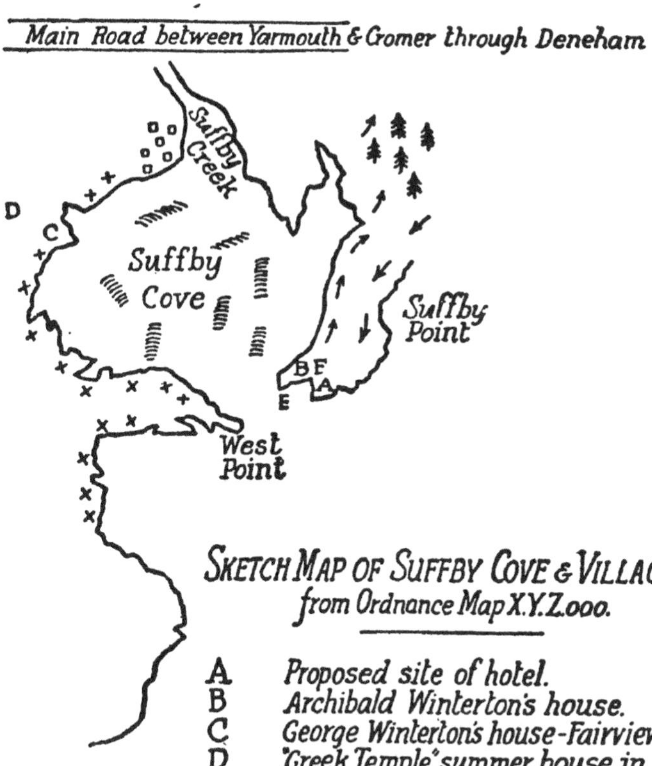

SKETCH MAP OF SUFFBY COVE & VILLAGE
from Ordnance Map X.Y.Z.000.

A Proposed site of hotel.
B Archibald Winterton's house.
C George Winterton's house-Fairview.
D "Greek Temple" summer house in Fairview Garden.
E Small sandy bathing beach whence Archibald Winterton started for his swim.
F Site of ruined lighthouse.
Sand banks in Suffby Cove visible at low tide.
Suffby village.
Site of proposed golf links.
Pines.
xxxxx Footpath along coast to Ighton Village

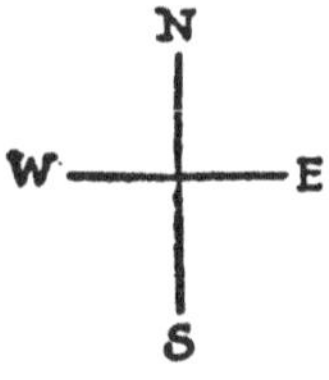

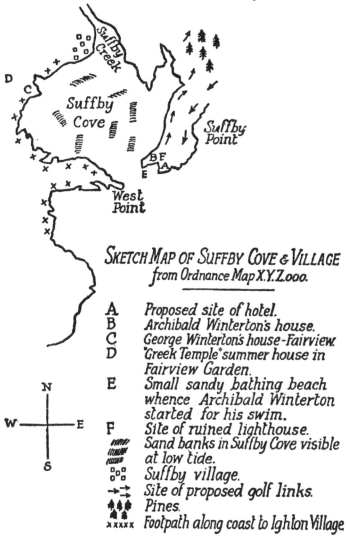

CHAPTER 1

Ye Olde Sunke Tudor Tea Garden

IT was one of the loveliest days of a lovely summer, and Detective-Constable Bobby Owen, B.A. (Oxon. pass degree only), as he jogged placidly along on a brand-new motor-cycle (Government property) at a quiet forty or fifty m.p.h., with an occasional burst up to seventy or eighty when he was quite sure there were no traffic police about, was almost able to persuade himself that after all there are on this earth, though rare, worse jobs than police jobs.

He was even not indifferent to the fact that he was wearing a new and expensive suit, cut by a first-class tailor and paid for by a generous country, whose head presumably had been a little turned by a recent announcement of a possible Budget surplus. Even the contents of the suit-case strapped on behind – dinner-jacket and so on, all very smart and new – had been provided for him in the same way; and, though he had no doubt his chief, Superintendent Mitchell, would jolly well make him work for them, at any rate he had no tailor's bill to fear – the happy, happy youth.

There appeared before him by the roadside Ye Olde Englyshe Petrol Pumpe Station for which he had been instructed to look out. He passed, and took the next turning north, a by-road that led to Deneham, the smart little east coast resort that had recently been winning favour by its stern refusal of hospitality to trippers – for whom, besides, its rather remote situation made it lack attractiveness, so there was no risk of hard feeling on either side. A mile or so along this road Bobby came to a small tea garden, a lonely, forlorn-looking little place, though bravely announcing itself as Ye Olde Sunke Tudor Tea Garden, presumably in a fine frenzy of rivalry with Ye Olde Englyshe Petrol Pumpe Station on the main road. Here Bobby alighted, parked his nice new motor-cycle in a convenient shed provided for the purpose, noted with a slight involuntary shudder that shrimps were fourpence a plate, sixpence shelled, and understood at once what strange subtle odour it was had mingled with the scent of the roses and the honeysuckle growing around. In the garden – why it was called 'sunke' did not appear – were half a dozen tables with attendant chairs, all in rickety wicker. He seated himself at one, and ordered tea and toast and eggs to satisfy an appetite his long ride from London had provided with a fine edge. But the toast was a mistake, toast in 'ye olde Tudor' days having evidently been chiefly used for roof repairs.

However, the eggs were new laid in the literal, not the commercial, sense – that is, they had come into being that same morning; and, if the tea were stewed, Bobby's young life, that had progressed from a well-known public school to an Oxford college and thence to London lodgings, had given him no knowledge or experience of tea that was not well and truly stewed.

So he drank it contentedly, enjoyed his new-laid eggs, and, if the toast baffled him who did not easily acknowledge defeat, he made a good exchange of it for plain bread and butter. This simple repast completed, he was about to light a cigarette when he heard a car approaching. Reflecting that Superintendent Mitchell smoked excellent cigars, and, since it was a fine day, since there was no specially trying case on at the moment, and since, above all, the Assistant Commissioner was away on a holiday, might well prove in a liberal and generous mood, Bobby hurriedly put his own gaspers away and hoped for the best. Then he rose respectfully to his feet as there entered the garden that redoubtable personage, his chief, Superintendent Mitchell, the biggest of the 'big four,' as the papers called them, who were at the moment in charge of the destinies of the Scotland Yard C.I.D.

Following him was a tall, thin man with a narrow, lined face, hair that seemed prematurely grey – for he did not look much more than half way between forty and fifty – and a complexion tanned a dull brick-brown by presumably a sun hotter than that this climate usually provides. Bobby guessed he would be Major Markham, formerly of the Indian cavalry, and now Chief Constable of Deneshire, in accordance with the happy rule that a thorough grounding in drill, especially cavalry drill, is the best possible preparation for police work. They came across to where Bobby was waiting, and Mitchell nodded pleasantly.

'Constable Owen,' he explained to his companion. 'He was with me in the sun-bathing case, and he was with me, too – or I was with him, I never quite knew which – in the Christopher Clarke case – "Hamlet in Modern Dress," as some of the newspaper wits called it.'

'Some smart work in those cases,' remarked Major Markham, with an approving glance at Bobby.

'Oh, I wouldn't say Owen was quite the thickest-headed of my men,' confessed Mitchell. 'Of course, we've got to wait and see what a few more years' red tape and officialdom will do to him. Ruin him, probably. Why, I used to be thought quite smart myself, and now you ought to hear what the junior ranks say about me when I'm not there. "Premature senile decay," when they're in their more kindly moods. Well, what about toast and an egg, Major? The young and greedy,' he added, with a glance at the remnants of Bobby's meal, 'probably have two and expect the British taxpayer to stand for their gluttony.'

Bobby hesitated for a moment between the dictates of a naturally kind heart and that profound instinct which leads us all to wish that others should fall into the trap wherein we ourselves have been taken. But his good heart won and he told them about that toast, compared with which cold steel and toughened iron were but as melting butter.

So they thanked him, and Bobby unostentatiously allowed his bill to drift away towards the Superintendent's plate, just in case Mitchell felt inclined to pay it and include it in that expense sheet which, when submitted by superintendents, suffers so little from the red ink that fairly floods those of lesser men.

Neither Superintendent nor Chief Constable seemed hungry, however, and, their brief meal dispatched, Major Markham produced his cigar-case and offered it to Mitchell, who, however, begged to be allowed this time to be excused, as his doctor had recently confined him to an allowance already exceeded. But he hinted benevolently that his young assistant, Owen, always enjoyed a good cigar. A little surprised at such thoughtfulness on the part of his senior officer, Bobby accepted one from the case the Major thereupon offered, and Mitchell smiled more benevolently still and offered a light.

'Import 'em myself,' said the Major proudly, and only then did Bobby realise that what he had accepted was a cheroot of almost unimaginable strength, a strength before which Jack Dempsey or Carnera would have seemed mere babes and weaklings. 'Nothing like 'em in the country,' added the Major, even more proudly.

'I tried to get some of the same sort,' confessed Mitchell. 'I was told they were hard to get, being chiefly stored for use to wake any of the dead who mayn't notice the last trump.'

Major Markham perpended.

'I don't see why,' he announced finally.

'I think Owen does,' observed Mitchell. 'Will you give him his instructions while he's enjoying his smoke? Do you know, I think I'll defy the doctor and have a cigarette. One little cigarette can't hurt me, and I can't stand seeing you two enjoying a smoke the way you are and me not.'

'I'll remember this cigar,' Bobby confessed, 'till my dying day.'

'I'll give you another before you go,' promised the Major, much gratified.

'About his instructions,' suggested Mitchell again.

'Well, it's this way,' began the Major, and hesitated. 'You see,' he said and stopped. 'The fact is——' he commenced again, and subsided once more into silence.

'Yes, sir,' said Bobby, laying down his cheroot with an air of intense interest.

'Now, now, Owen,' Mitchell warned him, 'don't get carried away and forget your cigar. A good cigar is spoilt by re-lighting.'

'Yes, sir,' said Bobby, with a malignant look at his superior that the superior returned with a sweet and gentle smile.

'What we actually want your to do,' Major Markham continued slowly, 'as Mr Mitchell has been good enough to lend you to us, is to go and stay for a month or six weeks or so with a Mr George Winterton. He's a retired business man; former stockbroker, I believe; quite well off, interested in crosswords and economics – he's writing a book on economics, he says, and crossword puzzles are his great hobby. He has a house overlooking Suffby Cove. Fairview, it's called.'

'As much bathing, fishing, boating as you like,' said Mitchell enthusiastically. 'Jobs like that never came my way when I was a youngster.'

'No, sir,' said Bobby, waiting patiently to know where the snag was.

'Mr Winterton's a bachelor,' the Major went on. 'There's a butler and housekeeper – man and wife they are – and there's a gardener whose wife helps in the house. A girl comes in every day from the village, and there's a secretary, a Miss Raby, who lives in the house and helps with the book. There are three nephews – Colin Ross, Miles Winterton, and James Matthews. Miles Winterton is an engineer, a P.W. man, but out of a job at present. He is staying with his uncle till something turns up, I suppose. Colin Ross is a racing man, and seems to use his uncle's house as headquarters, staying there when he's not attending race-meetings. I gather he pays for his keep by putting his uncle on a good thing occasionally. James Matthews seems the black sheep of the family, as he's an artist and lives in Paris.'

Major Markham evidently felt that, having said this, he had said all. But Bobby felt there must be more to come, for so far there seemed no reason why the assistance of Scotland Yard should have been invoked.

'Yes, sir,' he said.

'Well, you see,' continued the Major, 'it sounds rather absurd, but he's applied for police protection ...'

'And as he has a pal who's an M.P., sits for a London constituency,' observed Mitchell darkly – for, though he was a kindly man, and could run in a burglar or a pick-pocket as though he loved him, yet he did draw the line at M.P.'s, concerning whom his cherished theory was that as soon as elected they should be sent to serve their term, not at Westminster, but at Dartmoor. 'Then they couldn't do any harm or ask any questions either,' he used to say. He added now, still more darkly: 'You know what M.P.s are, getting up in the House and wanting to know, and then there's an urgent memo from the Home Office.'

'I don't think,' observed Major Markham, a little coldly – for he had visions of being an M.P. himself some day – 'that that affects the case. Every citizen has a right to ask for protection. As it happened, however, there wasn't one of my own men I could send very well. There would have been a risk of his being recognised; and then there is another reason as well. So I asked Mr Mitchell to arrange to lend me one of his best men——'

'I had to explain,' interposed Mitchell quickly, 'I hadn't one available; so he said, well, practically anyone would do, and so then I thought of you, Owen.'

'Thank you, sir,' said Bobby meekly.

'You're to be,' explained Major Markham, 'the son of an old business friend of Mr Winterton's. He hasn't met you before, but for your father's sake he is anxious to make your acquaintance.'

'I see, sir,' said Owen, 'but I don't quite understand what he wants protection against.'

'Against murder,' Major Markham answered; and the word had a strange, grim sound in the peace of that quiet garden, where the roses and the honeysuckle grew in such profusion, where it seemed the still and scented air should be troubled by nothing worse than the buzz of a passing wasp or the hum of a hungry gnat. 'Against murder,' Major

Markham repeated; 'it seems he thinks that last month, when he lost his brother, that was murder.'

CHAPTER II

Bobby Receives His Instructions

EVEN MITCHELL, a man not easily reduced to silence, whose career had made him familiar with many tragedies, seemed to feel the chill that word imposed upon the warm summer afternoon. He made no comment, but shivered slightly and sat quiet and still; nor was it now of set purpose that Bobby allowed that deadly cheroot of his to lie forgotten on the table. Not till this silence had lasted two or three minutes did Major Markham continue his story.

'The verdict was "accidentally drowned",' he went on then. 'On the evidence given, no other was possible. When Mr Winterton and his brother, Archibald Winterton – they were twins, by the way – retired from business, they settled at Suffby, George buying the house, Fairview, on the west shore of Suffby Cove and Archibald building one for himself across the Cove, at the southern extremity of Suffby Point. They lived in good style; had done well as stockbrokers, I understand. Suffby was chiefly Archibald's choice; he was fond of the sea, loved swimming, fishing, sailing. Every morning very early, he used to go down to a little beach near his home for a swim before breakfast. Bathing is perfectly safe in the Cove and quite safe off the Point, provided you don't go too far out, when, at the turn of the tide, there's a strong current runs down the coast. Archibald knew all that quite well, of course, and had the reputation of being a prudent as well as a strong swimmer. Two months ago he went for his usual swim, and never came back. Three weeks later his body was found by fishermen twenty miles down the coast.'

The Major paused, and Bobby asked:

'There were no marks of violence on the body?'

'Well, after three weeks in the water ...' Major Markham answered. 'Still, the doctors were all agreed that death had been caused by drowning, and that the injuries to the body had almost certainly been caused after death. Probably he had swum out too far; got caught in the current or had an attack of cramp. Impossible to say what really happened, but the jury returned the only verdict possible. There's one difficulty. The tide didn't turn that morning, and therefore the current wouldn't begin to run strongly, till more than an hour after he must have entered the water; in fact, not till some time after the alarm had been given and he had been missed. He had probably gone down for his swim earlier than usual on account of the state of the tide. He used to do that, apparently; he would go either earlier or later than his usual time, according to how the current would be running; he used to note the tides carefully every day.'

'Sometimes it is the most careful man who makes the worst slip,' observed Mitchell, 'like the story of the man who was always careful to wash his cherries before eating them, but one day forgot and drank the water he had rinsed them in, and so caught cholera and died. Besides, anything might account for it – cramp or heart failure or anything like that.'

'Both the brothers were exceptionally big, strong men, extremely healthy,' the Major observed. 'Still, the jury took the view that something like that must have happened. I certainly agreed with them. Also, there seems no reason why anyone should have wished to murder him.'

'Does Mr George Winterton give any reason for suspecting foul play?' Bobby asked.

'Nothing you can lay hold of,' answered the Major, a little hesitatingly. 'I admit he impressed me. I was inclined not to take him very seriously at first. But he meant it. He believes it all right enough. Then he looked at me and said "I'll be the next, very likely." Well, he meant that, too. But he wouldn't give any explanation. He seemed to me well, resigned, if you know what I mean. I asked him if he suspected anyone, and he said he didn't. He kept on talking about what a strong, experienced swimmer his brother was, and how careful. When there was any real risk, he never went far outside the Cove. I put it to him there was no way any foul play could have been carried out. There were no signs of struggle. An Airedale dog Archibald always took with him was found lying quite placidly on the sand waiting for its master to return. It's a dog that's very quiet and friendly with anyone it knows, but it barks its head off at the sight of any stranger. If it had barked at all, it would certainly have been heard at the house and certainly have started Mrs Winterton's poms barking too – she has two or three of them. His clothing hadn't been touched, either; and his gold watch – rather a valuable one – and a diamond ring he wore, but always took off before he went into the water, were quite safe. A thermos flask with hot coffee he used to take down with him for a warm drink after he came out of the water was there just as usual.'

'There was no footprint unaccounted for, I suppose?' Bobby asked.

'I can't be sure about that. The place had been well trampled over by people from the house and from the village, anxious to help after the alarm was given, before any of my men got there. But I think the evidence of the dog is conclusive that no stranger had been near. Finally, after a good deal of talk, it came out that he had had a dream – George I mean, of course.'

'A dream?' repeated Bobby.

'So he said,' answered the Major, almost apologetically. 'One can understand his brother's tragic death was a terrible shock to them all. The widow has gone to stay with some relatives. I don't much suppose she and the children will ever come back here. Probably the property will be sold; I've heard a London syndicate are after it to put up a big hotel and develop the place for golf and so on. Not that you would have expected a man like George Winterton – a fine, big, healthy fellow, as strong and active as anyone half his age; hard-headed business man, too – to start worrying about dreams.' The Major paused and smiled a little. 'Mrs Cooper did tell me she had given him crab salad for supper that evening,' he added, his smile broadening.

'Who is Mrs Cooper, sir?' Bobby asked.

'Oh, she's the wife of the butler, a very capable woman – runs the house like clockwork, and her husband too, and I think Winterton himself into the bargain. But he says it's worth putting up with a little bossing at times to have the house organised like an up-to-date factory. And then she's not like some housekeepers; she doesn't sulk if the routine's upset. Winterton told me once he thought she rather liked it if he brought back half a dozen unexpected guests from the golf-club to dinner. It gave her a chance to show her powers of resource – the artist exercising his functions, you know.'

'Must be a wonder,' observed Mitchell, with some slight show of emotion. 'Mrs Mitchell might allow me to bring home one man without warning, or even two at a pinch – but half a dozen. There's reason in all things,' he said.

'I understand, sir,' Bobby went on to Major Markham, 'that Mr Winterton doesn't give any grounds for his suspicions of foul play? Or for thinking he's threatened himself?'

'No; what actually happened was that he got a bit excited, and burst out that very likely what had happened to his brother would happen to him, too, if he wasn't careful. After that he calmed down and wouldn't say any more, and then he rolled up with this extraordinary request for police protection. I should have wanted to turn it down, even though he's willing to pay all expenses, except for one thing – a rather curious thing: an assault on one of my men that happened some little time before the accident to Archibald. Early in the spring we got word that a strange motor-boat had been seen lying off the entrance to Suffby Cove. Well, there's a certain amount of smuggling goes on now that, thank God, we've stopped being the world's dumping-ground. If you can run a consignment of cameras or Paris frocks through to London, it pays very well. Now and again, too, an alien tries to slip in without a passport, or an undesirable who's been expelled tries to get back. And there's always the drug traffic. So we have to keep our eyes open, and when, very early one morning last April, my man there – Jennings – saw a motor-boat lying in the creek that runs into Suffby Cove, he thought he had better have a look at it. But, as he was passing some pine-trees, someone from behind dropped a sack over his head. You haven't much chance when you've got a sack over your head, and, though I expect Jennings put up a good fight – and he's quite a hefty young fellow – they roped him up to a tree, and there he was found by his sergeant a little later. The motor-boat had disappeared, of course, though it had been seen leaving the Cove under sail. It was fitted up with mast and sail as well as its motor. And nothing's been seen of it since. We found out that the sack was of Dutch manufacture, but we couldn't trace it further. There were a few vague footprints, but none plain enough to be of any value, and no other clues that we could find; and no more's been heard of the motor-boat.'

'Sounds like a spot of smuggling,' observed Mitchell.

'It does,' agreed the Major, 'only – there's this. By a lucky coincidence a special watch was being kept on the roads that night. We had had word – as you may remember, Mr Mitchell; it was the O'Reilly gang – that London burglars were in the district. A specially sharp look-out on all roads was being kept, therefore, and we are fairly confident that no contraband was landed; anyhow, it was not taken inland that night, and next day the whole of the neighbourhood was thoroughly searched.'

'Easier to hide than to find,' murmured Mitchell.

'Agreed, agreed. But you don't land silk frocks or spirits or watches or cameras to stuff them up the chimney, or keep them buried in some hole or a hollow tree; and a very careful watch has been kept ever since. I don't think anything could be moved without our knowing it. I expect the whole lot of them down in the village would smuggle anything they got a chance at, but there's no sign of anything unusual there; no one suddenly more prosperous or spending money they can't account for; no gossip going on or anything like that. A reward's been offered and no one has tried to claim it. If there's been smuggling, I am pretty sure no one in the village knows anything about it. You must remember it's a very small community indeed – not more than a score of families; all of them know each other's business, and if one were in a smuggling game, all would be. But I think it's certain that's not the case, or somehow, somewhere, something suspicious would appear.'

'Could Mr Winterton, either the living brother or the dead one ...?' Bobby asked.

'It's possible; it's been considered,' the Major answered. 'But is it conceivable that two well-to-do retired business men of the highest reputation would go in for smuggling on a big scale at their time of life? Well-to-do people smuggle like blazes, of course, when it's a new silk frock for a woman, or when a man buys a new watch abroad and pretends he got it in London, or tries to slip a new camera past the customs house officer. But doing the thing on a big scale is rather different. No, I can't think the explanation's there. I'm inclined, for my part, to say that the motorboat and the attack on Jennings meant some undesirable slipping into the country – perhaps some refugee from Germany without money, but with friends here ready to shelter him. And Archibald's death was probably purely accidental and George's dream just crab salad, as Mrs Cooper hinted.'

'Who gets Archibald's money? Was it much?' Mitchell asked.

'Between forty and fifty thousand,' Markham answered. 'It all goes to the widow and children except for a few small legacies. George Winterton and the Town and Country Bank are executors. There is one thing. I managed to get out of the bank people that Archibald, some time before his death, realised securities for a large sum – between ten and twelve thousand pounds.'

'Nearly a quarter of his whole fortune,' Mitchell observed.

'It was transferred to Holland.'

'Where the sacks come from,' murmured Mitchell.

'After Archibald's death, the whole sum was repaid by George Winterton, by cheque. The explanation is that they had been speculating together in exchange – quite common nowadays – and Archibald's death resulted in the transactions coming to an end, without, for that matter, either great loss or gain.'

'I suppose, sir,' Bobby suggested, 'it isn't likely there had been quarrelling between the brothers over that? Or any possibility that George Winterton——?'

'You mean there may have been big profits, and George murdered his brother to keep the profits for himself? I think, out of the question, on score of character and opportunity alike. The brothers were good friends; retired, respectable, well-to-do stockbrokers don't turn into murderers. The evidence both of Mrs Cooper and of her husband is conclusive that George was in bed and asleep at the time his brother was drowned. It happens that Cooper remembers that at six o'clock when he got up, there was a strange cat – one from the village probably – on the sill of Mr George Winterton's window. It happened to be a black cat, and Mr Winterton has the common superstition that black cats bring luck. This time it brought bad luck, which is partly why the incident made an impression on Cooper. At the time he hesitated whether to drive the cat away for fear of its wakening his master or leave it there as a bringer of good luck. Finally he tried to shoo it away, but it wouldn't go, so he got a ladder and fetched it down, and in doing so saw his master in bed and asleep – the window open, as it always was. That was about six o'clock. At seven, as usual, he took in a cup of tea, and Mr Winterton was still asleep. That's a fairly complete alibi, if one were needed.'

'Yes,' agreed Bobby thoughtfully. 'Yes – ye-es.'

'Thinks he sees something,' observed Mitchell. 'Thinking it depends on Cooper's testimony, and can he be trusted, eh?'

'Oh, as for that, it's confirmed by Mrs Cooper,' Major

Markham said. 'She remembers the incident of the black cat perfectly, because of the bad luck it brought, instead of the supposed good luck. She says, too, that Mr Winterton slept a little later than usual, most likely because he had been sitting up late with one of his crossword puzzles. He is a crossword "fan," as they call them now, you know. And,' added the Major, a little slowly, 'I don't think either Cooper or Mrs Cooper would go out of their way to commit perjury for their employer's sake. He – well, he has the name of being a little mean about money, and of always suspecting other people of trying to cheat him. He makes sure he gets value for every penny, watches the books carefully, and so on. It's the same with them all. The gardener, for instance, has to account for all the fruit, and there's no doubt Mr and Mrs Cooper rather resent it; in fact, all the staff do. Archibald was quite the opposite; rather free-handed.'

'Not enough to make them want to murder him, I suppose,' Mitchell remarked. 'I suppose that isn't what's making our gentleman nervous.' He turned to Bobby. 'You've heard it all,' he said. 'Your job now is to look like a summer visitor having a good time at a friend's house by the sea, and meanwhile try to find out if Archibald Winterton's death was accident or murder, to see that neither accident nor murder happens to George Winterton, to find out who tied up Constable Jennings, and why motor-boats sail into Suffby Cove and out again without saying by-your-leave to anyone, what it was they landed if they landed anything, and where it is now. And when you've been as long in the force as I have, you'll learn that police work is generally like that – making bricks without straw. You haven't asked yet what sort of man Mr George Winterton is, apart from being a retired stockbroker of the highest character, as all stockbrokers have to be, because if they get found out, then they aren't stockbrokers any more.'

'No, sir,' said Bobby. 'I didn't ask, because I understand I shall be seeing him soon.'

'Wants to form his own judgments,' grunted Mitchell, 'instead of taking them from his official superiors, as all good juniors do. Well, time we were all moving. Report every day, Owen, whether you've anything to say or not, and be careful to send your reports to the private address given you. Don't want the local postman to spot there's a letter going every day to the chief of the county police.'

'No, sir; very good, sir,' said Bobby.

CHAPTER III

Mr Shorton's Threats

AFTER leaving Ye Olde Sunke Garden, Bobby rode quietly on his way, revolving in his mind the task that lay before him. On the whole he was inclined to think that Archibald Winterton's death was really one of those bathing tragedies every holiday season records in such tragic numbers, and that little importance need be attached to his brother's expressed suspicions. A formerly busy and active man, retiring suddenly from affairs, will sometimes let his mind play him strange tricks, as, missing its accustomed food, it seizes on any trifle in order to ascribe to it the significance in which life seems now so sadly wanting.

So George Winterton, having nothing now to occupy his thoughts formerly occupied with daily business routine, and having tried to find sustenance for them in crossword puzzles and so on, had allowed them to dwell on his brother's death till the tragedy appeared in heightened, exaggerated colours.

In the same way, Bobby thought, missing the importance his former position as partner in a prosperous and successful business had given him, he, or rather his subconscious for him (Bobby knew all about Freud and all the latest psycho-analytic theories), had tried to win back that importance by representing him to himself as the central object of some vast and dark conspiracy.

For, after all, who, Bobby asked himself without getting

any answer – who, in the light of clear, calm common sense, would want to murder two quiet, inoffensive, retired business men, ending their days peacefully by the seaside?

'Who gains?' is a good working maxim, and Bobby, crawling along at a beggarly thirty m.p.h., hardly noticing that practically everything on the road passed him standing, couldn't see that there was anything to be gained by anyone, either by Archibald's death or George's.

No doubt he would be able to feel more certain about that after he had had a chance of studying the last-named at close quarters, and perhaps a chance of a chat or two with Mrs Cooper, who, from what Major Markham said, seemed to be an intelligent woman. And, where the housekeeper has any intelligence at all, she probably knows more of her employer than any one human being ought to know about another – far more than mother, wife, or daughter can ever know, since emotion clouds insight.

There was certainly the odd story of the assault on the local constable, Jennings. But that was probably quite an unconnected affair; difficult to see any link between an assault on a policeman and an accidental drowning some weeks later. As for the hints about smuggling, it was hardly possible to conceive two respectable retired stockbrokers engaging in that sort of thing. There was certainly the story of the ten or twelve thousand pounds – a quarter of his total capital, apparently – that it seemed Archibald had been using in some transaction or another. But the explanation given – speculation in the exchanges – was reasonable in itself, and consonant with the previous habits and knowledge of the Winterton brothers; while so large a capital – especially if, as was likely, George had added an equal amount to his brother's contribution – would imply, if used in smuggling, operations on an extraordinarily large scale, far too large to be centred on little out-of-the-way Suffby Cove by the aid of one motor-launch. The smuggling story did not seem at all plausible to Bobby; drowning accidents are common enough, retired business men with nothing to do all day often get their mental life a little wrong, and as for the attack on the local man, Jennings, that might easily have been the work of someone who thought he owed the constable a grudge.

Thinking thus, almost persuaded already he had been detailed to find a mare's nest and would have little to do but enjoy a quiet holiday by the sea, Bobby turned from the road he had been following into one that ran between Yarmouth and Cromer, through Deneham, which lay eight miles north of the spot Bobby had now reached. Turning in the other direction – south – Bobby came soon to a belt of pine-trees beyond which lay Suffby Cove.

Here Bobby alighted from his cycle and stood for some minutes looking thoughtfully and admiringly at as peaceful, quiet, and lovely a scene as all the east coast could show; one, indeed, with which it seemed impossible to associate dark thoughts of crime and violence, even of murder perhaps. Bobby's half-formed conviction that Archibald Winterton's death must have been purely accidental received in his mind a confirmation of which he was quite unconscious.

It chanced to be high tide, and the Cove, which at low tide was apt to show disfiguring mud-banks, looked its best, lying like a golden lake in the sunshine, its surface breaking into tiny ripples beneath the breath of the softest and most languid of summer breezes. Almost entirely enclosed except for the narrow opening seawards at its southern extremity, it would have formed an ideal harbour but for its limited extent and for the shallowness of its waters, which prevented it from being used by any except quite small craft – and even they at low tide had to be careful to follow the recognised channels. In shape the Cove was roughly oval. The high ground of Suffby Point formed its east shore, and sheltered it well from easterly winds. At the southern extremity of the Point, Bobby could just make out a fair-sized house he guessed to be that formerly occupied by the unfortunate Archibald Winterton, and since deserted by his widow and her children. At the northern point of the rough oval the Cove formed was the mouth of a little creek that there emptied into its waters, and probably accounted for its extreme shallowness by the sediment, deposited throughout the ages, that had formed, too, the mud-banks apparent at low tide. On the west bank of the creek stood the few cottages that formed Suffby village, if village is not too imposing a word to apply to so tiny a community, and further still was a residence, low-built and comfortable-looking, dating, as Bobby afterwards learned, from early Georgian times, that he guessed must be his destination and the home of Mr George Winterton.

Remounting his cycle, Bobby continued on his way, crossing Suffby Creek by the smart, brand-new steel and concrete bridge recently put up by the local authorities to replace the mediæval 'trefoil' or 'threeway' bridge, dating from the fifteenth century but found now too steep and narrow for motorists in a hurry. A little beyond the bridge, a turning from the main road led to Suffby village on the left, and beyond that to the low Georgian house Bobby had seen from the high ground beyond the creek.

It stood close to the edge of the water; almost on the beach, indeed. A large garden, that must have covered two or three acres, stretched up the rising ground behind the house to a spot where was a small summer-house, built, after a passing fashion of the time, to represent the ruins of a small Greek temple. From this point there was a fine view over the sea, beyond West Point, though elsewhere the view was cut off by a growth of shrubs and the small, stunted trees that were all the strong air permitted to grow here, these sheltering the summer-house from observation on every other side, so that one came upon it almost unawares.

The house itself was approached by a wide, well-kept gravel drive, and Bobby, as he rode up it, was greeted by a furious outburst of barking from a big Airedale. The animal did not seem in any way vicious, but evidently did not mean any stranger's approach to go unnoticed, and though Bobby, who could usually make friends with any animal, called to it in his most coaxing tones, it was not to be beguiled from the path of duty and continued its loud announcement of his arrival till the door of the house opened and there appeared a manservant whom Bobby guessed must be the husband of the Mrs Cooper of whom Major Markham had spoken.

'It's all right, sir; he's only letting us know,' this man said; and, indeed, the dog at once grew quiet and, coming up to have a closer look at the new-comer, was quite willing to accept a pat on the head. 'He won't bark at you again, sir, now he knows you,' the manservant added; 'very intelligent dog, sir.'

Cooper was a tall, well-built man, and would have been distinctly good-looking but for a certain flabbiness of face and form and an awkwardness of gait due to the fact that he was what is called 'flat-footed.' One felt, indeed, when looking at him, that Nature had intended to make him extremely handsome, but had forgotten to give his features the finishing touches that would have made them distinctive. He had acquired, moreover, a deprecatory stoop that together with his flat-footedness took away from his height, and his fish-like, protuberant eyes of an indeterminate hue between blue and grey had an irritating trick of flickering eyelids that gave him at times an odd appearance of trying to wink at one. But he was an excellent servant, a really excellent judge of wine, on which his opinion could be trusted, and very hard-working, so that his employer counted himself fortunate in having been able to engage him. But just at first Bobby was slightly disconcerted by that flickering eyelid which seemed so much to suggest a confidential wink. He soon got used to it, though, and realised that it was nothing but a nervous trick.

'It's Mr Owen, sir, isn't it?' Cooper went on. 'Mr Winterton is expecting you, sir. I was to say he is so sorry he is unexpectedly engaged with a gentleman from London on business——'

They were standing now just inside the hall. Almost behind Bobby where he stood was a door through which at this moment there came a sudden roar of angry voices. Slightly startled, Bobby turned, and with that odd, disconcerting appearance of a wink his flickering eyelid gave him Cooper said:

'It's the gentleman from London, I think, sir. Mr Winterton was most unwilling to see him.'

The door opened and a round, small, red-haired man emerged – or, rather, bounded out, like a bristling cricket-ball. His face was crimson, his hair almost on end, his breath was coming in great gasps, his fists were clenched and gesticulating. He glared at Bobby and at Cooper as if his wrath included them in its ample bounds, and then swung round to face the room he had just left.

'It's a fraud – deliberate fraud, Winterton,' he shouted; 'a swindle, sir; nothing less than a swindle.'

There came to the door of the room a very big man, ruddy and blue-eyed, with fair hair just beginning to grow grey, stout and heavy in build. He said:

'If you say that again, Shorton, I'll take you into court for slander and libel. And if you come here again, I'll throw you out of the window. Now, take yourself off as quick as you know how. Cooper, Mr Shorton's hat, and if you see him here again, let me know, and I'll attend to him. If I'm out, set the dog on him.'

'Yes, sir; certainly, sir,' said Cooper impassively, though his flickering eyelid still gave him the appearance of bestowing upon Bobby confidential winks. 'Your hat and umbrella, sir,' he added to Mr Shorton in the best manner of the well-trained servant.

Shorton snatched them from him with a snort of rage – his social training was evidently not so well equal to the strain upon it as was the impassive butler's – included all present in one sweeping malediction, and then, as the big, fair-haired man made a step towards him, vanished through the door Cooper still held open, hurled an incoherence of oath and threat from the gravel drive, and departed down it, still with waving arms and rumbling threats.

'Little swine,' said Mr Winterton, and added to Bobby: 'You're Owen, I suppose? Sorry to give you such a welcome. That was a fellow from London I used to know – trying threats now, but they won't help him. Cooper, put Mr Owen's cycle in the garage and take his bag up to his room.' He added to Bobby: 'Come and have a drink and a smoke in my den, will you? It's where I spend most of my time, writing my "Justification of the Gold Standard." We've lots of time for a talk before dinner.'

CHAPTER IV

'Justification of the Gold Standard'

THE room into which Winterton led Bobby was long, low, and narrow; on one side three windows that commanded a view across the Cove to the high ground of the Point beyond, and at the further end a second door that led down two steps into the garden. By the window nearest the door whereby Bobby and his host had just entered stood a small writing-table with a typewriter on it, and near by a big card index cabinet. In the middle of the room was a much larger writing-table, covered with books and papers and an enormous pile of typescript, till hardly an inch of its surface was visible. Between the windows were big bookcases, crammed with volumes that from one of them had overflowed into a pile on the floor. By the revolving armchair, at the big central table, was one of those revolving bookcases presented to purchasers of a recent edition of the *Encyclopædia Britannica.*

Winterton invited Bobby to take one of the two or three comfortable armchairs in the room, and touched the bell by the fireplace. He had scarcely done so, had not had time even to take his own seat, when the door opened and a woman came in with a tray with whisky and soda-water.

'Ah, bravo,' Winterton exclaimed. 'Mrs Cooper always knows what's wanted.'

Mrs Cooper smiled very faintly, but did not speak. She was a tall woman, almost as tall as her husband, but with not a trace of his flabbiness about her. Her black dress, with white cuffs and collar, suited well an air of severe dignity she had, and her features were handsome and well marked, though somewhat expressionless. She wore her hair – intensely black in hue but already streaked with grey, though she was not yet forty – plaited close to her head, and her eyes, when she let you see them – for generally she veiled them behind heavy, swollen-looking lids – were of the same intense blackness. Though she gave at first an impression of being somewhat slow and deliberate in her movements, she went always so straight to her object, never wasting a turn of foot or hand, that whatever she was doing she would accomplish in less time than others whose activity seemed greater. Now, for instance, there was no sign of pause or time wasted on any attempt to clear a space on the hopelessly encumbered table. The tray was deposited instead on the top of the revolving bookcase, a touch put both bottle and glasses convenient to her employer's hand, a moment's pause while she waited, upright and still, in case anything else was required, and then she had gone with the same swift, clear decision that seemed to characterise her.

'Wonderful woman,' Winterton said as the door closed behind her; 'always knows just what you want and sees that you get it – runs the whole place like an automatic machine, and yet I can knock all her arrangements endways and she'll never say a word, but pick 'em all up again and have the whole thing running O.K. to the dot once more in quick sticks.'

'Has she been with you long?' Bobby asked, accepting the drink his host offered.

'Five years, she and her husband, in fact, ever since my brother and I settled here,' Winterton answered, his face clouding over as if the memory of his brother's tragic death were still as vivid as ever. His glance wandered out to where, through the windows, Bobby could see at the extremity of the Point the house he had already supposed must have been Archibald Winterton's. Beyond it he could see now what looked like a ruin of some kind, and he was about to ask what it was when, in tones quite different from those he had used before, charged as they were with a strong emotion, and even, Bobby thought, with a secret terror, his host broke out: 'Why should he have drowned? He was the strongest swimmer I've ever known, and the sea was quiet – calm as a mill-pond. That's what I want you——'

But Bobby interrupted him by jumping to his feet and going to the door. He opened it quickly. There was no one there; the hall was quite empty. He closed the door again, and, crossing the room, opened the door at the other end of the room, the one leading to the garden. There was no one visible, and nothing near where anyone could have hidden. Bobby closed that door, too, and went back to his host, who was looking surprised and somewhat indignant.

'Please excuse me, Mr Winterton,' he said, 'but it's absolutely necessary that when there is a possibility, even, of being overheard, we must talk as if I were in fact really what I am supposed to be – the son of an old friend in whom you are taking an interest. If you possibly can, I would like you to try to think of me like that. If you have some former friend you could, so to say, appoint to the position of being my temporary parent, and make references to at times, it would be a help. Perhaps you've heard that when an alibi's to be faked, a favourite trick is to select some real occurrence – a trip to Brighton or a visit to a pub, or anything – and transfer that actual event to the date the alibi's to be established for. You see the idea? Suppose, for instance, you had an old friend you went fishing with, or a walking tour, or anything like that. Make him my imaginary parent for the time. The only possible exception must be when we are out in the open air, with a clear space of a hundred yards at least all round – and then we had better talk in whispers.'

'But, hang it all,' grumbled Mr Winterton, 'there's no one in the house except ourselves. There are the Coopers, of course, but they're quite trustworthy.'

'I don't doubt it,' answered Bobby, 'but if they heard anything to make them think there was anything unusual about me, they might easily, without even meaning to, drop some remark outside that would start rumours and gossip, and all my chance of doing any useful work would be over. If I may say so, I hope and expect your suspicions are quite unfounded, but any hint of murder is serious, and it's police duty to take every precaution to make absolutely sure. So, if you please, try to think of me just as a guest, the son of an old friend. I shall try to do the same on my side. For example there are a lot of questions I shall want to ask you, but at the moment I'm merely trying to wonder what sort of time I'm going to have here, whether I'm likely to enjoy myself or be bored stiff, and whether you're the kind of older man one has to mind one's p's and q's with or not.'

'All right, all right,' Winterton agreed, though evidently still a little puzzled.

'Your workshop, I suppose, sir?' Bobby said, raising his voice a little, for before he had spoken in very low tones. 'I shouldn't want to go on swotting if I had chucked the office.'

The tones, the words, were so exactly what might have been expected from a youngster trying to make talk with an elder of whom he did not feel quite certain, that Winterton could not help smiling.

'Oh, well,' he said, playing up now very well, 'one doesn't want to rust. I'm turning author in my old age – writing a book, "Justification of the Gold Standard." I've always been interested in currency questions. I remember years ago going with your father to attend a big debate on bimetallism. He was rather keen on it at the time. I don't know if he kept it up.'

'I never heard him say much about it,' Bobby answered – quite truthfully. 'I suppose it's an awfully difficult question – about gold, I mean.'

'Not a bit,' declared Winterton eagerly. In his interest in his hobby he had evidently for the moment quite forgotten the fear that a moment before his expression had seemed to show. 'It's perfectly simple; in a word, "Gold's always gold." Getting back to gold is the only thing that can save civilisation. You must have a standard of value, and gold is the only possible standard because it is the only thing that doesn't vary. A pound of gold is always a pound of gold – it's an absolute. You can't tamper with it. It just Is. But a pound of produce some theorists want to base values on – why, it varies with every whim of fashion, with every change of the seasons. Take a pound of potatoes – their value depends on all sorts of things: their quality, their freedom from disease, whether their variety is popular or not, on the state of the market, on current medical fads, whether they're full of vitamins and everyone ought to eat a pound a day, or whether they're fattening and no one ought to touch them. What ship could make port if its compass was subject to all kinds of outside influences like that? But gold's always the same. You can't set a printing-press to work to turn out as many gold sovereigns as you happen to think you want, whereas any fool of a Government official can phone an order for the delivery of fifty thousand pound notes – or fifty million, for that matter. I tell you, young man, no country's safe, no man's safe, till we get back to gold.'

The door opened and Mrs Cooper came in, carrying a tray on which were various letters. But Mr Winterton was far too excited to take any notice. He held out his hand for the letters but did not take them, instead continuing his theme of the importance of a return to the gold standard.

'With all civilisation sliding to a smash,' he repeated, 'the only way to be safe is to have a solid reserve of gold you can always rely on.'

So far as Bobby understood the question, he was in entire disagreement with everything Mr Winterton was saying, since he could not see that there was in essence much difference between digging up a certain yellow metal, and saying that that represented food and shelter and clothing and all that men desire and need, and putting a piece of paper through the printing-press and saying the same thing of it. But he did not pretend to be an expert on economics, and what interested him – keenly, indeed – was the excitement Mr Winterton showed. He was on his feet now, his eyes alight, gesticulating dangerously with his full glass, the contents of which Bobby fully expected to see sent showering around. It was evident that for him his theme was the one thing that mattered, and Mrs Cooper said:

'The post, sir; it has just come.'

'Oh, yes, yes,' he said, taking the letters at last. 'Off on my hobby-horse again, you see, Mrs Cooper. But gold is always gold, and you can't say so too often.'

'Well, sir,' she agreed, 'there's something about the gold sovereigns we used to have before the war that does seem different – I have two or three still I've always kept.'

'Go on keeping 'em,' Winterton told her. 'So long as you've got them, you've got something real, and, Lord knows, with the way things are going, and a general smash likely any moment, when we shan't need solid gold again – Communists and Fascists and all the rest of 'em——'

'Yes, sir,' said Mrs Cooper, and retired with her deliberate movements that looked so slow and measured and yet in some way enabled her to cover the ground so quickly.

The interruption had served to check the full flow of Winterton's eloquence. He sat down now and drank off the contents of the glass he had been flourishing so dangerously.

'I daresay all that bores you, a young fellow like you,' he said.

'Oh, no, sir,' Bobby protested. 'I think it's frightfully interesting, and I'm like Mrs Cooper; I've got two sovereigns. An old uncle gave them me years ago and I've always kept them.'

'Keep 'em,' Winterton advised him, as he had advised his housekeeper; 'paper may some day be good for nothing but to light the fire, but gold's gold. Intelligent woman, Mrs Cooper, but I'm afraid she's heard me at it before. Like most people, she couldn't see the point at first, but I've made her understand it now.' He was looking at the letters that had just arrived, and now, with an impatient gesture, he tossed them on the table. 'Nothing there,' he said; 'only bills and circulars. She's had a hard life of it, too. She married a man during the war when she was quite a girl, little more than a child. He did very well, was given command of his battalion, distinguished himself handling it, and was appointed to a brigade. Three days afterwards he was killed, and then it came out he had a previous wife still living – magnificent soldier and leader, apparently, and at the same time a heartless blackguard. That left her without any claim to pension or any recognition, and his family refused to have anything to do with her. So she was left to get along as best she could with two children, one quite young and one not born then. The one died soon after birth and the other has died since, and altogether she had a pretty bad time of it till she met Cooper. He's quite a decent sort; had been batman to her husband – to the man she thought her husband, rather. The worst of her troubles were over then, but she had been through a good deal. She had a lot to do with getting her supposed husband's abilities recognised, I believe, so it's been rather a comedown – from a brilliant soldier already holding high rank, and marked for higher still, to a butler – and, though Cooper's a very good servant, he's hardly the stuff she can ever hope to make a success of. But she faces up to it very well.'

'Jolly hard lines,' Bobby said reflectively. 'Rather awful to feel yourself let down like that.'

'It's made her rather bitter in some ways,' Winterton observed. 'She doesn't say much, but now and then she lets something slip out that shows she hasn't much faith left in anything, and it's a little apt at times to make her forget herself – take rather a high hand with people. I had to give her notice once, her and her husband. Oh, good, there's Miss Raby back at last. Excuse me a moment.'

As he spoke he jumped up and crossed the room to one of the windows, on that warm day standing open. A girl was coming briskly up the drive. She was rather small and slight in build, with a vigorous, springing step. Winterton called to her, and she left the drive and came across to him. Bobby saw that she had small, dark, well-shaped features, with very bright, vivacious eyes, dark brown in colour, matching the dark brown of her hair. A distinctly pretty girl, Bobby decided, though a good deal of her prettiness depended as much on a certain bright vigour that seemed to hang about her as on any regularity or perfection of feature. She looked quick and capable, too, as if she could be thoroughly relied upon. As she came near she called out:

'I found the book all right, Mr Winterton. They only charged ten shillings.'

'Oh, good, good,' said Winterton. 'I'm glad.'

'It's in my suit-case,' she went on; 'two big volumes of it. I left it for one of the village boys to bring up from the bus stop.'

'You came by the 5.55, then?' Winterton remarked. 'I was going to send Adams with the car if you had missed that.'

The girl went on to the front door of the house and Winterton turned back into the room.

'That was Miss Raby,' he explained, 'my secretary; very clever girl. She does crossword puzzles for one of the London papers sometimes; gets a couple of guineas or so for each one they take, I believe. She's been to London to try to get hold of an old work on the French assignat issue I wanted, and she's found it, apparently. I thought she would have had to pay more for it,' he added, with considerable satisfaction.

'Is there a good train service?' Bobby asked. 'There's no station nearer than Deneham, is there?'

'No, and that's a good eight miles,' Mr Winterton answered. 'There's a train Miss Raby evidently missed that gets in about three. The next gets in at 5.55, and there's the last one at 8.20. If anyone comes by that I have to send the car, or they've got to walk, as the last bus has gone by then. The other two trains the bus waits for as a rule. Very convenient, too. Unfortunately, they're talking of taking them off or reducing the service. They say it doesn't pay; too little traffic. I'm glad Miss Raby got the 5.55, though; it's a bore sending the car.' He glanced at his watch. 'It's getting late,' he remarked; 'time to dress. We generally dress for dinner here. I like to keep it up even if we are buried in the wilds. Black tie, of course.'

CHAPTER V

The Missing Airedale

THE room assigned to Bobby was small but comfortable-looking, with a fine view from its one window out over the Cove to the open sea beyond. His suit-case had been brought up, and he was busy unpacking it and putting his things away when there came a knock at the door.

When he opened it he found Mrs Cooper there, composed and dignified, her strong white hands folded before her. She had come, she said, to know if he had all he needed.

'The bathroom is at the end of the passage,' she explained. 'There is only one; though Mr Winterton says he will have another put in some day.' There was, Bobby thought, the faintest touch of perhaps unconscious contempt in the tone in which she pronounced that 'some day,' as if it were an expression her clear-cut and determined mind held in utter scorn. She went on: 'Mr Winterton usually has his hot bath in the morning, at half past eight. Mr Colin likes one before dinner. I have it ready for him at half past seven, but he is generally late. If you wish it, I could have one ready for you every evening at a quarter past seven. When Mr Miles is here, if he wants one at night I usually have it ready for him at ten minutes to eight, but then he and Mr Colin generally get in each other's way. Dinner is at a quarter past eight. Mr Colin and Mr Miles usually go for a swim before breakfast. I will put a bath-robe and towels ready for you if you would like them. Or do you prefer a hot bath?'

'I think a swim would be rather jolly,' Bobby said.

'Would you require a swimming costume?' Mrs Cooper asked.

'Well, I hadn't thought of bringing one,' Bobby admitted.

'I will put one out,' Mrs Cooper said.

'Are you sure there's one to spare?'

'There are always some ready in case they are wanted,' she explained quietly, 'either for ladies or gentlemen. Mr Winterton does not care for sea-bathing himself, but most of his visitors do. Breakfast is ready at nine, but there are thermos flasks of coffee and biscuits every morning on the table in the hall, if required. Mr Colin always likes to be called at seven, in case he oversleeps and misses his swim. If you wish it, I will tell Cooper to knock at your door, too.'

'Oh, thank you,' Bobby answered. 'I expect I shall be awake all right. Is "Mr Colin" Mr Colin Ross, Mr Winterton's nephew?'

'Yes,' answered Mrs Cooper. 'Mr Miles, Mr Winterton's other nephew, is not staying here at present. That is Mr Ross coming now,' she added.

Bobby had heard nothing, but when he turned to look out of the window he saw a young man in a suit of plus fours, of a somewhat pronounced pattern, coming up the gravel drive with some golf-clubs swung over his shoulder. Bobby could not see his face plainly, but noticed that he seemed rather on the small side, and that he had a quick, slightly hurried step, like that of one who felt he never had much time to spare. And Bobby noted, too, that Mrs Cooper must have unusually good hearing to have caught already the sound of the newcomer's footsteps. Bobby himself had heard nothing.

'There's a golf-course near, then,' he remarked. 'One can get a game?'

'The nearest course is at Deneham, eight miles along the Cromer Road,' Mrs Cooper answered, 'but Mr Winterton and Mr Colin – and Mr Miles, too, when he's here – play on the Point for practice. They says there's a kind of natural course there. That is what the trouble was about.'

'What was that?' Bobby asked.

'It was in the London papers, I understand,' Mrs Cooper answered quietly. 'I expect Mr Winterton could explain it, if you asked him.'

'Oh, yes,' Bobby said, feeling slightly rebuked. 'I suppose the bathing is quite safe?'

'Perfectly safe in the Cove, though Mr Miles grumbles about its being too shallow at low tide in some parts. Outside the Cove it's quite safe for good swimmers except at the turn of the tide. There's a strong current then runs along the coast, about a mile out, it is dangerous to be caught in – as happened this spring to poor Mr Archibald.'

'Oh, yes, that was a sad affair,' Bobby said.

'We all felt it very much,' Mrs Cooper told him gravely. 'It was such a shock. Mr Winterton was greatly affected; he hasn't got over it yet. It made me thankful I've always felt too nervous of the water to be a swimmer. I will attend to the bath-robe and towels for you, sir,' she added, as she moved away down the passage.

Bobby went on with his dressing, and he was aware of an odd sensation that Mrs Cooper's real object in coming to him had been, in the common phrase, 'to weigh him up,' and that this she had done very thoroughly. That was why she had talked so freely. Well, he had talked freely, too, and for the same reason – the wish to weigh her up, as it was his business to weigh up everyone who might have any connection with the tragedy he was there to investigate. But he did not feel that, on his side, he had been very successful; there was some quality about the woman by whose virtue she seemed able to hold herself aloof, as it were, from common life, even while taking her full daily share therein. Perhaps, Bobby thought, it was the tragic experience she had known that helped thus to give her this manner of being set apart. He hoped, at any rate, that the clear sight of those disillusioned eyes of hers had not discovered that he had any connection with the police. He had been careful to fill his belongings with every kind of evidence of his public school and university years, so as to throw the curious off the scent and allay any suspicions that might be entertained in any quarter. No one who knew he was an old St. George's man would be likely to suppose that he was also a C.I.D. man, but the feeling did not leave him that Mrs Cooper was a person likely to see more than most.

When he was ready, he went downstairs to the study – or 'den,' as Mr Winterton called it – where he found his host waiting with the young man of the golf clubs, Colin Ross, who acknowledged Mr Winterton's introduction with a grunt and then went back to the evening paper, over which he was looking very ill-tempered.

'They've scratched Four Aces,' he announced. 'Dirty trick. They don't want her to win, that's all; keeping her back for next time.'

'Four Aces scratched,' Bobby exclaimed, with a great show of interest. 'I was going to risk a pound on her, both ways.'

' "Going to" is lucky,' Colin retorted. 'I have – a fiver.'

Bobby duly sympathised, and Colin grew more friendly in the realisation that Bobby also knew something of racing and was apparently interested in the sport. In point of fact, Bobby's interest in racing was entirely theoretical, but he knew well that the surest way of winning the confidence – and the confidences – of any Englishman is to have, and to be able to express, an instructed opinion on that great perennial question: 'What'll win?'

In fact, the discussion between the two young men grew quite technical and animated till Mr Winterton interposed with a dry suggestion that Colin had better 'go and wash his face and comb his hair' before dinner.

'How much have you dropped recently, Colin?' he added as the young man, acting on this tactful suggestion and muttering something about supposing old Mother Cooper would be raggy if he were late, was making his way to the door.

Colin looked sulky, as though the question did not please him.

'I'll pick up next week,' he declared. 'I'm on a good thing – try a tenner on Blackberry, Uncle George. You'll get a good price, because Gordon Richards is riding Sandboy. But Blackberry's a dead cert – even Gordon can't stop her beating Sandboy unless there's a dickens of a lot of rain between then and now. That might do it, but nothing else will.'

He vanished, and, as the door closed behind him, Bobby caught the oddest expression showing for a moment on Mr Winterton's face – of doubt and questioning, it seemed, and something that looked almost like a haunting terror, that in Colin's presence the older man had been at pains to suppress but that now peeped out the moment he was gone. Then Mr Winterton seemed to remember Bobby was there, and said hurriedly and nervously:

'I know those good things of Colin's – a pretty penny they've cost me. They do come off sometimes, though. I might risk a trifle, perhaps.'

He turned to make a note on the blotting-pad on the table, and when he looked round at Bobby again he had recovered his self-possession.

'Mr Ross seems to know a good deal about the game,' Bobby observed.

'A good deal too much. He'll burn his fingers pretty thoroughly one of these days,' Mr Winterton grumbled. 'I've told him more than once he ought to stop it; so did Archibald. A regular row they had about it. Of course, it's the boy's own business, really; he's his own master and it's his own money.'

'Is Mr Miles Winterton interested in racing, too?'

'Miles? Do you know him?' Mr Winterton asked quickly, and then, as if recollecting himself: 'Of course you would,' he declared; 'it was Miles's father who was with your father and myself on that walking-tour we all made in the Scottish Highlands.' He paused, and could not resist bestowing a wink on Bobby, as if to claim admiration for the way in which he had followed the advice given him of identifying Bobby's supposititious parent with some actual former friend. 'No, I don't think Miles goes in for racing much. I don't suppose you'll meet him this time; he's not staying here just at present.'

He said this rather shortly, frowning as he pronounced Miles's name, and Bobby made a mental note that if it almost seemed as though he held one of his nephews in secret terror, against the other he held some hidden, unexpressed anger.

The gong sounded presently, and they went into the dining-room, where Mary Raby was waiting for them. Mr Winterton introduced Bobby and plunged into talk about the book Miss Raby had been to London to secure. It had arrived now, having been brought up from the bus stop by someone from the village, and Mr Winterton was still talking about it when Colin appeared – after the soup had been served, for Mr Winterton would wait no longer, but having 'combed his hair and washed his face'; in other words, having had a bath and changed from plus fours to a dinner-jacket in something like record time.

'Miles still giving us a miss?' he remarked with a slightly malicious grin as he took his seat.

Neither Mr Winterton nor Miss Raby answered him, though Mr Winterton frowned and Miss Raby went red, and Colin switched off to tell them the solution to a clue in a crossword puzzle that had apparently been too much for both of them. It had something to do with a technical racing expression that neither Mr Winterton nor Miss Raby had ever heard of. But the proffered solution was ingenious, Mr Winterton was almost childishly pleased, and Miss Raby sighed and expressed a sad opinion that never, never would she be able to compose a puzzle so ingenious as those in this particular series. It seemed she had met the author of them, and she declared that he always made them up in bed, just before going to sleep, and apparently with very little trouble.

'They just come,' she said. 'I have to work and work, and then it's never anything like so good.'

'I've been trying my hand myself,' Mr Winterton remarked. He took a paper from his pocket-book and looked at it. 'It's interesting to try,' he said. 'I don't say this one I've been doing is technically very good, but I do think anyone who solved it would find it interesting – I might even say extremely interesting.'

He spoke with a certain emphasis that caught the attention of all of them. But he said no more – did not offer to show it – and, putting the paper back in his pocket, devoted all his attention to the meal. It was a very good one, too, quite worthy of undivided attention, doing equal credit to Mrs Cooper's cooking and to Cooper's serving, while the procession of wines placed before them was worthy of greater appreciation than it received – for Colin cared only for whisky, Miss Raby drank only water, Mr Winterton had sunk again into his own thoughts, and for Bobby wine was a thing to be avoided as an interference with a clear head and clear thinking. But Cooper, where wine was concerned, had something in him of the pure artist, and was content to know how right the port, the sherry, the hock, and the rest of them had been.

Afterwards they all went into a smaller room and played bridge; and Bobby disgraced himself by displaying a perfect ignorance of the fact that bidding four in clubs is a clear indication that the bidder holds not one card of that suit, as well as of other peculiarities of what once was a good game till the convention fiends fell upon it.

The bridge-party broke up rather early, for Mrs Cooper appeared to say that Jane was waiting. Jane was apparently a young woman from the village, engaged to help Mrs Cooper in the evenings, and, as Miss Raby lodged in the village, though she had all her meals in her employer's house, it was usual for Jane to escort her back to the village.

After that Colin became immersed in the racing news, and obscure calculations of weights and ages and distances, and Mr Winterton, after asking Bobby to help him with a crossword puzzle in that morning's paper, suggested that, as it was a fine warm night, with moon and stars shining, a stroll along the shore might be agreeable.

Bobby accepted with alacrity; it was indeed what he wanted, for there were questions he had to ask he did not care to utter in the house. But Colin looked up with something between a sneer and a smile.

'I thought you had given that up, uncle – taking strolls in the dark.'

Mr Winterton did not answer, though he looked vexed. When they got outside, he said:

'We'll take Towser.'

He whistled once or twice, but there was no reply. Bobby asked:

'Is that the Airedale I noticed? Fine-looking dog.'

'Yes, it belonged to poor Archibald,' Mr Winterton replied. 'When my sister-in-law moved, I took it over.'

He whistled again, but still there was no response, and Mrs Cooper appeared.

'Are you wanting Towser, sir?' she asked. 'We can't find him anywhere. I've been looking for him to give him his supper. Cooper's been all round the house, but he can't see him anywhere.'

'Oh, well, I expect he'll turn up,' Mr Winterton said, and began to walk down the drive Bobby noticed was lighted, and well lighted, by hanging electric lamps. The road to the village was lighted in the same way, and now Bobby could see lights in the cottages that seemed much more brilliant than those of the lamps or candles he would have expected to be in use there. He made some remark to that effect, and Mr Winterton laughed.

'Mrs Cooper's doing,' he said. 'When I bought this house, it was pretty old-fashioned – it was built a hundred and fifty years ago or more. I had a hot-water system put in and a bathroom – there ought to have been two, but that wasn't thought of at the time – and an electric light plant to supply the house. Mrs Cooper suggested that at very little extra expense we could generate enough to supply the village and light the road – most of the cottages belong to me; I had to buy them with the house. I said all right, I thought it a good idea; make me popular with the villagers and so on. But she had a battle royal with them before they would agree to have it put in; they thought it was a deep-laid plan to raise their rents or turn them out or something else equally villainous. I should have said, 'All right, if you don't want it, do without,' but she fairly bullied them into taking it, and in the end she got her own way. A remarkable woman in her own fashion, even if she is a little too fond of arranging everything for everybody. I think I told you I had to threaten to get rid of her once, she and her husband, but I was glad enough to keep them on all the same, once I had made them understand they couldn't have everything quite their own way.'

They had passed out of the drive now, and turned by an old wooden post standing in the shingle near a boat that was lying upside down. As they were passing it, Bobby was conscious that Winterton started suddenly and then stiffened. Bobby said:

'There's something there, isn't there?'

'No, nothing, no,' Mr Winterton answered, but all the same Bobby was sure he had seen a form rise from behind the boat and slip swiftly away into the darkness.

CHAPTER VI

Question and Answer

For a moment Bobby was tempted to follow, so sure was he that the gliding shadow he could make out in the distance was that of someone who had been startled by their approach. But there seemed no object to be served by such pursuit: Mr Winterton was already walking on in another direction, and it came somehow into Bobby's mind that to leave him alone might not be wise or prudent. He hurried after him accordingly, and as he joined him said:

'I am sure that there was someone there.'

'Are you?' Winterton said indifferently. After a pause he added: 'How dark the night is.'

This was hardly accurate, for in fact the night was very calm and clear, and, though there was no moon, the stars were shining brightly, their light reflected from the still water of the almost landlocked cove by which the two men were walking. Nor did Mr Winterton seem to find it dark enough in fact to trouble him, for he was walking briskly and steadily, putting down his feet without hesitation. All the same, he said again:

'How dark the night is.'

They had come now to a spot where the ground was higher as the shore sloped upwards to the cliffs that guarded the entrance to the Cove. It was bare and open here, too, with no shelter near for any eavesdroppers, and, as Winterton paused to look out across the Cove where the innumerable stars above shone in multiplied reflection, Bobby said to him:

'Mr Winterton, now we are alone, I want you to switch your mind over and begin to think of me again as an officer of police, investigating an extremely serious matter.'

'Oh, yes, there's that,' Winterton agreed, turning and looking at him. 'Yes, of course.' He added: 'I can't think what's happened to that dog. I've never known him go off like this before.'

'There are some questions I want to ask you,' Bobby said, slightly impatient, for that the Airedale was missing for the time did not strike him as a detail of importance. 'Do you mind telling me exactly what makes you think that the inquest verdict was wrong, and that Mr Archibald Winterton's death was not accidental?'

'I don't think; I know,' the other answered moodily. 'Do you never know things without knowing why you know them?'

'In the police,' Bobby answered with some emphasis, 'we are expected to know just exactly why we know what we know – no good talking about Bergsonian intuition to Treasury Counsel. I understand there was something about a dream ...'

'Oh, that,' Winterton answered, more briskly, rather as if rousing himself from the mood of abstraction into which he had fallen. 'Oh, yes, I had to satisfy Markham somehow. Yes, I had a dream all right, but I don't feel as I do because I had a dream: most likely I had a dream because of what I was feeling. But I had to shut Markham up somehow.'

'Why?'

'Because he made me tired, talking so much, worrying for reasons. Reasons are all very well. I've seen men on the Stock Exchange act on fool-proof reasons and drop a fortune, and others act without the shadow of a reason and romp home millionaires.'

'All the same,' Bobby said quietly, 'reason's our profession, and if you would tell me yours for thinking what you do, it would be a help.'

Winterton turned again and laid a hand heavily on Bobby's arm.

'Why should Archy have drowned?' he asked, his voice low and hoarse and shaken with a strong emotion that seemed half anger and half fear. 'I tell you he was as likely to drown as water is to burn or lead to swim. It was a warm spell just then; the night had been so hot I hadn't been able to sleep till I dropped off towards morning. It was perfectly calm; the tide didn't turn till later on. He left the house soon after six – there's proof of that; he would be in the water by half past six. The tide didn't begin to turn, to make the down coast current run with any strength, till half past seven – all that's on record. And Archy knew it all; it was to avoid the full strength of the current that he went down to the shore half an hour earlier than usual. He wasn't an ordinary swimmer; he was an expert – and as careful as he could be, too. The expert's always careful; it's only the amateur who takes risks.'

'You didn't give evidence at the inquest?'

'Yes, I did. I told them he was as likely to drown as a fish would have been. They wouldn't listen; talked about facts. I know better than their fool facts; cramp and heart failure and so on was what they babbled about, especially so on.'

'But couldn't cramp account for it?'

'No. Any doctor will tell you cramp is nothing for anyone to be afraid of; all you do is turn on your back and float till it's over. As for heart failure, Archy's heart was as sound as a bell. His doctor had to admit that; so had the other doctor fellow who examined the body after it was found.'

'I understand both doctors declared the injuries the body showed had been inflicted after death.'

'They admitted they couldn't be sure.'

'Had your brother any enemies?'

'No; no more than most people.'

'But if there was no motive ...' Bobby said patiently.

He was quite sure now that there was something his companion knew but did not wish to tell. Well, he supposed it was his business to get it out of him, but he had a feeling the process would be long and difficult. 'Information received' was always, according to the maxims of Superintendent Mitchell, what a detective had chiefly to rely upon, but here it seemed all information would be withheld as far as that could be done. 'Information extracted,' it was going to be this time, he told himself. Winterton was still silent, and Bobby repeated:

'You can give me no idea of any possible motive ...'

'That's what I want you to find out,' Winterton said then.

'Of course,' Bobby pointed out quickly. 'That means there is something you know – that you have suspicions ...'

'Not suspicions,' Winterton corrected him. 'There are certain facts. I don't know what relation they have, if any. I want to see if they strike you, and what you think.'

'Mr Winterton,' Bobby said gravely, 'if you deliberately withhold information in a case of this kind, you are interfering with the course of justice. You know as well as I do that that is a serious matter.'

'My good young man,' Winterton said irritably, 'I've been all over this with Markham and I don't want to go over it again with you. I'm not going to make what are possibly entirely unfounded accusations against other people, and I'm not going to betray third persons either. Other people's interests I'm bound to protect. I'm expecting a letter in a day or two that may alter things perhaps, but until then there's nothing I can say beyond what I've told you already. Meanwhile I want you to form your own opinion.'

Bobby felt profoundly dissatisfied, and yet felt it would be only waste of time to press Mr Winterton further at the moment. Later on perhaps. Or Mr Mitchell, or even Major Markham, might be more successful, with their greater weight of authority and standing. But, all the same, he made one more effort.

'Mr Winterton, if you really believe you are in danger from whatever destroyed your brother,' he said, 'you are making the risk much worse if you won't tell us what it is. We can't undertake to protect you from some threat we know nothing about – either its nature or what direction it may come from.'

'I don't know that myself,' Winterton answered, 'only I know – just know, that's all – that Archibald was murdered, and I suppose it may be my turn next. But it mayn't. What happened to Archibald may have nothing to do with me – or it may. Sleeping dogs may lie still; they say it's best to leave them sleeping, but sometimes they won't stay that way themselves. What I told Markham I wanted was someone to try to find out all he could about my brother's death and at the same time to do what he could to see that nothing happened to me. That was what we agreed was to be your duty here.'

'That's all very well,' Bobby grumbled, 'but it's like asking me to make bricks and refusing me not only straw, but clay as well. I shall have to report to my superiors that I can't possibly accept responsibility for guarding against a danger when all information about it is flatly refused.'

Winterton made no reply to this. Bobby, after waiting a moment or two to let his remarks sink in, continued:

'Going back to Mr Archibald's death, have you any idea how murder could have been carried out? I don't quite see at present how murder was possible in the circumstances. It is agreed, I suppose, that his wife and the servants are above suspicion, besides there being the evidence of all of them that none of them left the house that morning. And the children are all quite young, and there were no visitors. It did strike me there might just possibly have been something wrong with the coffee in the thermos flask he took down to the beach with him, but that's hardly likely in the first place, and, in the second, I think the evidence showed it hadn't been touched. It was there unopened with the clothing and dry towels, according to the evidence at the inquest, wasn't it?'

'Yes, that's so,' Winterton agreed.

'Also the dog was there – it's the same one I saw, isn't it? Towser, you call him.'

'Yes, I told you I took him when my sister-in-law moved.'

'He would have been heard barking if any stranger had approached?'

'He would have barked the place down,' Winterton agreed. 'No, I don't know how a murder could have been carried out. But I am sure it was, all the same.'

'I believe a strange motor-launch has been seen in the Cove ...?'

'Oh, that was weeks before,' Winterton answered. 'Careful inquiries were made; it was one of the first things thought about. It was fairly well proved that no strange boat of any kind was anywhere near at the time. It was very fine, calm weather; full moon, too; any strange craft would have been seen.'

'There was an assault on the local constable at the same time, wasn't there?'

Winterton did not answer for a moment, and Bobby was conscious that he was smiling faintly to himself. When he spoke, there was a touch of amusement in his voice:

'Oh, yes,' he said; 'poor Jennings, our wireless expert; yes, he had a sack thrown over his head and was tied up to a tree. Beastly shame. But I daresay he bears no malice.'

Bobby found himself wondering what amused Mr Winterton. Was it merely the idea of an officer of the law having been treated in so undignified a fashion, or was there some local joke behind – some jest that Winterton knew of but did not care to repeat? Or some not-jest, perhaps? Anyhow, apparently, it could not be connected with any foul play that might have taken place, since Archibald Winterton's death had occurred some time later.

Bobby tucked it away in his mind as a point possibly worth consideration later on, but for the moment he felt it would be useless to question his companion more closely. It would be better to wait a little; he might another time be in a more communicative mood, and Bobby, too, might presently have more facts to go on. He tried another line of inquiry.

'You have three nephews, Mr Winterton. There are Mr Colin Ross I met to-night, Mr Miles Winterton, and Mr James Matthews, I think?'

'Yes. What about them?'

'You are on good terms with them all?'

'I caught young Miles flirting with my typist the other day – Miss Raby,' Winterton answered. 'I told him to get out; I wasn't going to have that sort of thing going on. I didn't want him to play the fool with her or go marrying a girl whose father's a railway porter or something like that. She's a clever girl and all that, excellent typist and a great help, and a really remarkable *flair* for crosswords. But I don't want her for a niece.'

'I see,' said Bobby, deciding that it might be worth while to look up Mr Miles's record and recent movements. 'There was no ill feeling between him and Mr Archibald, I suppose?'

'Oh, dear, no. The boys generally stay with me because I've more room at my place than Archy has – had. And then his wife was a little inclined to be strict in some of her ideas; liked early hours and so on. But if they generally stayed at Fairview, they were often over at Archy's place during the day.'

'And Mr James Matthews?' Bobby asked.

'Oh, he's in Paris; he has a studio there; does all his work in Paris. We only see him occasionally; he hasn't been over since Christmas, I believe. If he can make a living painting, it's all right, but I'm not going to support him.'

'He has asked you for money?'

'Well, he's always wanting me to buy his pictures. I don't pretend to know much about art, but I do know what I like, and I told him I wouldn't touch his stuff with a barge pole. Archy took one or two things. I wanted to know which was right side up, and James had the cheek to say a pattern remained a pattern whether you stood on your head or your heels. I told him he had better get back to the city where you always stand on your heels. But he has a little money of his own, and so long as that lasts I expect he'll go on with his painting. If you ask me, he's no taste for work.'

'Mr Colin Ross seems very interested in racing?'

'Makes a business of it,' Winterton said. 'I think he's a fool to waste his time like that. But he's of age and his own master.'

'Do you know if he has lost money? Has he tried to borrow any, for example?'

'He didn't get it – not from me. Archy lent him some, I believe, but it was paid back all right.'

'He owed none, then, at the time of the accident?'

'Murder,' corrected Winterton grimly. 'You don't believe it now, but you will.'

And this prophecy he uttered was one that Bobby was destined to recall upon a certain occasion now not far away.

'Can you tell me,' he asked, 'where all your three nephews were at the time – it – happened?'

'Miles was in London. He had gone up to see Frazer's, the big contract people. Miles is a P.W. man – public works, that is – you know. Frazer's have promised him a job at Liverpool, but they won't be starting for some time yet. Colin was attending some race-meeting somewhere. I don't remember which, but whatever racing was on that date, he would be there. James was in Paris, I suppose. He didn't come over for the funeral; laid up with a cold or influenza, I think it was.'

'None of them had any expectation of benefiting under Mr Archibald's will?'

'They each had a small legacy of two hundred and fifty, duty free. That's all. Most of his money went to his wife and the children, naturally.'

'May I ask about your own will?'

'Well,' Winterton answered, a little slowly, a little uncomfortably, and yet evidently feeling the question was one that ought to be answered, 'I suppose the fact is, I ought to make a new one. I've been meaning to for long enough, but I've kept putting it off. When my brother and I started in business, we made wills leaving everything we had to each other. That seemed fair at the time, because of our business relations when the death of one might have ruined the other. Archy made a new will, of course, when he got married. I ought to have made a new one, too, but I kept putting it off.'

'Do you think your nephews know about that?'

'They might; I don't suppose so; they may perhaps. I've never said anything about it, and of course they haven't either.'

'In the event of anything happening to you, then,' Bobby said slowly, 'I take it the will would be void, the person to whom you left your property having died before you?'

'I don't know; I hadn't thought of that,' Winterton answered. 'No, I think the lawyer who drew them up for us put in something about the money going to heirs and assigns. I think I remember now. We both wanted to avoid any intestacy; there was a relative we were on bad terms with at the time. We wanted to make sure he didn't cut in. But he's been dead these twenty years or more.'

'Then I take it that means none of your nephews stand to benefit by your will unless you make a fresh one?'

'You mean, perhaps, I had better not make one just now?' Mr Winterton asked.

'That is for you to decide, sir,' Bobby answered gravely.

From where they were standing the village and the road leading from it to Fairview were plainly visible. Hitherto, the electric lights had been shining along the road and in the windows of some of the cottages, but now they all went out together. Mr Winterton gave a little laugh.

'That's Mrs Cooper,' he said, 'and half past ten by her kitchen clock. She thinks no one in the village ought to want a light after then, and no one at all ought to be out of doors any later. So out go the lights. She would like to do the same thing for Fairview, too, I daresay, but I drew the line there. Well, shall we go back now?'

It was a question that made Bobby feel not quite certain that Mr George Winterton was not rather more subject to the authority of his housekeeper's clear, direct mind than he himself either realised or would ever have acknowledged. For indeed there are so few of us who really know what we want that the influence of a mind and will that does is often very great. Without waiting for a reply, Mr Winterton began to walk back towards the house, and when they had gone a yard or two they heard someone calling. Mr Winterton paused.

'That's Cooper,' he said; 'he's calling the dog.'

'Towser?' Bobby asked.

'Yes; he can't have got back. Funny; he never goes far from the house alone.'

They both stood still and listened. Again they heard the call, and this time the name 'Towser' was quite clear. It was a woman's voice, and it sounded very clear and a little strange, a long-drawn, wailing cry.

'That's Mrs Cooper now,' Winterton said. 'I wonder what can have happened to the dog?' He shivered slightly. 'Come on,' he said; 'it's growing cold.'

CHAPTER VII

The Shorton Scheme

THERE was one other point on which Bobby wished enlightenment, but he had been careful to leave it till the last, for he was not quite sure how any mention of it would be received.

They were hurrying a little now, for Mr Winterton had increased his pace as they returned along the rough path that ran by the shore of the Cove, and Bobby was indeed inclined seriously to believe that his host was being subconsciously affected by his housekeeper's expressed disapproval of late hours and late rambles. A born ruler, organiser, director of men and things, Mrs Cooper seemed, he told himself, and then he said aloud:

'Mr Winterton, there's one thing I would like to mention, if I may. Very likely it's of no importance, but when I reached your house to-day I couldn't very well help hearing ... it was a Mr Shorton, I think, and he seemed very upset about something.'

'Little bounder,' Winterton answered. 'He thinks he's badly used; got a grievance and all that. Not my fault; it was all his own doing; and, as Archy's executor and trustee till the kids come of age, I wouldn't think of going against his wishes, even if I wanted to, which I don't.'

'It was something your brother was concerned in – something that happened before his death? Have you any objection to telling me the details? Anything that can throw light on any detail connected with him might be useful.'

'There's no reason why you shouldn't know all about it, I suppose,' Winterton answered, though with some slight apparent reluctance. 'Anyhow, it's no secret; you could easily find out all about it if you wanted to. Sometimes old business friends used to come down here to stay with one or other of us. Archy and I both liked to keep in touch with the City, and a week-end by the sea sounds all right to most City men, so most of them were willing enough to run down here now and again. Shorton, the man you saw, came once or twice. He took a fancy to the place, and got out a scheme for developing it into an up-to-date resort. The idea was to build a big seaside golfing hotel, rather on the lines of Gleneagles in Scotland, only not quite so swell; rather more for the fairly well-to-do business man, the class that's prepared to spend fifty pounds on a holiday or a fiver on a week-end now and again. Shorton said there was a big market there. On the Point itself there is what is very nearly a natural golf-course. A little expenditure would make it one of the best in the world. Suffby Cove itself would make a splendid swimming-pool. Shooting rights were to be bought over land near, and there would be lots of fishing and boating, and, of course, a first-class jazz band and a good dance-floor; even an ice-rink was thought of. Shorton was quite enthusiastic; swore it would be a gold-mine. Archy didn't see it that way. More did I. It was a promising enough scheme on paper, but you can never tell if that sort of thing will catch on, and we didn't feel sure we could compete with the big seaside places. And we didn't much wants crowds of holiday-makers and trippers swarming all over the very place we had come to for quiet and peace. My sister-in-law liked it still less; hated it, in fact. We all felt if the scheme went through we should have to leave, and we weren't so sure as Shorton was that there was big money in it. Anyhow, the money wouldn't begin to come in for years, and we were neither of us so young we could afford to wait years for results. So we came down flat against it. Shorton argued we couldn't possibly lose. He said the public would subscribe the money if we got out an attractive prospectus. If the thing was a failure, the public would stand the racket, and if it was the success Shorton expected – well, naturally there would be lots of cream for us, as the promoters, to skim off before we passed on the rest of the profits. Of course, we knew all that already.'

'Of course,' murmured Bobby, though a little startled by this side-light on the workings of the Limited Liability Act.

'The more we thought of it,' Winterton went on, 'the less we liked it. We had found Suffby; we were nicely settled and quite comfortable; it suited us very well; we felt a big hotel planted down like that, next door almost, would spoil the place for us altogether. I shouldn't have had much peace for getting on with my book. Shorton's an obstinate little devil, and he really had got it into his head that the scheme promised big money. He had got others interested, too. When we told him we didn't like it, he got huffy, and said it would go on all the same. He had it all worked out. He had arranged for a motor-bus service; he had an idea for collecting guests, free, gratis, and for nothing, from their homes, and bringing them direct to the hotel in a big Rolls-

Royce with a chauffeur in livery. As he said, people do love to think they are getting something for nothing, and you can always make them pay through their noses afterwards. Archy saw it was serious. We arranged that I was to let Shorton talk. I wasn't to commit myself, but I was to let him talk, and he could think what he liked from my being ready to listen and promising to consider his figures. Meanwhile Archy made inquiries. He found Shorton had already bought up a lot of land, and had options on more. He had bought nearly all Suffby Point, except, of course, the house Archy occupied and its garden. He didn't want them. The site of the hotel was to be almost next door, and I suppose he reckoned that when Archy had had enough he would be willing to sell, and the house would come in nicely as an annex. But by this time rumours were getting about, and one man who had two fields reaching right across the Point was holding out for a big price. Shorton thought he was being had, and that put his back up. He had an option on the fields, but by way of a bluff he let it run out. He calculated that would make the owner of the fields come down. But Archy was watching. The option ran out at twelve one day, and at one o'clock Archy bought those two fields. When Shorton found out, he was furious. He called Archy a blackmailer. Archy said all right, now he wouldn't sell those two fields for the amount of the American debt. He couldn't close the fields altogether, for there was a right of way along the cliffs, but he said he would put up a corrugated iron fence twelve feet high all round them, with an iron turnstile for admission to the right of way path, and he would prosecute anyone for trespass who left the path by as much as a yard, and what would become of Shorton's precious golf-course then, and who would go to an hotel you could only get at through an iron turnstile? So then there was another row, but Archy was within his rights, and a good many people sympathised with him. There was quite a general feeling that Archy was putting up a public-spirited fight to protect the amenities of the peaceful countryside against London exploiters, and that he was saving the simple fisher-folk from corruption – not so much simple about the fisherfolk if you ask me. It was generally felt that if Shorton had chosen to sink a lot of money in his scheme, well, that was his affair. If he was going to drop a packet, he had done it all himself, and he had had plenty of warning. Then poor Archy was drowned. I heard Shorton had the indecency to send out for champagne when he knew. I was told he drank a toast to "the North Sea, and may its tides never grow less." He said that wasn't true when he came to see me, but anyhow it put my back up pretty thoroughly. He had got a notion, from the way I listened to him, that I was quite in favour of the idea. He had been to see Mrs Archy – who hadn't heard the champagne story – and got her consent, and of course the bank, who are co-trustees with me, didn't object, if I were willing. I wasn't. If for nothing else, that champagne story settled it once and for all. And I'm not going against what I know were Archy's wishes. I don't like, any more than he did, the idea of the whole place swarming with summer visitors, and everything turned upside down. When Archy's oldest boy comes of age, he can do what he likes, but till then they can wait – eleven years. Shorton came down again to-day to have another try to get me to change my mind. He thinks I'm trying to squeeze them out to take the thing on myself. That's nonsense; I'm not; but it's what he thinks. He says he's sunk fifty thousand that I'm making him lose. I don't suppose it's as much as that, but I daresay he stands to face a loss. That's his look-out. Finally he offered me all his rights and so on for ten thousand, which may be about what he has really spent. I told him I wouldn't touch it with a barge-pole. Then he began to lose his temper, and you turned up in time to hear the rest of it.'

'Thank you,' said Bobby, who had listened intently, with a certain rising excitement indeed. 'I can quite see it looked a very promising scheme from their point of view, and I can quite see your objections to it. Do you know, I have a sort of idea that the name Shorton is familiar somehow.'

'Perhaps you heard about the rag on the Stock Exchange

over a Channel swimming stunt they got up a year or two ago. The *Daily Announcer* got to know about it, and turned one of their funny men on the story – quite good his articles were. Shorton actually started. He's a first-class swimmer; Archy and he met first on the committee of the City Swimming Club. Of course, he's not up to Channel form, but he got more than half way, and won some money for *Help Yourself* – the Stock Exchange charity annual, you know. Everyone thought he had done very well; he got quite a reception next time he went to the House.'

'He must be a jolly good swimmer,' Bobby remarked. 'I suppose I'm right in saying that your brother's death offered him and his backers – or seemed to – a chance of getting back their money they must have given up as lost?'

'That's just what they did think,' Mr Winterton agreed, 'only they had forgotten me.'

'That,' observed Bobby thoughtfully, 'is just what I am wondering – whether they have forgotten you.'

Mr Winterton stopped abruptly.

'My God,' he said in a shaken voice, 'what do you mean by that?'

The surprise, the sudden agitation in his voice, were sufficient proof to Bobby that, whatever secret fears his companion might have entertained, they had not been inspired by Mr Shorton.

'What do you mean?' he repeated. 'Why do you say that?'

'As I understand it,' Bobby said slowly, 'certain persons have sunk ten thousand pounds – which is a large sum – in a scheme promising, they think, big profits. Only there is an unexpected obstacle in the way – your brother. He dies. The way seems clear again. Then another unexpected obstacle appears – yourself. The scheme is again held up. But please note that I'm drawing no deductions at present. I am simply stating the facts as I understand them to be.'

'But, good God!' Winterton protested, his voice still shaken and astonished. 'Good God!' he said again.

Bobby said nothing. They walked on a few steps, and then once more Winterton halted.

'But Shorton's perfectly well known; business man and all that,' he protested; 'offices in Gracechurch Street. I've been there myself.'

'Yes,' said Bobby.

'City men – business men – don't commit murder.'

'I suppose not,' agreed Bobby; 'it's so seldom necessary in the City. But I have not said anything about murder. I have stated certain facts. It is police duty to consider every fact. Personally, I don't accuse Mr Shorton or anyone else. I am merely here to collect facts and report them to my superior officers. Of course, I quite agree Mr Shorton doesn't in the least look like a murderer, and murder and business are quite different – as different as playing poker and using a poker on someone else's head. The whole technique is so different, isn't it? Naturally you won't attach any importance to what I'm saying. I don't myself. It's only facts that count.'

He made as if to walk on as he spoke, but Winterton did not follow. Very plainly he was still greatly shaken and excited. He was muttering indistinctly to himself, and then he said aloud:

'No, no, you're on the wrong track there.'

'Well, I don't admit that, you know,' Bobby answered pleasantly, 'because I don't admit that I'm on any track at all at present, wrong or right.'

They went on again towards the house, and when they were nearer, Bobby spoke again.

'Now, Mr Winterton,' he said, 'if you don't mind I would like to ask you to switch your mind back once more, entirely forget that I'm police, and even in your thoughts regard me again as an old friend's son. We've chatted a bit about golf during our walk to-night, and I've asked your advice about going on the Stock Exchange. I may have a chance of getting in with Hobbs & Sutcliffe. Jolly good, old-established firm, aren't they?'

'But,' protested Winterton, slightly bewildered, 'that's a real firm. I know them quite well; everyone does.'

'Exactly,' Bobby answered, 'and if you mention to them

that a young fellow, Robert Owen, has been recommended for a job with them, you'll find they know all about it. My chief, Superintendent Mitchell, has arranged that. He knows one of the partners, and there's a letter on file in the office any of the clerks can see, recommending that same Owen, and mentioning your name as an old friend of the family.'

Mr Winterton grunted.

'You do things thoroughly,' he observed.

'At the Yard, sir,' Bobby answered, 'we find we have to. Often everything hangs on detail. In the last case I was employed on, the angle at which a woman wore her hat proved the clue to the whole thing. Now, sir, please forget the Yard and police and just look on me all the time, even in your own thoughts, as the young fellow you are taking an interest in and have been giving advice to.'

'Oh, all right, all right,' Mr Winterton said, rather irritably.

'Especially,' Bobby ventured to add, 'when Mrs Cooper or her husband are about. Mrs Cooper strikes me as the sort of woman who would notice anything at once.'

'I'm not in the habit of talking about things before Mrs Cooper,' retorted Mr Winterton, now plainly vexed, so that Bobby decided it would be prudent to say no more.

They went up the drive, and when they entered the house Mrs Cooper met them in the hall. Mr Winterton greeted her amiably, as if to impress on Bobby that he knew quite well how to deal with her.

'Hullo, hullo, how's this?' he said. 'Not in bed yet? I thought you were always in bed by now.'

'I'm just a little worried about Towser, sir,' she explained. 'We can't find him anywhere. I thought perhaps he might have joined you.'

'No, we've not seen him,' Winterton answered, 'but he'll be all right – gone back to Mr Archibald's place again, perhaps.'

'I thought myself it might be that,' Mrs Cooper said with an appearance of being a good deal relieved to find her employer had the same idea. 'I've put the tray in your room sir, as it's a little late. It's rather damp by the sea, sir, to-night, isn't it? I hope you didn't feel as if it might bring on your rheumatism again?'

'No, no, no, quite all right,' Winterton assured her hastily, and when Mrs Cooper had gone he said to Bobby: 'It has got a bit late – nearly eleven. We keep early hours here, you know; not like London. The youngsters are generally up early for a swim, and that makes a difference, I expect. How do you feel? Like to go up to your room, or would you care for a nightcap and a chat first?'

Bobby declined the suggestion of a 'nightcap' – he never touched spirits if he could help it – expressed entire willingness for bed, and, as he said good night to his host, noticed that the promised thermos flasks and biscuits were ready ranged on a table in the hall. An idea came into his mind; he rejected it; it came back, and he told himself it might be as well to keep it tucked away in his memory. It was not likely that a thermos flask could bear the meaning that had suggested itself to him and yet perhaps it might, and in a thoughtful, troubled mood he went upstairs to his room. The window was wide open this warm night; and as he went across to it he heard once more a low wailing cry floating out across the still water of the Cove. It was Mrs Cooper again, calling for the missing Airedale, and now it seemed there was in fact a certain chilliness in the air, for, as he listened, Bobby found himself shivering a little.

CHAPTER VIII

Thoughts and Reflections

WHEN Bobby went to his room, he made first a few preparations for bed and then sat down by the window with fountain-pen and paper to write out his first report.

But he found himself both with so much to say and so little idea of how to disentangle the significant from the unimportant that presently he put his paper by, returned his fountain-pen to the pocket of the coat for which he had changed his dinner-jacket, and set himself instead to review in his mind all that he had learnt and seen and heard since his arrival.

Of one thing at least he was certain. His host, George Winterton, retired stockbroker, peacefully occupying himself in his retirement with a study of currency theory, on whose brother a strange and sudden death had recently descended, believed that he himself went in deadly imminent peril of a like fate.

For that Mr Winterton's fear was genuine Bobby was by now well convinced. There was no mistaking that look of terror in his eyes, the occasional nervous twitching of his muscles. And the look Bobby had seen him throw after Colin Ross when that young man left the room was just the look Bobby had seen show in other men, when swift terror gripped them and their eyes betrayed it.

It would seem to follow, then, that young Colin was the source of this terror that his uncle was experiencing, and yet it might well not be so. He might merely typify it, or be simply the unconscious channel through which it threatened.

Then, again, why on the one hand did Mr Winterton apply to the authorities for protection, and yet on the other hand refuse to give the information required to make such protection effective? That might mean there was something he felt it was necessary he should keep concealed, but then in that case why had he gone to the police at all? It was true he said something about some letter he was expecting, the receipt whereof would allow him to talk more freely. But that might be mere bluff, a device to keep Bobby quiet and patient. Bobby's own feeling was that Mr Winterton should be told plainly that either he must be entirely frank and open or no help could be given him. On the whole Bobby hoped his superiors would take that view, which for his part he intended to recommend strongly.

Then, again, there was the possibility that the whole thing might be mere hallucination. Mr Winterton's fear might be real enough in itself and yet founded on illusion. In other words, Mr Winterton might not be quite sane on that point. Possibly the shock of his brother's death might have overthrown his mental balance; and yet, even in formulating this theory, Bobby doubted it. More than once already in his police work he had come across cases of insanity, and he had grown to recognise symptoms of it that all seemed to him quite absent from his host, who indeed appeared to him perfectly sane.

But, all the same, it was a possibility to remember; and still, as Bobby gazed now from his open window across the Cove out to the open sea, where a man's life shortly before had left him, he seemed to himself to grow conscious of a sense of threat, of menace somehow, implicit in the scene.

It was as though the Cove, the sea beyond, were waiting for another victim, patiently, calmly, certainly, knowing their hour must come. The feeling came to him that they were watching; watching him perhaps; and so strong did this sensation grow, of secret eyes aware of every movement he made, that he turned to switch off his light that he might be the less easily seen if there was anyone out there watching him, for now this feeling had passed from the vague impersonality of sea and cove to the more concrete idea of some living man or woman hiding out there in the shadows of the garden, or further out by the shore, in order to keep him under observation. Indeed, once he even thought he saw a movement among some bushes at a little distance, but that, he decided, was only his imagination. All the same, he denied himself the solace of a cigarette lest the sight of its glowing tip, or the smell of the burning tobacco, might reveal to any possible watcher that he was still alert and wakeful.

By the open window, then, behind the curtain, he sat quietly, his thoughts very busy. The night was very still; the vague disquiet he had experienced before began to leave him; his sense of reason and of logic woke once more to tell him that it was a thousand to one Archibald Winterton's death was merely one of those unfortunate accidents that darken with their tragedy every bathing season, and that

George Winterton's unease and fear were merely subjective, without reality, a result of the shock he had experienced in losing his brother.

But in that case it followed there was nothing to investigate – no threatening, obscure danger to be guarded against; nothing, in fact, for Bobby to do but enjoy a quiet and peaceful holiday by the sea.

However, that was not his business here, and he supposed his only course was to assume that murder had really been committed, that Mr Winterton was really threatened by some danger or another, that every conceivable line of inquiry must be followed up till his superiors decided they were leading nowhere and withdrew him. Better, evidently, to run no risk through too hasty assumptions of neglecting what might prove in the end to have been a terrible reality.

At any rate, one fact was certain – Archibald Winterton was dead: a little strangely dead, indeed, for there was always the question why an expert, experienced swimmer should drown upon a calm, warm, sunny morning.

Chin resting upon clenched hands, his eyes staring intently into the calm and luminous night, Bobby set himself to consider a solution that had been lying at the back of his mind for some time and that now thrust itself forward. Could it be that George Winterton himself was his brother's murderer? Was that the reason for the strange fear that so evidently had him in its grip? If he himself had called in police aid, was that a result of the restlessness criminals often know that forbids them ever to feel themselves safe, that makes them pile precaution on precaution till the very excess brings about exposure? More than once, even in Bobby's brief experience, he had known criminals themselves take the first steps towards drawing attention to the crimes they had themselves committed.

If George Winterton were himself the murderer, might he have argued that for him to call in the police would be the best means of turning suspicion away?

But, then, the dead man was his brother, and, though fratricide occurs, it is not common, at any rate not without strong motive, and in this case no motive at all was discernible. The two brothers had, it seemed, always been on friendly terms; there was no known cause of quarrel. True, there had been recently large and presumably important financial transactions between them, and in such affairs bitter disputes have been known to arise, but these seemed to have followed a perfectly normal course – though there was always the possibility that more lay behind such dealings than appeared on the surface. Further, there was the evidence of Mr and Mrs Cooper that at the time of the accident or murder, George Winterton was fast asleep in his own bedroom, which seemed conclusive, unless the actual deed had been carried out by an accomplice or unless the evidence of the Coopers was in some way mistaken.

Then there was the little red-haired, angry Mr Shorton. Motive enough was there, apparently, for murder has been done for a smaller cause than the loss or gain of ten thousand pounds – more, indeed; for the scheme Mr Winterton had outlined had obviously very considerable speculative possibilities.

Only it seemed difficult to imagine ordinary City men planning and carrying out a cold-blooded murder. But then Bobby saw he had been using there a question-begging phrase: How did he know Mr Shorton was an ordinary City man? Shorton might be very far from 'ordinary,' and, though murder is foreign to City methods, the temptation to remove a life standing obstinately and irrationally before the realisation of a big scheme involving many interests might prove irresistible to some tempers.

In that case it would follow that George Winterton was now the obstacle in the way, and, if he realised that, then that might prove to be, after all, the cause of these fears he was suffering from.

Then there were the three nephews, and first of all Colin Ross, and the puzzle of the fact that it was he of whom his uncle seemed so fearful. Did that mean, Bobby wondered, that Winterton suspected Colin of being the murderer, and feared to meet the same fate at his hands?

But there again it seemed difficult to imagine any motive. No suggestion, apparently, of any quarrel or ill feeling, nothing that Colin stood to gain in any way by the death of either of his uncles. Rather would he lose, apparently, since Archibald had been willing to lend him money at times, and George, it seemed, provided him with free quarters when he needed them. There was the possibility that he had borrowed from his uncle Archibald more than he could repay, and that he was being pressed for it, but of that there was no tittle of evidence. Undoubtedly a man who was to all seeming an almost professional backer of horses might easily be desperately hard up for money without anyone knowing it, but the death of Archibald brought him no gain, only the loss of a possible source to borrow from.

Then there were the other two nephews, James Matthews and Miles Winterton. Of these, the first had apparently been in Paris at the time of the tragedy. The second, Miles, was, it seemed, in disgrace for having been flirting with Miss Raby, but there was nothing in that to suggest any connection with the murder.

Then there was Miss Raby herself, apparently a harmless little typist-secretary. She seemed intelligent and good-looking and possibly had not been averse to the flirtation that had got Miles Winterton into trouble with his uncle, but there was nothing to suggest she had any connection with the tragedy of Archibald's death. All the same, Bobby decided it would be as well to try to find out something more about her.

Then there were the Coopers, butler and housekeeper. A tragic story, Bobby reflected, it was that he had been told about the woman. No wonder there was something aloof and strange about her, as of one who had experienced more than others ever know. Evidently a woman of much strength of character, too, with abilities and powers at war, so to say, with her environment, and seeking expression in every possible way, as in dominating her employer and the village affairs. Bobby found himself smiling a little as he remembered how she had gently urged her employer bedwards by informing him that the tray with his 'nightcap' – a whisky and soda, probably – had been put in his bedroom, and equally gently had put a stopper on further late rambles she apparently didn't approve of by casual references to chills and damp sea air. Mr Winterton would probably think twice before rambling about late at night again. Yes, a clever woman, and one who might have made something of her life had it not been wrecked by the treachery of the man who had tricked her into a sham marriage. A pity she had been forced to ally herself with her present husband, who did not look as if he had much in him or was ever likely to be anything but a butler.

'I expect she runs him all right, though,' Bobby thought, half smiling; 'if she gets half a chance she may run him into something after all. But I bet he'll never call his soul his own any more, though very likely he doesn't know it.'

In any case, it seemed impossible to think of any motive they could have either for compassing the death of their employer's brother, or for threatening the safety of that employer himself. There was nothing, so far as Bobby could see, that they could hope to gain in either case. If they wanted a change, all they had to do was to give notice and go, though Bobby had a strong suspicion that Mrs Cooper would much prefer to work for a bachelor or for a widower than take a place where there was a mistress. Then, again, if their testimony cleared Mr George Winterton of all suspicion of being concerned in his brother's death, since it proved he was in bed and asleep at the time, it also in a way cleared them as well.

Finally, there were the people in the tiny village with whom Bobby promised to make himself acquainted in the morning, but not a touch or shred of suspicion seemed at present to point towards any of them. Also there were Adams, the chauffeur and gardener, and his wife, who apparently came to the house to help Mrs Cooper with the housework. They occupied a cottage in the village, and it was with them, Bobby gathered, that Miss Raby lodged.

So far as Bobby could see, no reasonable suspicion could

be entertained against any of them. And if it was murder that had been committed in the early hours of that calm spring morning, why had the Airedale made no sound, shown no sign of agitation? It seemed clear proof no stranger or intruder had appeared. Odd, by the way, that to-night the dog was missing, but no doubt it would turn up again all right in the morning.

A clock somewhere in the house struck two. The time had gone quickly for Bobby, absorbed in so many and such baffling thoughts. He yawned and thought of bed, and he was rising slowly to his feet to seek it when he stiffened to quick attention, alert and eager, as he saw a light shine out there in the garden a little distance away, flash out and vanish, and appear again three times in succession.

A signal, evidently, Bobby thought, with a quick sensation of relief that now, it seemed, the time for puzzling, bewildering, baffling thoughts had gone by, and that for action had arrived. With swift and silent movements he turned to his suit-case. There was a false bottom to it, holding one or two things there was no need for any servants' eyes to catch a glimpse of, and one of them was a long, thin, knotted rope of woven silk, very light and strong. One end Bobby made fast with a double hitch to the bed; the other end he let fall gently from the window. It reached very nearly to the ground. The window was wide open, so that fortunately there was no need to raise the sash, and the curtain he had already pulled to one side. Now he swung himself across the sill, and, hand over hand, slid down the rope to the ground beneath.

CHAPTER IX

Nocturnal Interview

In the distance he thought, but was not sure, that he heard a door closing. If so, it must have been either the back door or the garden door leading from Mr Winterton's study. The front door of the house was near where Bobby stood, and no one could have issued from it without his knowledge. Unfortunately, this seaside garden offered very little cover. There were no trees. A few ornamental shrubs would give shelter to anyone crouching behind them, but provided no continuous concealment. The night was clear, too, luminous with the light of the many stars in a sky still cloudless overhead, though in the west heavy storm banks were piling up. It was very quiet, too; even the restless murmur of the sea seemed still, so that every faintest sound was audible instantly for long distances.

Bobby began to understand that, if any secret interview were being held here, the task of approaching unperceived near enough to acquire any useful information was going to be one of extreme difficulty. So far as he could tell, the spot where had shown the light he had imagined to be a signal was about half way between the house and the entrance to the drive. Presumably someone had come up the drive, and half way along it had stopped to flash the light it must have been expected some inmate of the house would be on the look-out for.

Only was this person, whoever it might be, waiting there in the drive, or was he seeking admittance to the house?

Bobby dared not leave the shelter of the shadows that lay by the side of the building. Hugging the wall as closely as he could, he ran to the south-east corner, and thence, swiftly, in a wide circuit, crouching low, upon his hands and knees often, sometimes crawling, he made his way towards the spot where the light had been shown.

A clump of bushes gave him shelter and protection for a few yards, but beyond it lay the open lawn, and now there came to him a sound of footsteps and soon a low, faint murmur of voices. At a little distance, right in the middle of the lawn, he was able to make out the dim shape of two forms standing there, two vague shadows in the night.

Though eagerness consumed him like a fire, though he felt that here almost within his grasp might be the clue to the whole affair, yet he could not see how he could approach even an inch nearer without incurring almost certain discovery. A heart-breaking experience to be held thus, as it were, dangling upon the very edge of knowledge and yet unable to grasp it. A few yards nearer, and the issues of life and death could be determined; he would know the truth of Archibald's death, whether accident or murder; he would learn what danger, if any, threatened the life of the dead man's brother.

Impotent, he raged internally, and yet knew he must control himself. One incautious movement and any hope would be gone of bringing murder to justice, if murder there had been, or of giving the protection he claimed to a threatened man, if indeed he were threatened. The truth was there perhaps, almost certainly, and yet how to reach it across this bare expanse of closely shaven lawn, in this still night air, when he feared even the ticking of his wrist-watch might be heard, so loud it seemed in that tremendous silence?

The idea came to him to end the suspense, to show himself, to demand of these two who they were, and what was the meaning of their nocturnal interview. But if he did that he would have to give his authority, and so disclose his own identity, and that would be to go against his instructions. Besides, they would very likely refuse to answer, or answer falsely, and he would be no further forward, and they would be warned.

Yet he felt it was imperative to ascertain who and what they were. To let this nocturnal visitor slip away without finding out all about him would be abject failure. Bobby felt that if that happened he would never dare face Mitchell again.

Crouching there, watching intently but able to make out only two almost formless shadows, straining his ears to catch every sound but able to hear only a low, indistinguishable murmur, consumed with the devouring impatience of his helplessness, Bobby tore at his mind with almost physical effort to wrench from it some practicable course of action. An incautious movement he made – it was hardly more than the angry straightening of his arm, as if to seize by the throat the problem that baffled him – appeared to attract the attention of those he watched, for at last two words that were audible came to his hearing, as one of them exclaimed:

'What's that?'

He lay very still. He held his breath. He would have stilled the beating of his heart had that been possible. He turned the face of the wrist-watch he was wearing against the grass in an effort to smother its boisterous ticking. Apparently reassured, the two on the lawn began their colloquy again, and Bobby was not sure, but thought he heard a rustling sound, as of paper being handled. He wondered if that meant that money was passing from one to the other.

Very carefully and cautiously he began to withdraw, abandoning as hopeless any idea of drawing near enough to be able to overhear what was being said or to have any chance of recognising the speakers. One of the shrubs behind which he was sheltering he saw move suddenly, and then he heard a rustling sound coming from it. For a moment he almost imagined someone else must be hidden there, watching like himself. Then he saw it was a prowling cat, busy on its own occasions, and he instantly resolved to make it a sacrifice to his needs. He found a clod of earth and flung it with force and good aim. The startled animal scampered away, fortunately taking its course across a corner of the lawn close by the two who were talking there. Startled in their turn by the animal's sudden rush, they jumped apart, and then, realising that it was only a cat, resumed their talk, while, profiting by their distraction, Bobby hurriedly retreated. Any slight noise he made now he hoped would be attributed to the wandering cat, and be disregarded, and, running and crouching from shelter to shadow, from shadow to shelter, he made his way to the entrance to the drive.

The gate was half open, and he hurried through. The wrist-watch he was wearing had a luminous dial, and, not without a pang of regret at the sacrifice he was making, he took it off, and let it fall gently by the wayside, making sure that the luminous dial faced towards the entrance to the drive, so that anyone coming out could hardly fail to notice the watch as it lay there.

This done, he ran back lightly through the gate and looked about for a place of concealment. The best that he could find was an angle of the garden wall at a little distance, where at any rate a shadow fell.

There he took his post, and was hardly in position when he heard footsteps coming down the drive – a light, rapid, almost running step, as though whoever came was in haste. A moment later a swiftly hurrying, shadowy form became dimly visible, and in a moment was gone, passing with the same secret speed. All Bobby could make out was that it was someone of no great height or size, wrapped in a cloak or long, loose coat. He thought it might be a woman, but was not sure.

Whoever it was passed quickly through the gate. Bobby left his corner in the shadows and was just in time to see the unknown pause to pick up his watch from where he had left it by the wayside and then hurry on; becoming soon lost in the night which now, Bobby noticed, was growing darker as the clouds spread overhead.

Slowly, still taking every precaution against being seen or heard, Bobby made his way back to the house. Which of the inmates was it, he asked himself again and again, who had taken part in this secret colloquy of the night, and what, he wondered still more, had been its purpose? His thoughts turned again to the strange motor-boat reported seen in the Cove shortly before Archibald Winterton's death. Had it appeared again, and was this a messenger of some sort landed from it that he had seen? And, if so, was some equally tragic *dénouement* portended?

And who had been the other party to the interview?

George Winterton himself? His nephew, Colin Ross? Or one of the Coopers, perhaps; either Mrs Cooper or her husband? Which of the four?

Bobby was near the house now, though still going slowly and with as infinite a precaution to every step, almost, as if the whole garden were full of hidden watchers it was necessary to avoid. He heard a door shut. This time the sound was quite plain. The next moment he saw lights go up in that room to the right of the front door which he knew was George Winterton's study.

The light remained on for two or three minutes, and then was extinguished, and to Bobby it seemed clear evidence that the second party to the interview he had just witnessed must have been Mr Winterton himself. Any other inmate of the house might easily have made use of the study door for secretly leaving the house, but only Winterton himself, familiar with the room and no longer thinking secrecy essential since his own presence in his room would hardly require any special explanation except sleeplessness, would have been likely to switch on the light. He indeed might have done it automatically, finding himself in his familiar surroundings. No one else would have been likely to do it at all.

'Only what's he up to?' Bobby asked himself wonderingly and doubtingly, and with resentment wondered, too, how he was supposed to be able to protect from an unknown danger a man who indulged in these nocturnal and secret excursions.

'Might easily have found him there in the morning in the middle of the lawn with his head knocked in and a knife in his back,' Bobby thought discontentedly, 'and then, of course, I should be told I had failed.'

He made his way, still with the same caution and care, to the study door. There might be footprints there, possibly, he thought, or he might make some other useful discovery.

But in the darkness, now growing more intense all the time as the oncoming clouds obscured the stars, there was little chance of that. A drop or two of rain was already falling, and Bobby decided it was time he returned to his room by the means by which he had quitted it. Turning the corner of the house again, he was just in time to hear, rather than see, the front door closing, and then, as he stood and listened, he heard its bolts cautiously pushed into place.

It seemed, then, there had been another wanderer in the garden, another witness to the secret meeting that had just concluded, and who could that have been, and what his motive?

Colin Ross? Cooper? Mrs Cooper? Or was it possible, some other person altogether?

And had this further unknown been aware of Bobby's presence, or had he been as ignorant of that as Bobby had been of his? Unpleasant to reflect that, while he had been so intent and careful in his watch, another might have been as carefully and intently watching him. It was not comforting to think that perhaps every movement he had made had been spied upon and was known – but to whom?

Troubled and worried, Bobby made his way back to the spot where the rope still dangled from his window. He was a little relieved to find it still in position; he had been half afraid it might be gone. He climbed up easily enough, and was scarcely in his room when heavy rain began. His intention had been to keep watch and vigil to see if any mysterious motor-boat came gliding into the Cove to take off any emissary it had landed. But this darkness that had now come on, and the heavy rain like a falling curtain, made all observatiom impossible, as it also, Bobby hoped, would make the always difficult navigation of the Cove quite impossible. The wind was getting up, too, and it was plain that any footprints or tracks left in the garden would be soon obliterated. So, as there was nothing else to do, Bobby went to bed, to sleep and dream of his lost wrist-watch and the small chance there was of his ever seeing it again.

KEY WORD: 'GOLD'

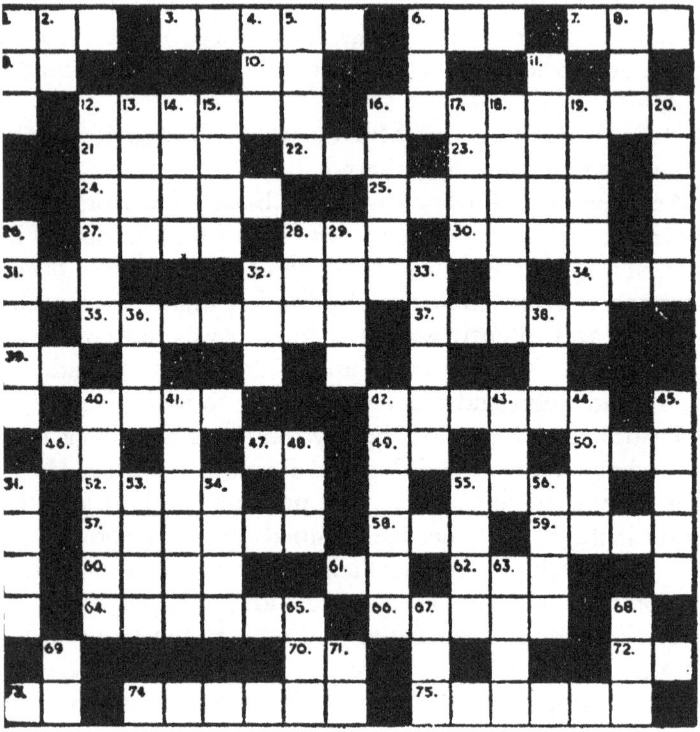

CLUES TO CROSSWORD PUZZLE

ACROSS

1 The End: strike it

3*Some say Lord This cost US U.S.

6*Better, said Sydney Smith, live in a cottage with this than in a palace without it

7 '—— was I weary when I toiled at thee'

9 Add to 2 down to make a goddess

10 A Chinaman's first name sometimes
12 Here lived a great emperor after his abdication
16 Poet's epithet for an aeroplane doubtless
21 A rum name for a flower
22 Liberty? Oh, the reverse. Equality? Certainly. Fraternity? A sign of
23 Here cook and P.C. meet, so say the comic writers
24 Straits with a masculine beginning
25 Once had many wives, now he's wiser
27 Association with apples – and soap
28 Palindrome. But is it a girl's name or a town in Europe?
30 When Sir Ralph the Bold was hurt in a this, it was a 37 across who was called for
31 Pray in Latin
32 Prickly. But sometimes you need it stiff and straight
34 High toned, this
35 Donkey's dinner: not yours, I hope
37 See 30 across
39 Sounds like a number, but isn't one, anyhow
40 One needs this in life but not in an engine
42 Good eating, these
46 The boxer's hope – and dread
47 This is just simply It
49 ' "Charge, Chester, charge, ——, Stanley, ——" Were the last words of Marmion'
50 'Here? No, look there' (Hidden, but if help is needed try a glass of effervescence)
52 A poet's woe: a merchant's joy: fire! fire!!
55 Ah, that was before the motor age
57 A little affects all, the Scripture says
58 Another palindrome, but ask the Poet Laureate
59 These came in March, as Cæsar knew
60 Ireland in a muddle, as usual
61 Seems a busy insect has lost its tail, though it never had one
62 Initials of a great country
64 One must walk before one runs, they say, but one must this before one walks
66 Very silly to fall into one of these
70 Printer's measure
72 We must learn to say this, the wise tell us
73 And in life, how often we have cause to say this
74*'——, take care, she is fooling thee.'
75*Good gracious, I hope you aren't this

DOWN

1*Mr John Ball (the late) wanted very much to know who was the gentleman when Adam this: use present tense and modern form

2 Add to 9 across to make a goddess

4 The colours this when the thing was washed

5 Just as 47 across is simply It, so this is That

6 Initials of terror to a Russian; but the little dog seems to have got its tail in front

8 Initials of a Society, very learned and apparently very antiquated

11 The Provost of this college should put it in order: look how the window projects

12 Add a man's name to a kitchen utensil to make a boat

13 Hills of France

14 If you add a tic to this, you get a lunatic, obviously

15 Sounds as if a Persian poet wants his mother badly

16 You have certainly two or three or even more of these (reversed)

17 Anyhow, can't well be more than the whole

18 Ladies and judges go fine in this

19 A prophet in a muddle apparently, or is he trying to hide himself from the king's anger?

20*Nothing can go faster, yet never wins a race

26*Those who can go this in winter to seek the sun

28 What would the crossword puzzle maker do without this useful animal?

29 A this of ham and eggs is a welcome sight to a hungry man

32 Christopher was a tinker, the bard tells us

33 Hard rock: has to do with the fairy folk

36 When thick, the boxer's hall-mark

38 You this if you will, they say. Hum!

40 It would be tame merely to drink from this, quaff instead

41 Far, far from the restless sea

42*Where the naughty child stands, but don't this wheat, please

43 What would they say in the tea shop if you asked for two boiled this?

44 This time comes before harvest

45*The snail carries his on his back

48*Economical Romans used one letter for this

51*When a policeman's, the subject of much wit

53 A very modern prefix

54 Well, this is a backward plunge

55 '—— the Joiner': you will be this in bed to-night, I hope

56 Sounds like those ladies wear, but are quite different, really

63 This is only half

65 Always in poetry

67 Hot this is what one often thinks the politician deals in

68*It is pleasant when the friendly Cockney gives you his this

69*Why, here's the Foreign Office for a change reversing not its policy but itself

71 Well, anyhow, not you

N.B.—Clues marked with a star require further consideration as being either too obvious or not obvious enough. Attention to them, Attention.

CHAPTER X

The Crossword Puzzle

In the morning the wind had fallen, but there was still rain, though less heavy than during the night, and Bobby had to give up the idea of the early swim he had been looking forward to.

When he went down to the breakfast-room he found the atmosphere there, too, distinctly on the stormy side. Colin Ross was looking sulky over a plate of ham and eggs to which, nevertheless, he was doing full justice; Miss Raby, just arrived from the cottage where she lodged, was looking slightly scared; and Mr Winterton, the morning paper in his hand, was delivering a passionate harangue on the general critical condition of world affairs and the imminent danger of civilisation collapsing into a Bolshevist chaos. Bobby's entry made but the slightest diversion. Miss Raby, it is true, looked a trifle relieved, as if hoping his appearance would serve to check her employer's excited eloquence. But Colin nodded only the briefest and curtest of greetings, and Mr Winterton scarcely interrupted his flow of general denunciation to wish Bobby good morning and wave him to a seat.

'As I was saying ...' He continued his lurid prophecies. 'Universal confiscation,' he declared, 'that's what it comes to; seize everything you possess, from your wife to your last pair of trousers, that's their game. Nationalise everything; put it in their own pockets, they mean. Well, they'll find some of us have taken our precautions.'

'What precautions, uncle?' asked Colin, through a mouthful of ham.

It was a simple question enough; natural, too, Bobby thought; and yet it shut down Mr Winterton's passionate discourse like a hand clapped upon his mouth. He even went a little pale; he peeped at his nephew over the top of his paper, and then suddenly turned his attention to the toast and grumbled that it was burnt, which wasn't true.

Taking advantage of the pause, Bobby told of the loss of his wrist-watch.

'Must have happened while we were out last night,' he said, addressing his host and thinking to himself that the remark was strictly accurate – more accurate than Mr Winterton would guess.

Mr Winterton and the other two expressed a conventional concern. Colin remarked there wouldn't be much left of any watch left out in such rain as they had had during the night, and he said this with a touch of malice, so that Bobby was again aware of an underlying hostility he had thought before he perceived in the young man's attitude.

It was a point to remember, he told himself, for he did not see that, on the face of it, his appearance in his ostensible character of a passing visitor should have disturbed Colin at all. Was it, he wondered, that Colin had some suspicion of his real character and of the true capacity in which he was present, and, if so, did that hint at a guilty conscience?

Miss Raby remarked that they were all very honest folk in the village, and if the watch were found it would certainly be restored. Bobby said he valued it greatly; he would willingly offer two or three pounds' reward to get it back (but would the almost sub-human niggards who checked expense-lists pass a reward like that for a watch that had only cost as much?). To explain the liberality of the reward, Bobby remarked that the watch was a present (and, indeed, the shopkeeper who had sold it him had described that process as 'simply giving it away'), and Miss Raby observed that for the chance of earning such a reward every boy and girl in the neighbourhood would search every square inch of beach and shore.

'You think you dropped it on the beach?' she asked.

'Well, all I can say for certain,' Bobby answered with scrupulous accuracy, 'is that I was wearing it when Mr Winterton and I went out for a stroll, and when I was getting ready for bed I found I hadn't it.'

With that the subject dropped, though Bobby could not help wondering, as he addressed his considerable energies to the excellent ham and eggs before him, and to the equally excellent coffee, evidently made by someone who had taken the trouble to learn how, whether that missing watch of his was not at this very moment reposing safely in Miss Raby's handbag.

For the more he thought about that figure he had seen slipping so swiftly by him down the drive, the more he was inclined to believe it had been a woman's. And, if a woman, was it not most likely Miss Raby herself? So far as he knew at present, there was no one else in the neighbourhood with whom the unknown could reasonably be identified. There was, no doubt, the possibility that it had been someone landed from a motor-boat repeating its former visit. But that did not seem very probable to Bobby, though also he found it difficult to imagine why a secretary, who had unlimited opportunities of private talks with her employer during the day, should come for a secret interview with him in the middle of the night.

Glancing round the table – spread as it was with the bountiful breakfast of the well-to-do English, bright and gay with flowers, with freshly laundered linen, and shining, polished silver – he thought how typical it was of an ordered, prosperous, established civilisation that one could hardly conceive would ever pass away. Yet, to judge by Mr Winterton's harangue, that civilisation was threatened by an immediate collapse he judged it necessary to take secret and hidden precautions against; so secret and so hidden, indeed, that he found even the least reference to them by his nephew oddly disconcerting.

Were those precautions, Bobby asked himself, the source of the hidden danger he thought threatened him?

And of the four of them sitting there, busy with their breakfast, exchanging trivial remarks, how many had spent at least part of the night before, wandering about in the darkness outside on strange and doubtful errands? He himself had, for one; and Mr Winterton for another; since to

Bobby's mind at least the evidence of the light turned up in the study seemed sufficient proof of identity. That whoever had re-entered the house by the front door was Colin Ross was at least conceivable; and Bobby was still inclined to the belief that the second party to that odd colloquy on the lawn had been Mary Raby. Yet who, seeing them all sitting there, could have dreamed that doubt and mystery sat with them, that the dark form of murder hovered threateningly in the background, as yet uncertain whether to pass away as an unreal dream or to materialise into a dreadful actuality of the past – perhaps of the future, too?

Mr Winterton had been very quiet after his nephew's apparently simple question, but now he began to talk again, still on the same theme – of the imminent danger of revolution, of the approaching chaos, of the necessity of being prepared for it (he did not use the word 'precaution' again). None of the others said very much. It was not Bobby's business to discuss politics. Miss Raby did not appear much interested, but, possibly in fulfilment of her secretarial duties, made occasionally vague sounds that might have been meant for agreement – or anything else. Colin's only comment was to the effect that he would jolly well like to see any Government, red or white or any other colour, interfere with racing, and, for the rest of it, he didn't give two hoots; one Government was as bad as another.

'You'll care two hoots,' retorted his uncle, 'when the smash comes. Look at the state of our finances. Bits of printed paper driving out good honest gold. But it won't be so long before the paper will just be good for what paper is good for – lighting fires. But gold's always gold; and people will be glad enough to come back to it some day.'

'Government will be confiscating it most likely,' Colin observed.

'If they can find it,' retorted Mr Winterton. 'They can't search every house in the country or dig up every garden, can they?'

No one tried to answer this conundrum. To change the subject – for Bobby was privately growing a little tired of threatened chaoses and the merits of the gold standard – he asked if the Airedale had returned yet. Neither Mr Winterton nor Colin had inquired, and Miss Raby had not heard of the dog's disappearance. Cooper entering at that moment with the fresh supplies of ham and eggs necessitated by the gross under-estimate made of Bobby's appetite, was appealed to, and answered that nothing so far had been seen of the missing animal. Mrs Cooper, indeed, had already, in spite of the early hour and the rain, been down to the village to inquire if it had been seen there, but had learnt nothing. She was getting quite worried, and was beginning to be afraid something must have happened.

'She's got quite taken up with the dog,' Cooper explained, 'and felt so safe like with him around, knowing the way he barks at any stranger, and it is queer he hasn't come for his food.'

'Oh, the brute'll turn up all right,' Winterton answered.

'Yes, sir, I hope so, sir, I'm sure, if only to stop Mrs C. worrying,' Cooper answered as he retired.

Bobby applied himself with thoughtful diligence to his new helping of ham and eggs. Was it only a coincidence, he wondered, that the dog, with its reputation for announcing so loudly the presence of any stranger, had vanished just before that interview on the lawn of which he had been a witness – and not a solitary witness, either, to judge from that closing front door he had caught a glimpse of? But, then, that would go to suggest he was wrong in identifying the second participant in it with Miss Raby, since apparently the dog never barked at anyone it knew, only at strangers. A little dispiritedly Bobby told himself the thing was getting too complicated for a comparative novice like himself. He wished Mitchell were at hand, so that he might consult him. The Superintendent, with his greater experience, might be able to detect some co-ordinating link of which up to the present Bobby could make out no faintest trace.

Colin, having finished his breakfast, got up with the remark that there were a lot of figures he wanted to go through that morning. A good racing man had to be a good mathematician, he announced, though ignorant that there he was establishing a connection between the good racing man and the latest fashionable conception of Divinity. As he was leaving the room he added over his shoulder:

'No chance of you changing your mind about buying Butter and Eggs I suppose, uncle?'

'No, not a scrap,' snapped Mr Winterton, and Colin scowled and shrugged his shoulders and retired without another word.

Mr Winterton, muttering something ill-temperedly to himself, followed, and Bobby, left alone with Miss Raby, said to her in a somewhat surprised tone:

'Butter and Eggs? I had no idea Mr Winterton did business like that.'

Miss Raby laughed a little.

'Oh, that's only a racehorse Mr Ross wants Mr Winterton to go shares with him in buying,' she explained. 'He's always wanting to buy racehorses, and Mr Winterton never will.'

'I suppose he would like a stable of his own,' Bobby remarked. 'Has he got any horses?'

'Just one or two,' Miss Raby answered; 'at least, I think so. He was telling us the other day that if he had enough capital he would soon get together the best stable in the world. He knows an awful lot about racing and horses and things.'

Bobby asked one or two more questions, but Miss Raby, apparently afraid she was being guilty of gossiping about her employer's relatives, would say no more, discovering that it was time to begin work and that Mr Winterton was probably now waiting for her, ready to dictate another chapter calling on mankind to cling to gold as the one sure rock and refuge in a tumultuous sea of varying exchanges.

So she vanished, and Bobby lit a cigarette and walked to the window. The rain had almost stopped now, and he decided to go out and make the inquiries for his wrist-watch he was anxious to begin in the village. He went into the hall, and saw coming down the stairs Mr Winterton, who stopped to tell him he must amuse himself as best he could.

'Come into the study,' he said, 'and I'll give you a guide-book that'll tell you about one or two interesting places near here. There's a good map, too, if you're fond of walking, and of course you can get a boat in the village if you like. Are you fond of fishing?'

Bobby said there was nothing he liked better, though he did not know much about the deep-sea variety. Once he had spent three gorgeous days upon a salmon river and had caught two big fish, as well as a superb cold and a ducking when he went head first into a deep pool he only knew was there when he found himself five feet under water. Mr Winterton chuckled at this reminiscence, capped it with another, and then led the way into the study, where they found Miss Raby sitting at her typewriter, and looking severe because the chapter she had been expecting to type was not ready.

'The fact is,' confessed Mr Winterton, 'I spent all the time you were up in London busy working at that crossword puzzle I was trying to make up. The wretched thing won't come right.'

'Perhaps I could help,' Miss Raby suggested. 'I got an order for twelve more last night from the *Daily Announcer*,' she added with a touch of pride.

'I've never tried to make one up,' Bobby observed. 'I suppose it's jolly difficult?'

'I expect it's more practice than anything else,' Miss Raby answered.

Mr Winterton was taking some half-sheets of paper covered with words and letters in squared spaces from a drawer he had unlocked. He hesitated for a moment and looked at Bobby, as if debating what to do, and then handed him what seemed a nearly completed crossword.

'Take any interest in crosswords?' he asked. 'Have a look at that one.'

Bobby took the paper with a show of interest he did not

altogether feel. He noticed that there were a great many blank spaces, that the blanks did not seem to be arranged in any pattern, that the words were apparently all very short. He looked idly down the list of clues and read a few of them. Some of them seemed more than obvious, he thought; almost childish, indeed. He noticed that several were marked with an asterisk, and that the asterisk apparently referred to a note to the effect that clues marked with it required revision and attention.

'Looks jolly interesting,' he said, with all the enthusiasm he could muster for something that in reality did not interest him in the least.

'Perhaps you'll find it so some day,' Mr Winterton said enigmatically.

He took the paper back from Bobby and put it away carefully with the other papers he had taken from the drawer, in a pocket-book he placed with equal care in the breast pocket of the coat he was wearing. Miss Raby, watching him, repeated her offer of help, with some remark to the effect that often just changing a letter or two made all the difference, but he shook his head.

'No, no, I'll work it out myself,' he said with emphasis.

'Is it a new kind of crossword, sir?' Bobby asked. 'I noticed it was headed: "Key word, Gold." Crosswords haven't a key word generally, have they?'

'This one has,' Mr Winterton answered. 'I suppose in a way it is a new kind. The clues I've marked are what need attention though. If ever you try to work it out, don't forget that – and don't give up too soon.'

'No, sir,' promised Bobby, though a little bewildered by the earnestness with which had been delivered what seemed a very trivial injunction.

He lingered a little in the room, hoping something more would be said. But Winterton and his secretary plunged into a discussion of a recent pamphlet on the importation of gold, part of the argument of which was to be criticised in a new chapter of 'Justification of the Gold Standard,' and presently Bobby took his guide-book and departed for the village – if that is indeed not too big a name for the tiny collection of houses clustered about the mouth of the creek where it emptied itself into Suffby Cove.

Most of the men were away at their various occupations, fishing or working on neighbouring farms, but a few were busy with their boats or nets, or with nothing at all, on the beach. Bobby soon got talking to them, and told his tale of his lost wrist-watch for whose recovery he promised a couple of pounds reward. Nor was it without a pang of conscience that he observed a steady trickle of youngsters – and some oldsters, too – drifting off along the shore in obvious search for that watch Bobby had every reason to believe was all the time safe in the possession of – of whom?

CHAPTER XI

The Dead Airedale

DAWDLING about the beach, chatting first to one and then to another, dropping judicious hints here and there about future boating and fishing excursions, gravely discussing the prospects of the inevitable three-thirty at to-morrow's meeting, distributing many cigarettes and a consolatory penny to a babe that had tumbled down and damaged its nose, Bobby soon found himself on friendly gossiping terms with half the inhabitants of the little village and the possessor of a large and varied fund of information of less and greater interest. His inquiries seemed particularly addressed towards assuring himself that the bathing was safe. He was informed emphatically that it couldn't be safer if only you were careful not to swim too far out beyond the Cove at the turn of the tide, as apparently poor Mr Archibald had done and paid the penalty for his rashness. But that was the only accident that had ever happened to a bather in living memory, and it could only have happened through over-confidence. Fortunately no one else, either at Fairview or in the village, was a strong enough swimmer to be likely to suffer from that failing. Mr George Winterton never entered the water. Mr Miles was a good swimmer, certainly, but he was careful, and Mr Colin, though fond of the sport, had never been known to venture outside the Cove. Miss Raby was an enthusiastic but indifferent performer, and had nearly drowned Mrs Cooper – or been drowned by her; no one seemed quite clear which – in an effort, never since repeated, to teach her swimming. Mrs Cooper, it seemed clear from the story told by one or two of the villagers with a good deal of amusement, did not display in the water that calmness, poise, and authority which she seemed to exercise by right on land.

All the same, Bobby could not help being struck forcibly, and even with a certain amount of amusement, by the extraordinary way in which Mrs Cooper had managed to impress herself upon the community. It was as if her austere and dignified presence assisted at every enterprise, directed every activity. A chat about the best bait for conger eels developed into a burst of gratitude to Mrs Cooper for having succeeded in securing a scholarship for the speaker's boy at a neighbouring school. A remark on the sandbank that made the navigation of the Cove a little difficult, and even threatened to silt it up altogether, turned into an angry protest at the way in which she had, apparently by sheer force of personality, settled some obscure quarrel about pigsties in back gardens. One man, inclined to be a rowdy nuisance to his neighbours, had been, it seemed, just simply cleared out, obeying Mrs Cooper's warning that, unless he went, worse things would befall him. On the whole, public opinion in the little community seemed in a state of balance, ready to crystallise into regarding her an as intolerable nuisance and busybody whose interference with everyone and everything must be put an end to, or, on the other hand, into accepting her as a kind of local dictator who could be trusted to bring about many benefits at the price of an implicit obedience. It was a revelation to Bobby of the way in which a personality, by sheer force of will and character, could impress itself upon others, for of course Mrs Cooper had no advantages of money or social position to help her. One of those he talked to, an oldish man of evidently contemplative mind, remarked on this fact.

'Only the dear Lord knows where we would be,' he remarked, 'if she were the real missus up there at the house; we wouldn't none of us dare wash our faces except the way she liked. Good thing for Mr Winterton she's got a man already, else next thing that's what she would be – the missus. And the way it is, he's the master, but he has to do just what she tells him.'

However, it was information bearing more directly on the twin problems facing Bobby – whether Archibald's death had been a murder, whether the same fate threatened George – that the young detective was in search of. One thing he soon discovered was that George Winterton was, on the whole, respected but not much liked, while his dead brother, Archibald, had been very well liked but not greatly respected. George Winterton had acquired the reputation of being 'mean,' the sin that among the commonalty of England is without forgiveness. He bargained about payments; if he tipped it was on a small scale, which is worse than no tip at all; he let it be seen that he considered sixpences and shillings as important; and it was, of course, firmly believed that he made a very good thing out of the electric light with which the village was now supplied – thanks to the initiative of Mrs Cooper. As a matter of fact, there was extra expense, with little compensating gain, but the village wasn't going to believe that; not it. But, then, he never interfered, or worried anyone, gave himself no airs, and could be friendly and pleasant without being too familiar, and was known to be writing a book, a strange, rather awe-inspiring pursuit that no doubt accounted for little eccentricities he showed. One day, for instance, he had grown quite excited on hearing that an old woman in the village had dug up five golden sovereigns she had kept buried in her garden for years and had exchanged them, very satisfactorily, for pound notes.

He had actually gone to the trouble of hunting up the old lady in question – a Mrs Shipman – to tell her she had been a fool to part with good solid gold for bits of paper, and to say that if anyone else in the village had any gold put away, they had better keep it against a day, surely not far distant, when gold would be seen to be just gold, and paper just paper. Only let them, he had said – and the advice had been fully in accord with their own way of thinking – let them keep it well hidden, or else they might find a Government official suddenly swooping down to confiscate it.

'He said as over in America,' observed the aged man who told Bobby all this, 'they've started doing that already – making it against the law to keep your own gold your own self.' He added the profound and unanswerable reflection: 'But what I says is, America ain't us and we ain't them.'

Towards the dead Archibald the general feeling seemed to have been the reverse; he had been well enough liked but not at all respected. He had been free with his money; free, too, with his talk; and a little too forgetful of the reserve and dignity villagers are generally inclined to consider should accompany any intercourse between themselves and their social superiors. For instance, he had not been above telling or listening to a bawdy story, and, though the story might be appreciated, and have no great harm in it for that matter, the thing was not approved in a gentlemen of Mr Archibald Winterton's wealth and standing. More serious was the fact that his friendly interest in his humbler neighbours had been more specially marked when they happened to be of the sex once called the weaker, and were also young and pretty.

This last piece of information, that came out rather slowly and reluctantly – first a hint and then in fuller detail in response to Bobby's clever, indirect questioning – he was inclined to think interesting; more than interesting, perhaps. Was it possible that here lay the sought-for clue? Had that interest been pushed too far in some particular case, and had it been resented – resented perhaps to the last extremity? Bobby tried his best to find out if any such suspicions had been aroused, but without success. It did not seem as if Archibald had ever gone much further than showing a partiality for stopping to talk to any pretty girl he met, and assuring her of her good looks, and a tendency to buy his fish, or hire his boats, or employ on odd jobs, members of the families which could boast the pretty girls among their members. On the surface, harmless enough, if a little undignified; but Bobby wondered very much if something more might not lie behind. One thing at least was soon apparent – that Archibald's death had given rise to much gossip and comment. It seemed the general feeling that there was something about it not quite natural, not very easily explicable. Everyone knew he had been familiar with the sea in all its moods; a good sailor, an excellent and cautious swimmer. His death by drowning on that calm, tranquil sunny morning, was hard to understand. Apparently there had been a good deal of discussion as to what had actually happened, but so far no satisfactory theory had been advanced.

'Cramp,' most people were content to say in order to have some sort of satisfactory solution they could rest their minds on; but then Bobby had been assured on good authority that cramp was no danger in itself to any practised swimmer.

'Something must have happened somehow,' remarked a younger man who had joined them. 'With the sea, you never know what'll happen. If it hadn't been along of me seeing old Mother Shipman's unlucky black cat, and hurting my leg the way I did, I should have been out there about when he must have got carried away, and very like I should have been able to help him.'

'You mean if you hadn't run after the poor brute to stone it,' observed the older man, 'you wouldn't have tumbled over Ted Davis's anchor, and got laid up with a cut leg for your pains.'

'I thought seeing a black cat meant good luck,' observed Bobby.

'Not that there wicked beast of old Mother Shipman's,' retorted the young man. 'Bad luck that beast brings, if any ever did, more especial when you're going to the fishing.'

'The same day she got it,' explained the other man, 'the *Suffby Belle* went down with three of our lads that were never seen again, and folk remembered how that black cat had been walking round and round, miaowing and crying, all the time they was getting off. No one else here has ever cared to have a black cat since, nor wouldn't dare, but Mother Shipman thinks the world of hers.'

'If it hadn't been for she,' the young man asserted, 'I should have been out there in my boat when the poor gentleman was drowning.'

'You can't tell that,' the other objected.

'It was just six exact when I cut my leg on that anchor Ted Davis ought to be summonsed for leaving lying about the way he does,' the young man said, 'for I heard Miss Raby's alarm go off in Bob Adams's, and she always sets it for six. That means,' he repeated obstinately, 'but for the cat prowling and miaowing around, just as it did that other time and me trying to drive it away, I should have been out there just in the nick of time.'

Bobby left them arguing the point and strolled on to chat with another ancient he saw mending nets a little way away. He was growing excited; his mind was very busy; it was almost as though a flash of light had passed for a moment across the black chaos of his thoughts. But he wanted another point of view, and from the aged mender of nets he got confirmation of the story that Archibald Winterton had been inclined to show himself a little too friendly towards some of the village girls. Jealousy and resentment might, Bobby thought, account for much, and yet he could get no hint that Archibald's philandering had either been meant or taken very seriously. It had not apparently been considered anything more than silly and undignified. And, when Bobby dropped the question casually, he learned that Archibald's dog, the missing Towser, had always regarded all the villagers as intruders and potential enemies, and certainly would not have allowed one to approach his master without very loud and fierce protest. The animal's silence seemed fair presumptive proof that none of the villagers at least had been near the scene of the tragedy on that fatal morning.

Presently one or two more men strolled up – probably, like Mrs Cooper on Bobby's first arrival at Fairview, anxious to form their own impressions of the new-comer. Bobby managed to turn the conversation on motor-boats, and found there was a strong prejudice against them as being unreliable and lubberly. A new theory was put forward concerning Archibald Winterton's death – that he had been run down by one, which had then gone on without stopping; 'just as them motorists do,' interjected one of the group.

To this it was objected that no motor-boat had been seen or heard of in the neighbourhood since considerably earlier in the year. At this there was a good deal of smiling and winking, and Bobby finally succeeded in discovering that what amused them was the fate which had on that occasion befallen the unlucky police constable, Jennings, who had, as Bobby knew, been assaulted and tied up to a tree the morning of the motor-boat's arrival.

Bobby asked what the boat had come for, and no one seemed to have any idea. He asked straight out if it was a case of smuggling, but no one seemed to think that likely.

'No way of getting the stuff away from here,' was the general verdict, and Bobby felt pretty sure they meant what they said, while it was fairly clear that in that small and closely connected community none of them could have engaged themselves in such an operation without everyone else in the village knowing all about it.

Indeed, it seemed the general opinion that smuggling was a game not worth the trouble and the risk involved.

'If you do have a bottle or two of brandy or a pound of 'baccy to sell,' observed one man who sounded as if at one time he had had some experience, 'you get asked questions till you don't know where you are, and then the police come along and turn everything upside down – it ain't worth it.'

Another man put forward the theory that possibly the motor-boat had come from abroad and had landed some refugee, and this seemed to be accepted as a more likely explanation. Two or three of the men agreed that in almost any Continental port offers were often made of liberal payment by persons who for one reason or another wanted to enter the country without the knowledge or permission of the immigration authorities.

'If it was only that,' Bobby observed, 'I don't see why it should have been necessary to attack the policeman and tie him up the way you say happened.'

No one had any clear explanation to offer, except that it was to give the hypothetical refugee a chance to get away safely. It was not an explanation that seemed very satisfactory to Bobby, for why assault and tie up a man it would have been perfectly easy to avoid? The conversation drifting on, Bobby discovered that two of the group were enthusiastic wireless amateurs and really knew something about the subject – a good deal more than Bobby did himself. One of them, a man named Gates, was quite learned about atmospherics and so on, and in this connection the name of the ill-treated Jennings cropped up again. It seemed he, too, was an enthusiast, and was the happy possessor of a marvellous and expensive new set, recently purchased.

'Must have cost pounds,' declared Gates enviously, 'pounds and pounds. My old woman would have something to say if I spent all that on a new set.'

'So did his; fair gave it him, she did,' declared another man, grinning broadly. 'He said he saved it out of his 'baccy money – as if she would swallow a yarn like that. He had backed a winner, if you ask me, though naturally, of course, he didn't want to say.'

'Why not?' asked Bobby. 'Doesn't Mrs Jennings like betting?'

'Oh, it isn't that,' explained Gates, 'only he's in the police. Of course, they all do it; pass a slip to a bookie themselves one minute and run him in the next, they will. But they mustn't say they do it; betting, I mean.'

'Has he had the set long?' Bobby asked carelessly, and learnt only a few weeks.

It was drawing on towards lunch-time now, and Bobby strolled back to Fairview, where he found all the household – Mr Winterton, young Colin Ross, Miss Raby, the Coopers, Mrs Adams, and the day-girl, Jane – all clustered round the dead body of the Airedale. It had been found floating in the sea, its head battered in and a deep knife-thrust in the side that must have reached the poor brute's heart.

One of the searchers for Bobby's watch had found the dead animal floating in the sea near the shore and had brought the news. Much disturbed, Mr Winterton had called Colin to help him – Cooper was out of the way at the moment – and they had gone down and brought in the body. Bobby joined the group, heard the story of the discovery, and listened to the different theories that were being put forward. Colin thought someone in the village the dog had either bitten or frightened must be responsible, but Mrs Cooper was sure none of the villagers would do such a thing. Cooper thought it must have been some tramp, though tramps were rare in that lonely place and none had been seen lately. Miss Raby said nothing, but looked scared and ill at ease, and Mr Winterton also had little to say. He seemed very puzzled, and declared moodily he could not understand it, and, though Bobby asked a good many questions, he elicited no new fact.

A heavy blow with a club or stone had smashed in the animal's head, and a knife-thrust had then done the rest. That the body had been in the water some time was evident, so that the thing had probably happened the previous evening. At any rate, no one seemed to remember having seen the dog after the boisterous greeting it had given Bobby on his arrival.

Mr Winterton talked of offering a reward for the discovery of the guilty person, and Bobby, standing looking at the creature's body lying there in the middle of the lawn, was aware of a profound unease. A sense of dread and depression was upon him; he felt alone and afraid, for it seemed to him this thing was ominous. It was as though he sensed a warning, a warning of a darker tragedy to come.

He took an opportunity to draw Mr Winterton aside. He said to him:

'I don't understand this, Mr Winterton, and I don't like it either. I think we had better be careful. If you don't mind, I wish you would promise me not to go out alone at present; to be as little alone, in fact, as you can. I'll phone my chief this afternoon, though not from here, to tell him what's happened. And I think to-night you had better have the door and window of your room well closed.'

Mr Winterton, a little pale, promised all this, and Bobby noticed that his appetite at lunch was very poor.

CHAPTER XII

The Recovered Watch

LUNCHEON was indeed that day a somewhat silent and gloomy meal, as if the shadow of coming catastrophe lay heavily upon them all. For once Colin seemed to have something else to think of than odds and weights and starting-prices. Mr Winterton hardly spoke, and Miss Raby had entirely lost her appetite. Bobby, too, was oppressed by the dim menace he felt somehow implicit in the killing of the dog, and once, when he looked at Mr Winterton, he had the strange impression that he saw him sitting there as a dead man.

The illusion was so strong that he nearly cried out aloud, but at that moment Mr Winterton turned and spoke and Bobby was ashamed to think that he, a member of the C.I.D., whose first duty is to be hard-headed and clear-thinking, should have given way to such childish fancies. Yet for the moment it had really seemed to him that a corpse was sitting there, and, though he struggled hard to thrust the impression aside, none the less he knew that it had profoundly shaken him.

Even Cooper seemed to feel the general unease, and

showed himself nervous and forgetful. When he was pouring out some wine for his master, his hand shook so that he spilled some on the table-cloth, and when presently he came in with a telegram it might have been a sentence of death he had on the tray he carried, so ghastly pale was his face, so uncontrolled the nervous twitching of his eye and a new trembling now showing at the corners of his mouth.

But Mr Winterton, after he had opened and read the telegram, and told Cooper there was no reply, seemed suddenly to grow much more cheerful and composed. The telegram itself he put away very carefully in his pocket-book, and then grew quite animated, asking Bobby how he had spent his morning, asking Colin what good tips he had to give away for all of them to make their fortunes with, and telling Miss Raby they would have to try to put in a good afternoon's work.

'We've been making very poor progress,' he declared; 'we'll have to brisk up if the book's to be published this side of Christmas.'

To this new mood of his the others did not respond very well, and then, just as they were rising from the table, Cooper appeared again to say that a young woman from the village would like to see Mr Owen, as she had found a watch on the foreshore and thought it might be his.

'Ah, good,' exclaimed Mr Winterton. 'Who is it, Cooper?'

'Laura Shipman, sir,' the butler answered.

Bobby noted the name; he remembered it was that of the old woman who was the owner of the supposedly unlucky black cat the villagers didn't seem to like and who had also been the first recipient of Mr Winterton's general warning against our parting with gold. Also he had seen Mr Winterton start perceptibly when he heard the name given, though he had recovered himself immediately and was now making a joke about drinking a glass of wine to a 'happy return of the day.' All the same, Bobby was fairly sure the name had meant something to him.

In the hall Bobby found waiting a tall young woman, of somewhat striking appearance, and with handsome, well-formed features. She had dark hair, and dark, flashing eyes, and a skin, naturally dark, that had been further tanned by the sun and the sea air, and, though Bobby was like most young men, and found it difficult to believe that a pretty face could hide a soul anything but pretty, or a charming smile to be false, yet he found, or fancied he found, something eager and greedy in those black glittering eyes and something very hard in the set of those thin lips. But he thought that might be merely preconceived prejudice, and he tried his best to be very amiable, even to appear a little struck with her charms, as he thanked her for returning the watch and fumbled to find in his pocket the reward he had promised.

Intensely did he wonder as he did so what errand it was had brought this village girl here in the middle of the night and what it was had been discussed in that strange interview upon the lawn.

There was Colin Ross, too. Did he know, or suspect, this girl had been the other person present? That was, of course, assuming that it was really Colin who had been the second witness to whose presence the cautiously closing front door that night had testified. Certainly Colin had not seemed to show any sign of recognition when the girl's name had been mentioned, but, then, Bobby had been too taken up watching Mr Winterton to have had much attention to spare for Colin.

Quickly he made up his mind it would be more prudent not to make any attempt at present to question the girl. It would be better to know more about her first, and then he would have a better idea of how to approach her. Perhaps, too, his superiors might prefer to take over themselves the task of questioning her, allowing Bobby still to stay in the background. After all, a good deal of caution and discretion would have to be shown. The mere fact of a nocturnal meeting might have some perfectly simple and natural explanation, and, in any case, it was not one that itself came within the reach of the law.

So he contented himself, as he handed over the two pound

notes he had promised, with saying again how glad he was to get his watch back, and with asking casually what would seem, he hoped, the very natural question where she had found it.

The answer she gave was that she had picked it up on the shore early that morning, and this answer was obviously false, since if the watch had lain exposed to the rain all night it would certainly have shown some sign of that fact, while it was not on the shore, but just outside the entrance to the drive, that he had deposited it.

There was, of course, the possibility that she was not the person directly involved, but only an intermediary, and for the present it seemed to Bobby better to let her suppose her story was accepted and believed. So he thanked her again profusely, offered her a compliment on her good looks she showed no disposition to resent and that he hoped might induce her to think it natural if he tried to follow up their acquaintance, and then let her depart with her two pound notes while he went back to join the others and show off his recovered possession.

Colin, however, had disappeared back to his study of the *Racing Guide* and his excursions into the higher mathematics of weights and ages and starting-prices and so on; and Miss Raby had returned to her typewriter, and a fresh copy to be made of a much-corrected chapter in the new book on 'Hidden Gold Reserves: Their Power and Influence.'

But Mr Winterton was still in the dining-room, and Bobby suggested a stroll in the garden his host did not seem much inclined for till Bobby whispered that he asked for it as a police officer, not as a guest.

'Oh, very well, very well,' Mr Winterton said in a slightly vexed tone; 'but I'm hoping there'll be something soon I'll be able to tell you about that'll put things in a clearer light.'

'If there is anything you can tell us,' Bobby said gravely, 'I think you would be well advised to do so. We cannot give you much help when we are kept so much in the dark.'

'That'll be all right soon,' Mr Winterton retorted, 'but I

can't tell you what I don't know, and I can't tell you other people's business I've promised to keep to myself.'

They left the house by the door that led from the study to the garden, leaving Miss Raby regarding disapprovingly an employer who so sadly neglected his work. When they were a little distant from the house, Bobby said:

'I could not help noticing you had a telegram at luncheon. It seemed to me it might have some connection ...'

Mr Winterton hesitated, flushed a little, and then answered:

'My brother has lost his life already. That may have been quite accidental. I don't know. But I don't mean to risk anything of the sort happening to anyone else. I'm not going to take that responsibility. I'm not thinking of myself. There is someone else who might be in very great danger indeed if it got out what that telegram meant. It might be a matter of life or death for him, too. All this is someone else's business just as much as it is mine, and I've got to think of him.'

'Then, Mr Winterton,' Bobby said firmly, 'I shall apply to my chiefs to withdraw me. I can't feel that there is any justification for asking me to accept responsibility when I am kept so much and so deliberately in the dark.'

'You aren't asked to accept responsibility,' Mr Winterton snapped. 'I pay for you to be here, and I take all the responsibility.'

'There's another thing I want to make clear,' Bobby went on, disregarding this. 'I don't know who killed your dog, and I don't know what it means, but I feel it may mean something pretty serious. You have asked us for protection. It is our duty to do what we can to protect any person who seems to be threatened in any way. I want, therefore, to ask you to adopt every possible precaution, especially during this afternoon, as I shall have to be out of the house till late perhaps.'

'You mean you want to ring up and ask for help?' Winterton demanded.

'To be relieved,' Bobby corrected him, 'on the grounds

that you are refusing co-operation by keeping back material facts. But until I am relieved I remain more or less responsible, and, as I don't at all like this business about your dog being killed, I'm asking you to promise not to leave the house on any account till I get back, and to be alone as little as possible. In short, to be as careful as you can. Probably you know better than I do where the danger is and what precautions to take.'

'I wish I did,' Mr Winterton answered, 'but I don't. I don't even know if there is any real danger, any more than I know for certain whether my brother was murdered or whether it was just an accident. But, anyhow, you may be quite sure I'll be as careful as I can. I shall spend most of the rest of the day in the study, and I can't very well be dragged out and knocked on the head like poor Towser. I'll keep Miss Raby with me till you get back, and I have a revolver. And to-night I'll lock my door and barricade it, and the window as well, and if you hear anyone trying to break in and you aren't too sound asleep ...'

'I don't think I shall sleep very soundly. I hope you will,' Bobby answered in tones as grave as the other's were light. 'If I hear any noise I shall come at once.'

'Oh, I shall sleep sound enough,' Mr Winterton answered.

As if tired of the subject, he began to talk about the various shrubs and flowers he was trying to grow. The strong sea air and a certain poverty of the soil made gardening somewhat troublesome, and Mr Winterton grew quite eloquent about the difficulties encountered. He seemed, Bobby thought, in better spirits than previously, and he chatted in quite a lively, friendly manner. The garden was on a long slope rising upwards from the house, that was quite close to the shore of the Cove. On almost the highest spot, at the very end of the garden, nearly two hundred yards from the house, they came to the small stone summer-house in the form of a miniature Greek temple that, when he first saw it, had attracted Bobby's interest and attention. It was now in a somewhat dilapidated condition, and the door had been secured by a padlock.

'The roof was getting to look dangerous,' Mr Winterton explained, 'and so I had it shut up. I can't make up my mind whether to have it repaired or pulled down altogether. It's a fine view out to sea from here, isn't it?'

Bobby agreed that it was. They strolled on a little further, and then Mr Winterton said he must be getting back to work or Miss Raby would be talking about another wasted day.

Bobby accompanied him back to the house and took occasion once more to impress upon him the necessity of exercising every care, for indeed Bobby could not get out of mind the Airedale's inexplicable death. It seemed to him a plain warning; indeed, a warning so plain it seemed also hardly genuine. At any rate, if mischief were intended, it would probably not materialise till night, since only during the night was the Airedale's protection of special value.

Deep in thought, he walked back through the garden towards the Greek temple summer-house. He had noticed footprints near it on the ground made soft by the recent heavy rain, and in his present mood of perplexity and apprehension there was nothing that he felt he dared neglect. That a woman had made them he soon convinced himself, and when he looked at the padlock fastening the door he saw at once fresh marks to suggest that it had been recently opened.

He had some skill as an amateur locksmith, and by the aid of a pocket-knife supplied with one or two useful little tools he soon had it open. Inside, the little building had a very neglected appearance, and the roof certainly looked somewhat insecure. The webs of various spiders festooned the walls, and plainly the place had not been used for some considerable time. Nevertheless, the floor was still damp from what seemed a recent swilling down, and Bobby asked himself wonderingly why anyone should have taken the trouble to wash over the floor of this neglected place and yet leave those webs and that general dirt upon the walls.

It seemed to him a puzzle, and there flashed into his mind a sudden idea that perhaps the answer to that puzzle, if only he could find it, was the answer also to all these other events that seemed to him so vaguely sinister, in whose bewilderment he felt his mind caught up in amazement and in fear.

CHAPTER XIII

The Telegram

BOBBY's motor-cycle was still in the Fairview garage, but he did not get it out. It would be better to walk to-day, he thought; there would be more time then for that lingering and chatting so alien to the true motor-cyclist's conception of life but so natural and wise a method of arriving at the truth of things. At a brisk pace he set off, accordingly, and on his way through the village he noticed specially the small cottage, a little apart from the others, which had been pointed out to him as that occupied by Mrs Shipman, the owner of the 'unlucky' black cat, and, presumably, by Laura Shipman as well.

A tall, thin, somewhat untidy old woman was in the doorway of the cottage as he passed, and gave him a malevolent glare, though he fancied her ill will was more for the universe in general than for him in particular. He responded with a cheery greeting and a remark on the beauty of the day, and she muttered something in reply and went back into the house.

'Pleasant old party,' he thought. 'If I can manage to start a flirtation with Miss Laura, it'll have to be without giving the old woman a chance to butt in.'

The problem of the connection of this girl, Laura, with Mr Winterton, and of the reason for the extraordinary interview she had had with him on the lawn in the middle of the night, was one with which his mind was very busy. Yet he could not imagine how she could be connected either with any danger that might threaten George Winterton or with the foul play of which Bobby was growing more and more to believe the brother had been a victim.

'Only how could murder, if it was murder, have been carried out, and what possible motive can there have been?' he asked himself bewilderedly, and found no answer.

Four miles' brisk walking brought him to Suffby Horpe, a village not much larger than Suffby Cove, but boasting a post office and a police station which was also the residence of Police-Constable Jennings, the victim of the mysterious assault committed on the morning of the appearance of the equally mysterious motor-boat.

Bobby's first visit was to the post office, an establishment presided over by a pleasant-faced, chatty, middle-aged woman, who also sold everything – from tea in packets to cigarettes, chocolates, and film periodicals – that this age demands, whether in Mayfair, Whitechapel, or the most remote country village. Bobby began by buying a packet of cigarettes, and was pleased to find the post-mistress knew all about him as a friend of Mr Winterton's staying at Fairview. A full report of him, his appearance at Fairview, his lost watch, had already been received by the good lady, and so Bobby had not the trouble of explaining who he was as he went on to inform her that Mr Winterton would like repeated the telegram he had just received. There was, Bobby explained, a possibility that a mistake had been made in one of the words, and, as it was, he remarked carelessly, a code telegram dealing with business ('Stock Exchange transaction,' observed Bobby with indifferent impressiveness), it was important to be sure of absolute correctness.

The post-mistress hesitated a little, evidently not quite clear about rules and regulations. But, then, Bobby had come straight from Fairview, and he was a very pleasant-spoken, good-looking youngster, possessing also what is so graphically described as a 'way with him.' Moreover, there was a candour in his eyes, a curl in his hair, a quality in his smile, the post-mistress would in any case have found it hard to resist, especially when he was so plainly contemplating purchasing that large salad-bowl with a picture ('hand painted in colours') of Suffby Cove on it she had had for years and never yet been able to get rid of. So the request for a repeat duly went off, and Bobby paid for his salad-bowl, arranged for it to be delivered at Fairview, and then departed to interview Police-Constable Jennings.

Jennings himself was out on patrol, but in the doorway of their residence, that served also as the local police station, Mrs Jennings was nursing a baby. Bobby's excuse for calling was that he had recovered his lost watch, and wanted any story the police might hear that it had been stolen to be disregarded. Though evidently a little puzzled by this emphatic contradiction of a suggestion no one seemed to have made, Mrs Jennings promised to give the message to her husband on his return. By good luck, the famous wireless set was in full action, and Bobby, after making a prudent approach by way of admiring the baby and saying how different it looked from London babies (but he drew the line at kissing it; there are some sacrifices, he felt, not even stern duty may demand), he remarked on the excellence and clearness of the tone of the set. Mrs Jennings, he soon found, was torn between pride in its possession, for it was something of a social asset to be the owner of the best wireless set in the neighbourhood, and resentment at money having been spent on it she could have put to other household uses. Bobby declared it was so good it had evidently been bought in London, and Mrs Jennings said, with some slight, secret scorn of London, that, on the contrary, it came from a certain Norwich establishment. So Bobby confessed meekly that Norwich shops must evidently be fully equal to London establishments, and thanked her and went back to the post office, where the repeat message had just been received.

Short as it was, Bobby read it over twice, told the post-mistress there had been no mistake, and undertook to deliver it himself to Mr Winterton, chatted with her a little longer, and then resumed his walk. Reading the telegram before the post-mistress, he had tried to appear totally indifferent, but now he looked grave and troubled, for the message seemed to him to be capable of dark meanings, even though its receipt had apparently brought considerable relief to Mr Winterton – another apparent contradiction it was not easy to understand.

'Anyhow,' he thought, 'it'll be dead easy to follow up and find out what it means and, once that's done, most likely we shall have the clue to the whole thing in our hands.'

A motor-coach came along, and he hailed it and went on to Deneham, where he alighted at the station, which, as is the way of English country stations, was a good two miles outside the place itself. As he did so, he caught sight of Mrs Cooper. She did not seem to have noticed him, and he went across behind one of the station buildings out of sight. In a moment or two she was joined by Adams, the Fairview chauffeur and gardener. Apparently they had come for some parcels waiting for them which they brought out and put into the car in which they had arrived. Then they drove off, and when they were out of sight Bobby strolled into the station to make some quite unnecessary inquiries about the trains. The station-master he found to be an intelligent, well-spoken man, who seemed much superior to the position he held in charge of this small and remote place. At one time, indeed, he had, Bobby learnt later, been in charge of a big junction in the north, but apparently he had found the responsibility of the work rather too much for him, and he had experienced something in the nature of a nervous breakdown, and had at his own request been transferred to this little backwater of a place, where he seemed quite happy and content in the quiet and tranquillity that lay between the country and the sea.

'Though if Mrs Cooper has her way,' he remarked, after he and Bobby had been chatting a few moments, 'it won't be quiet much longer.'

Odd, Bobby thought, how almost any conversation turned sooner or later on something Mrs Cooper had said or thought or done. It was a striking tribute to the force of her dominating personality. The station-master and Mrs Cooper and her husband had grown quite friendly, it seemed, often exchanging visits, and lately she had been somewhat disturbing the poor man by holding forth on the undeserved neglect in which this lovely corner of the coast had so long lain. That had been understandable, she thought, while the only access to it had been by a branch line on which few trains ran, but now, with the coming of the motor-coach, all that was altered. A district offering such facilities for all sea sports, as well as for golf and for field sports, was, according to her, a perfect gold-mine waiting for anyone with sufficient intelligence, character, and energy to develop it. 'Winter sports' was a slogan, she argued, that drew thousands to Switzerland every year. 'Sea sports' was, she declared, another slogan that could draw even more to this spot, once it was scientifically organised and developed.

'She says,' remarked the station-master, half smiling, half worried, 'that a good thing's no good without a good slogan, and a good slogan is only wasted without a good thing behind it, but with the two together you can sweep the world, she says; and she would too, if she had the chance.' A touch of enthusiasm had come into his voice, as if he had been affected by the vision she had shown him. Then he stopped, and laughed in a shame-faced sort of way. 'I told her,' he said, 'if that ever began to happen here, I should have to apply for another transfer. Only, as she says herself, it never will; not yet, anyhow.'

'I suppose the idea is to make a new Blackpool or Margate,' Bobby remarked.

'Well, I think her idea was more to attract better-class people,' the station-master explained; 'not the real tip-toppers, because there aren't enough of them, but the people who are just smart enough to want to be a bit more smart than their neighbours.'

Bobby reflected that Mrs Cooper seemed to know a good deal about human nature, and then, to explain his visit, went on to inquire about the times of the trains and the connections with the London expresses, and also as to the cost of sending back his motor-cycle by goods train.

'I rode down yesterday,' he explained. 'I managed to

miss the train I meant to take, and I thought the next would get me here too late, though if I had known Miss Raby was coming by it I would have waited.'

'Miss Raby came by the afternoon train,' the other answered. I remember telling her she must hurry to catch the bus for Suffby Cove, and she said she would walk along the cliffs. I sent her suit-case on by the next bus.'

'Rather jolly walk by the cliffs. I must go back that way,' Bobby observed, and, after a little more talk, went off to the call-box which stood at the entrance to the station, just outside it.

But then, as he was approaching it, he heard his name called softly, and, looking round, saw a hand waving to him from a car that had just drawn up. He went towards it, and saw in the driving-seat his chief, Superintendent Mitchell, who told him briefly to jump in.

'Bit of luck meeting you like this,' Mitchell remarked as he drove on. 'Major Markham's been worrying; got the wind up; I don't know why. He was afraid of compromising you if he tried to get in touch direct, so he asked me to have a try as being less known about here. Well, got anything to report?'

'Heaps, sir,' Bobby answered. 'I was going to ring you up.'

He began to tell the whole story of his experiences since his arrival at Fairview. He told it in detail, omitting nothing; no incident, however trivial; no theory, however quickly discarded; he told all, and Mitchell listened intently, his face growing very grave. When Bobby at last finished, he was silent for a time, and then said slowly:

'Do you know what I am wondering? Whether it was George Winterton himself put his brother through it. There seems to have been some sort of big money deal between them.'

'Yes, sir, but,' Bobby pointed out, 'the evidence of the Coopers seems to provide an alibi for him. Unless they are lying – and I don't see why they should lie simply to protect him – he was in bed at the time his brother was drowning.'

'I had forgotten that for the moment,' Mitchell admitted. He had been taking notes while he listened to Bobby, and now he referred to them. 'There's this Mr Shorton, the City man,' he remarked. 'So far as I can see, he is about the only person with any motive for wanting Archibald out of the way. Apparently he had sunk a good bit of money in this scheme of his for a seaside hotel Archibald Winterton was holding up, and apparently he had some reason for thinking he hadn't been treated very fairly. Archibald seems to have got in ahead of him with buying the land lying across Suffby Point, and he may have suspected the real object was to squeeze him out and carry on afterwards. Perhaps it was, too. But you don't often get murder in the City, though you do get sharp practice all right. There seems to have been a good deal of money at stake, though, that Shorton is threatened with losing.'

'Yes, sir,' agreed Bobby; 'and, now that Archibald is dead, George is the obstacle in the way. If anything happened to him, I suppose the scheme would go through at once.'

Mitchell stroked a reflective chin and looked more worried than ever.

'Did you say,' he observed presently, 'that Shorton was a champion swimmer?'

'At any rate, exceptionally good,' Bobby answered.

They had halted the car, for their talk, at a spot whence a good view out to sea was to be had. Gazing at it reflectively, Mitchell murmured, half to himself:

'It keeps many secrets; perhaps it means to keep this one, too. Drowning or murder, I wonder which?' He roused himself from his thoughts and said: 'We shall have to check up on him. About this nephew, Colin Ross. You say you think Mr Winterton seems afraid of him?'

'Once or twice I've thought I saw him looking at him in a funny sort of way. I thought perhaps it meant he was afraid or nervous of him in some way. That's all.'

Mitchell made a fresh note.

'Betting man,' he said. 'We'll have to try to find out if he is pressed for money. But it doesn't appear that his uncle's death – the death of either of them for that matter – was going to be any benefit to him. Then there's this secretary girl, Miss Raby. You say the other nephew was cleared out for flirting with her?'

'Yes, sir; but she seems a very quiet, gentle sort of girl.'

'Sometimes they're the worst when they once get going,' observed Mitchell. 'God help the man who comes between a woman and the thing she wants when she wants it bad. An elemental lot, the women. If she was really keen on this nephew – what was his name, Miles Winterton? – and the uncle came between them, that might account for a lot.'

'But Archibald had nothing to do with all that,' Bobby pointed out.

'She may have thought he had,' answered Mitchell; 'anyhow, we shall have to try to check up on her and on Mr Miles, too. You say she came back from Town by the afternoon train but pretended it was the late one she had arrived by?'

'Yes, sir. The station-master told me that when I was talking to him just now.'

'May mean something or may not,' Mitchell reflected. 'Probably not; but you can never tell. But somehow or another we must find out what this Laura Shipman was doing talking to Winterton in the middle of the night. That must mean something. You can't suggest what?'

'I can't even imagine any explanation, sir,' Bobby answered. 'There's no suggestion he ever takes any notice of the village girls, as it seems Archibald used to do, and there would be plenty of opportunities of meeting in the daytime if they wanted to.'

'Seems to be all cross purposes, this case,' sighed Mitchell. 'Some of it must mean something, but a lot of it can't, but how on earth to pick out what matters, I can't see. Though I don't say the Assist. Commish., when I tell him how you identified the Laura Shipman girl by that trick of yours with the watch, won't put a good mark against your name – unless he forgets. Wonderful poor memory a man develops, somehow, when he becomes Assist. Commish. Owen,' he added, with a sudden change of manner, 'I'm worried about the killing of that dog.'

'I don't like that part one little bit myself,' agreed Bobby, 'only I don't understand it either. ... If the poor brute gave no alarm when there happened whatever did or didn't happen to Archibald, why should it be necessary to knock it on the head now? It seems going out of the way to put us on our guard.'

Mitchell nodded.

'The dog's silence the one time and it's being killed now are both hard to understand, hard to fit together,' he repeated, still worried. 'The worst is, if Archibald was drowned by accident, there may be no fitting together needed and we may be merely beating the air. Anyhow, I think we shall have to have a talk with Miss Laura. To come back to Jennings' wireless you were talking about, you say it was bought in Norwich somewhere.'

'Yes, sir,' said Bobby, and gave the name of the shop he had been careful to note.

'It's a long shot,' observed Mitchell, 'but we'll see what they have to say. The attack on him was made before Archibald was drowned, wasn't it?'

'Yes, sir. He bought the wireless set a fortnight after the attack on him, and nearly a month before Archibald's death.'

'I think those are the chief points,' Mitchell remarked, again consulting his notes. 'There's the swilling down of the summer-house, too, but I don't see that that concerns us – unless you have a theory that the dog was killed there and the swilling down was to remove any signs of blood.'

'There's that,' agreed Bobby, 'but why should anyone use an old tumbledown summer-house, with a dangerous roof to it, for killing a dog in? Besides, I saw no tracks of any dog, and those I did see had been made after the rain, while the dog was almost certainly killed before.'

'Difficult to see where swilling the floor of an old summer-house comes into the picture,' repeated Mitchell, 'and yet

I've a sort of feeling that it does. About the telegram Winterton received at lunch. You say you got them to repeat it?'

'Yes, sir. The good lady didn't much want to, I think, but I suppose she decided it was all right. I think she wasn't quite sure whether it was regular.'

Mitchell looked at him.

'I daresay she would have done it for me, too,' he remarked, 'when I was as young as you and just as beautiful. But I never had a permanent wave like yours in my hair. Personally, I am rather inclined to call a curl like that just plain cheating; hardly fair, at any rate.'

Bobby wriggled. He always wriggled when anyone talked about that curl he had done so much, and so ineffectually, to straighten out by means of soap, combings, and brushings *ad lib.*

'She knew I was staying with Mr Winterton,' he protested. 'It was that did it.'

'Not it,' said Mitchell with decision. 'Let me look at the thing again.'

Bobby took the telegram from his pocket, and Mitchell smoothed it out thoughtfully.

' "*You know who released gaol yesterday morning; you can expect him soon*",' he read aloud. 'Handed in at Charing Cross, where there's no chance of its being remembered. Well, anyhow, it gives us a clue we ought to be able to follow up easily enough. We'll check up on every living creature who was let out of gaol in these British Isles yesterday and find out which of them has anything to do with Mr George Winterton, and, when we know that, it ought to put us on the right track. Nothing else?'

'No, sir.'

Mitchell fell into deep thought again.

'Well,' he said, rousing himself, 'there's one thing you've noticed that must mean something, because a discrepancy always does.'

'Yes, sir,' agreed Bobby gravely.

'Well, then,' said Mitchell, 'remember it, and now you

had better get along back to Fairview. Your instructions are,' he added, his voice suddenly stern and official, 'so far as possible, don't let George Winterton out of your sight. Be on your guard every moment – more especially to-night.'

'Yes, sir,' said Bobby once more, and this time more gravely still.

CHAPTER XIV

Murder!

MITCHELL put his young colleague down at a lonely spot on the road and then drove on alone, so that no inquisitive eyes might notice them together. The rest of the distance to Suffby Cove Bobby accomplished, therefore, on foot, hurrying a little now, for an obscure apprehension drove him on.

Likely enough, he supposed, that in fact no real danger threatened, and yet he felt he would be easier in his mind, once he were back at Fairview and knew that nothing had happened during his absence, and knew that if anything threatened in the future, it would be while he was on the spot to check and meet it. Yet still it remained likely enough that Archibald's drowning had been purely accidental; and, indeed, how could murder have been carried out with no sign left and the Airedale lying there and making no sound? Besides, who had benefited in any way whatever by his death? A possible hint about as yet unproved semi-flirtations with one or other of the village girls was no sufficient background for so grim a picture as premeditated murder makes. And yet there was always the difficulty of understanding why the sea should have had its way with so strong a swimmer on so quiet and calm a morning.

At any rate, Bobby reflected, there was now a good solid clue to work on. Mitchell's methods were thorough, the C.I.D. organisation complete; soon there would be a separate report on every living creature, man, woman, or child, released from any gaol in the British Isles during the last day or two, and it would be a very funny thing if they could not find out to whom the recent telegram referred. Once that was known, progress would be easy, and it would be possible to form some idea of what all these happenings meant, if indeed they meant anything at all. For that, Bobby's sense of logic and reasoning powers, and his sense of the reality of things, led him to doubt, while yet some instinct, deeper and more profound than logic, told him that things evil and horrible were brewing. There came into his mind a memory of the opening scene in *Macbeth* where the three witches brew mischief together, and he fancied that perhaps, somewhere very near, that same scene was being repeated, though it might be in a different shape and form, with all the difference there is between the society of to-day and that of a thousand years ago. Nor could he quite get rid of the teasing memory of the recently swilled floor in the half-ruinous summer-house built like a Greek temple, for somehow he still had the impression that if only he knew why that had been done, then he would know all.

Then, of course, there was the 'discrepancy,' as Mitchell called it, so noticeably occurring in his narrative of his experiences. He supposed that must have some significance, and, as now he was near the village, he left the main road to take the path leading through the cottages. One or two of his acquaintances of the morning he met and nodded to, and he noticed old Mrs Shipman standing on her threshold with her 'unlucky' black cat in her arms. But she scowled when she saw him, and went indoors, and he walked on till he came to the cottage occupied by Adams, the Fairview chauffeur and gardener, and his wife, with Miss Raby for a lodger. Mrs Adams, of course, knew who Bobby was, and as he saw her in her garden he stopped to chat for a moment. Turning the conversation on to sea-bathing, he learnt that Miss Raby, though no great swimmer, generally went for a dip in the sea before breakfast. Her alarm-clock roused her at six every morning, Mrs Adams explained in answer to a leading question of Bobby's, and, when he suggested that perhaps she kept it slow on purpose, Mrs Adams laughed at the little joke and explained that they 'had the wireless' and that Miss Raby's alarm-clock and their own and the kitchen clock were put right by it every evening. Bobby made one or two other little jokes and aimless inquiries so that Mrs Adams should not suspect any special meaning was hidden in his questions about the alarm-clock, and then took his leave. In his pocket-book he made a note in the private cypher he used, to remind him to put in his report that he had checked up on Miss Raby's alarm-clock and had evidence that it was always kept right.

When he reached Fairview, he found Mrs Cooper in the hall in the act of taking into the study, where Mr Winterton and Miss Raby were still at work, a tray with tea and a plate of freshly baked scones of most appetising appearance, so golden-brown and crisp they looked.

'They look jolly good,' Bobby commented; 'make my mouth water. I say, if I drifted into the study should I stand a chance of getting some?'

Mrs Cooper laughed a little, evidently not ill pleased at the compliment.

'I made them specially for Mr Winterton,' she said. 'I can't always find the time, but he seems to enjoy them when I do.'

'They look scrumptious,' Bobby repeated, and then made a wry face. 'Only I don't know if I dare eat anything at all,' he said. 'I'm half afraid a hollow tooth I've got is starting off again.'

Mrs Cooper was interested. She was always interested in other people's troubles or difficulties, and always knew just what ought to be done. In this case she knew a very good dentist; only a young man certainly, but very clever and careful, who visited Suffby Horpe once a week. Mr Owen would do well to see him, she said, and Bobby thanked her and made a note of the name, but confessed he was an awful coward where dentists were concerned. However, those scones looked so jolly he decided that if he could cadge one he would risk its setting that exposed nerve going again, so he followed Mrs Cooper into the study, where he received a smiling greeting from Mr Winterton.

'While you've been wandering over half the country, young man,' he said, 'looking for a chance to get into mischief most likely, we've been sitting here with our noses to the grindstone, haven't we, Miss Raby, with nothing to disturb our labours?'

Bobby smiled faintly, understanding that these last few words were meant specially for him, and were a teasing reference to his fears and nervousness and warnings about taking every precaution possible. Miss Raby, busy clearing a table of a mass of books and manuscript, that Mrs Cooper might have somewhere to put down her tray, responded to her employer's remark with some sort of muffled sound between a word and a grunt that might have meant anything, and Mr Winterton laughed a little.

'Miss Raby's cross because I've spent all afternoon over my crossword puzzle I won't let her help me with,' he said smilingly. 'But I don't want any professional expert butting in; this is my own little effort – my ewe-lamb of a crossword. Interested in crossword puzzles, Owen?'

'I try them sometimes,' Bobby answered. 'I think the clues are often a bit far-fetched, though.'

'You can't make them too obvious,' protested Miss Raby from the professional point of view.

'Some of the clues in this one I'm working on might interest you, Owen, some day perhaps,' remarked Mr Winterton, repeating an observation he had made before, and its struck Bobby that though he had taken every care to inform Mitchell of every detail, even the most insignificant, he was not sure that he had said anything of Mr Winterton's interest in crossword puzzles, or of his efforts to construct one to rival Miss Raby's professional concoctions.

However, crosswords were only a harmless pastime, without, Bobby supposed, any reference to the strange impalpable fog of threat and menace into which it seemed they were all caught up, and Mr Winterton was now devoting his attention to the scones.

'Ah, your own special make,' he said beamingly to Mrs Cooper. 'They're always first rate.'

'I'm sure I hope you'll enjoy them, sir,' Mrs Cooper said.

'You can be perfectly sure I shall,' declared Mr Winterton, 'they're always delicious'; and, after Mrs Cooper had withdrawn, he remarked: 'She makes them from a secret recipe of her own, and very good they are, too. I only get them when she wants to be specially nice to me.'

Bobby, in spite of his expressed fears about that tooth of his, did them full justice, and found them delicious. Miss Raby expressed a considered opinion that their secret consisted in the use of honey and cream, and afterwards Bobby got a book and sat in the garden, close to the study door, so as to be at hand in case of need, for he was still troubled by a kind of dim, unacknowledged apprehension that kept his attention less on his book than on every sound or movement near. It was always a relief to him when the steady tap, tap, tap of the typewriter, or the sight of Mr Winterton's figure passing to and fro near the window, told that all was still quiet and normal within.

Once Bobby, weary of sitting still and unable to keep his attention on his book, took a stroll round the house, and looked for a little time and very thoughtfully at the spot upon the lawn where he had seen the dead body of the unlucky Airedale laid down. It was, he noticed, by a coincidence almost exactly the spot where had taken place that strange and still unexplained midnight interview of which he had been an unseen witness – he and another of whose presence he had then been unaware, of whose identity he was still ignorant. He wondered whether this other witness had been equally unaware of his vicinity, was still equally ignorant of his identity. Neither suggestion seemed to him probable, and he felt himself at a heavy disadvantage.

He went back to his seat till it was time to prepare for dinner. Dinner that evening consisted of sole cooked in Madeira, roast duck served with green peas done in butter, and so young and tender they vanished almost as they touched the tongue and left only their flavour lingering behind like a blissful memory, and apple tart with cream, followed by coffee obedient to the maxim of the Eastern sage that coffee should be 'as sweet as love, as black as night, as strong as death, and as hot as hell.'

No wonder that, with such a dinner, Mr Winterton seemed in good spirits as he put forward a reasoned argument that this dinner was the best dinner that in an imperfect world could be made manifest to imperfect man.

He sent his compliments to Mrs Cooper by Jane, the day-girl doing the waiting in place of Cooper, who had asked to be excused from duty that evening on the plea of a bad headache.

'He hasn't seemed quite himself the last day or two,' Mr Winterton remarked. 'I don't know if that's the reason why Mrs Cooper has been so good to us to-night. Perhaps she wants to make up for his absence; she doesn't often give us a dinner like this.' Then he looked at Bobby and began to chuckle. 'Or perhaps there's another reason,' he said, still chuckling. 'The women are all the same – a straight nose, good teeth, and a wavy sort of curl to the hair, and where are they? Miss Raby will have to be careful.'

Miss Raby tried to combine an air of extreme contempt of this with an air of not having heard a word of it. Bobby went very red and longed passionately to be bald, since, he supposed, nothing else would prevent people making idiotic remarks about that curly hair of his. Colin observed thoughtfully that he didn't care who made the running so long as they all got to the winning-post together, and Mr Winterton, very pleased with himself, or the dinner, or both, chuckled again.

Afterwards they all played bridge. Bobby managed rather better this time, avoiding worse trouble by making as few bids as possible, and deciding that the secret of contract was to let the others do the bidding and come the inevitable croppers. Colin was on the winning side in each rubber, and with undisguised satisfaction collected ninepence winnings from all the others. Miss Raby observed acidly that such skill in cards was conclusive evidence of a university career put to other than its proper uses, and Mr Winterton fell asleep twice, once when dummy, and once when Bobby was dealing. Each time he put the blame on Mrs Cooper's dinner.

'A meal I shall remember all the rest of my life,' he declared solemnly.

The party broke up a little earlier than usual. Miss Raby, escorted by Jane, departed for the village. Colin retired to bed, remarking that he wanted to be up early as he was attending a certain race-meeting next day. Mr Winterton observed that he, too, was ready for bed, and with him Bobby went upstairs.

'You won't forget, sir,' he whispered to his host, 'to lock your door to-night and make your window fast?'

'Oh, come,' Mr Winterton protested, 'you don't really think it's necessary to take precautions like that?'

'No, I don't,' Bobby answered, 'not in the least; precautions are almost always unnecessary. You can cross the street without looking a hundred times, but the hundred and first time ... and I don't want this to be the hundred and first time.'

'Oh, but——' Mr Winterton began.

'There's always what happened to the dog, sir,' Bobby reminded him. 'I shan't be easy till we know a bit more about that.'

'Oh, all right, all right.' Mr Winterton yielded. 'You mean you think it's a case of trying it on the dog?'

Bobby smiled gravely, and Mr Winterton, pleased with his joke, did not object to Bobby's attending himself to the fastening of the window, which he accomplished by the aid of a small wedge so that it could not possibly be opened more widely without considerable effort and resultant noise. He looked at the door, too, and made sure that the lock was in working order. Mr Winterton promised to be sure to turn the key.

'Then I shall be quite safe against anything except a battering-ram or a poison-gas bomb dropped down the chimney,' he said teasingly.

Bobby took this chaff well enough, but all the same lingered in the corridor outside till he heard the key actually turned in the lock, and the line of light beneath the door vanish as a proof that the electricity had been switched off and that Mr Winterton was now at last safe in bed.

Bobby went back then to his own room, but all the same, in spite of all this care, he was still aware of a dim unease. He opened the window and looked out. The night was calm, the stars shining, the murmur of the sea as its tiny waves caressed the shore seemed only to increase the tranquillity of the night, the peacefulness of the scene. Yet it was in just such tranquillity of nature, in just such peace and quietude, that Archibald Winterton had perished, and more and more the apprehension grew in Bobby's mind that behind all this there hid and waited strange, sinister activities. It was as though the very stars cried to him a warning, as though the murmur of the seas was telling him to beware.

He was half undressed, but, instead of completing the task, he slipped on his dressing-gown and in his slippers stole silently down the corridor, though not until he had thrown one last long, lingering look at his bed that had never seemed so soft and warm and inviting of appearance.

At the door of Mr Winterton's room he paused, and then, on the threshold, he curled himself up. Entry by the window he had made impossible without considerable noise and effort. Entry by the door was now impossible, too, except across his body; and now, he told himself, surely he could defy those dark forebodings that had hung so unaccountably in his mind all the long day through.

Yet a threshold, though a useful and indeed a necessary thing, has but few advantages as a bed. As for floor-boards, they have a fiendish knack of prying out each soft and tender spot upon the human body. And, even on a warm and still night, it is wonderful how chilly can be the draught blowing the length of a corridor.

By midnight Bobby was extremely uncomfortable and weary and sad. By one o'clock every bone in his body ached with a distinct and separate ache. From two till seven minutes past he slept, and woke when his nodding head banged against the door-post. Between five minutes to three and three he slept again – uneasily. At half past three he was sorry he had ever been born. By a quarter to four he would hardly have wished even a sergeant or an inspector to be in his place, and at four he woke from a nightmare. At half past four he got up and walked about a little, very softly, so as to stretch his cramped and aching limbs, and soon after five he made up his mind he could abandon his self-imposed vigil, for it was daylight now and surely all danger must have passed.

Accordingly, stiffly and yawningly he returned to his own room, wondering whether to try to snatch a couple of hours' sleep or to see what a swim would do towards overcoming the effects of his night-long vigil he made up his mind very firmly he would say nothing about in his report. No need to expose himself to the unmerciful chaffing he might expect if that story got about.

He went to the window to see what sort of a morning it was, and when he looked out he saw upon the lawn below the dead body of a man, supine, the head no more than a tangle of blood and brain, a knife standing out just above the collar-bone, across the green and dewy grass a long red stream spreading out fanwise; and, even in the first bewildering shock of the horror and amazement he experienced, Bobby had no doubt but that there lay George Winterton, foully murdered.

CHAPTER XV

Dew

For a time – how long a time he never knew – Bobby stood there at the window, staring, watching this dreadful thing that lay there on the lawn in the soft morning light.

A kind of lack of apprehension had fallen on him, so that, though he saw and knew that he saw, yet what he saw seemed as if it lacked power to make entry to his mind and understanding. For he knew he had spent the night watching on the threshold of the door, locked from the inside, of the room in which slept the man who was at the same time lying dead without, and it seemed to him that this thing could not be and yet it was.

Fascinated he stared, motionless he stood, and his bewilderment, and the blank chaos of his thoughts, would scarcely have been increased had what he watched vanished away into nothingness while he still stared.

But it did not; the grisly thing lay there still, hard and clear of outline, real with its own terrible reality, and still, like a cry to heaven, there stretched that straight and crimson stream of blood, half way across the green verdure of the dewy lawn. The word 'dead' formed itself in Bobby's mind, almost with a shock of surprise. There came back into his mind an odd, disconnected memory of the first dead man he had ever seen – Sir Christopher Clarke – in what had come to be known, in newspaper jargon, as the 'Hamlet in Modern Dress' murder. This still form lying out there on the lawn had about it that same air of a deserted thing, from which all lending it significance had fled, he had then remarked. He remembered how, when the coroner, the well-known Mr James Adoor, had asked him how he had known at once the body was that of a dead man, he had tried, stammeringly and ineffectively, to explain this, and how Mr James Adoor had told him sharply he was there to give information, and for nothing else, and how he had flushed and, silenced, hung his head in meek acceptance of authority's stern rebuke. But this dead body on the lawn had about it somehow just that same air of emptiness; void and empty it lay and yet at the same time terrible and daunting.

This odd flash-back of memory, this first moment – interval – it might have been one moment or many – of sheer amazement passed. All at once, hardly knowing how he got there, he was in the passage just outside his room, shouting an alarm. He ran to Mr Winterton's door. It was still locked. He shook it violently and shouted, half expecting, such was the confusion of his mind, the tumult of his thoughts, to hear a response from within.

He bent down and saw the key was in the lock inside. Door and window were still securely fastened from within, and yet the inmate of the room lay dead without, and that could not be and yet it – was.

'Well, it's impossible; it can't be that; there's some explanation as simple as A B C,' he thought.

He heard doors opening and shutting and voices calling. Plainly the alarm he had cried had been heard. He ran down the stairs. The front door was locked and bolted. He tore it open and ran out.

By the side of the lawn he stood still, for the first time remembering, in the shock he had experienced, that he was an officer of the law, a guardian of the King's peace that had been this night violated, and that upon what he did during the next few moments much might depend.

During the night there had been a heavy dew that lay sparkling in crystal-clear drops upon the grass, and clearly outlined in this showed a trail of footsteps to and from the body, between it and the edge of the lawn near where Bobby was now standing, on the gravel path.

It was the murderer's trail, apparently, that he had never dreamed he had left behind him so plainly stamped upon the dewy grass, and on it Bobby focused his attention in an almost fierce concentration of every thought and sense. It was a man's, that was plain; and then from behind the clouds that till now had hidden it there shone forth the sun in full and sudden power.

Even as Bobby stooped in close, intent examination of that so clearly outlined double track of footprints to and from the dead man's body, the hot and splendid sun-rays began to drink up the dew. He saw the track begin to waver under his very eyes, to dissipate itself and vanish, as the hungry heat sucked the moisture up. Where, a little before, they had lain so clearly, offering their mute evidence of the coming and the going of the murderer, soon there was nothing left; and above shone the sun in splendour, a murderer's protector.

All that Bobby could do was to mark with twigs the exact spots where the track had left the gravel path and returned to it; and both points were almost exactly before the front door of the house. He heard someone behind him, and, turning, saw Colin Ross standing there.

'It's murder, murder!' he was stammering. 'Uncle George ... murdered ... like Uncle Archy,' he said in a whisper.

He was pale, shaken, aghast. That was natural enough. But Bobby noticed that he was dressed, except for his coat and collar, and he saw, too, that Colin's shoes were damp with fresh drops of moisture, as it were drops of dew. He said to him:

'You knew ... you knew what had happened ... you have been out here before?'

'No, I haven't. What do you mean?' Colin answered vehemently. 'I heard you shouting, that's all.'

'There is dew upon your shoes,' Bobby said.

Colin looked down at them.

'It's from the grass border; I must have walked on it,' he said.

'You did not. You came straight down the front door steps from the house,' Bobby answered.

'Well, I have now,' Colin said, and began to walk across the lawn.

But a little way away from the dead body he stopped short and put both his hands up to his face, as if to shut out the dreadful sight. It was evident the composure he had assumed at first, or trusted to, was breaking down. Bobby had the idea that, if he were guilty, it was an even chance that he might confess it then and there, or, if not guilty, at any rate tell frankly everything that he thought or knew. Bobby sought in his mind for something compelling to say that would force some such statement from Colin, but all he could think of was to call out loudly:

'Who did it? What do you know? What do you know?'

Colin did not answer. He had begun to tremble violently. From the path a woman's voice shrilled loudly:

'Oh, look, look, look! It's Mr Winterton! Oh, what have they done to him?'

It was Mrs Cooper. Close behind her was her husband. He was still in pyjamas, his feet thrust into bedroom slippers. Mrs Cooper had pulled on a dressing-gown. She began to walk across the grass towards the two young men, but Cooper himself sat down on the steps leading to the front door and looked as if he were going to faint or be ill. Mrs Cooper said:

'First it was Mr Archibald and now it's this. ... What has happened? ... Oh, who could have done such a thing?'

'Did you hear anything in the night?' Bobby asked.

'Nothing,' she said; 'nothing.'

She folded her hands before her and stood erect and grave, adding somehow a touch of dignity to that strange, gruesome scene. Then she said an odd thing.

'I am glad, at any rate,' she murmured, 'he enjoyed his last dinner.'

Bobby turned to Colin.

'Did you hear anything?' he asked.

'No, till I heard you shouting,' Colin answered. 'Did you hear anything yourself?' he added truculently.

'Nothing,' Bobby replied, 'and I was awake nearly the whole night.'

Colin looked up. Bobby's window was open, and almost directly overlooked the spot where the body lay.

'You were awake,' Colin repeated. 'A man was knocked out with a blow like that right under your window and you heard nothing?'

Bobby did not answer. Excess of precaution had once more proved its own undoing. He had heard nothing because he had been crouching in the corridor, keeping his absurd and foolish vigil outside Mr Winterton's door. Had he been content to stay in his own room, surely he would have heard something, seen some signal, as on that previous occasion, heard some murmur of words, or else the sound of that fierce blow which had crushed the victim's head, or at least caught an echo of the murderer's movements as he fled away. All that, however, he had no wish to explain just now. He knelt down and very carefully moved one of the dead man's limbs and felt the ground below, and also the ground beneath the body, as far as he could get his hand under.

'What are you doing?' Colin asked loudly and suspiciously, and then: 'We must do something. We must get help.'

'The ground under him is quite dry,' Bobby said. 'I think he must have been lying here before the dew began to fall.'

'Oh, well,' Colin muttered. 'Well, help me carry him inside.'

He stooped to take hold of the body, but Bobby checked him.

'I think we must not touch him,' he said. 'I suppose we ought to leave everything just as it is till the police come.'

'I suppose so,' agreed Mrs Cooper, 'but we can't leave him lying there like that, poor gentleman. I'll get a sheet to cover him.'

'We had better not even go into the house,' Bobby said. 'I think we had better all wait here for the present.'

'Oh, that's all rot,' Colin cried angrily.

Mrs Cooper was looking steadily at Bobby, a faint ironic smile at the corners of her mouth. He had the idea that she was thinking he was taking a good deal upon himself, that he was doing it all very badly, and that if she chose to take matters in hand – if she had the wish and the right to do so, that is – then it would all go much better. All that was a good deal to read into so faint and small a smile, but Bobby thought it was all there, and he was not sure, moreover, that she was not right. He could not help a slightly sulky expression his features assumed involuntarily, and then he had the ridiculous idea that really he was like a naughty little boy standing before his nurse or teacher. But when Mrs Cooper spoke it was in her housekeeper's smooth, deferential voice. She said:

'I think Mr Owen means the police may suspect us all. I think he is quite right. I expect they will. I expect it will be their first idea.' She looked down steadily at the long, crimson trail their eyes were all otherwise a little apt to avoid. 'I suppose, whoever did it, there would be blood on his clothes most likely. The police will want to be sure there's no blood on anything belonging to us.'

'Oh, that's all rot,' Colin repeated, though with less assurance. He looked angrily and doubtfully at Bobby. 'There's no blood on anything of mine, anyhow.'

'But there was dew on your shoes,' Bobby said slowly. 'It may be that means as much.'

Colin made a quick movement, and for a moment Bobby thought he was going to attack him. But if Colin had had that intention he mastered himself and turned away, muttering angrily. Bobby said:

'We've got to use the phone, though. That ought to have been done before.' He looked round. Cooper was still sitting on the doorsteps, looking very white and ill, but his wife made him a sudden gesture and he stood up and came a step or two towards them and then stood still again. He seemed indeed, Bobby thought, the most affected of them all. To Colin, Bobby said: 'I'm going into the house to ring up the police and a doctor. I will ask you and Mrs Cooper to stay here. You will be a guarantee, each of you, that neither of you touches the body. If Cooper will come into the house with me, he and I will each guarantee that neither of us touches anything but the phone.'

'You seem to think you've got to do it all,' Colin said to him ill-temperedly.

'I was the first to find the body,' Bobby answered. 'As you said, my window is just above, and I heard nothing. I think, in a way, it is my job.'

'What kept you awake?' Mrs Cooper said to him, and he thought there was a slight touch of suspicion in her voice.

'Oh, you know, those scones,' he answered; 'very jolly and all that, but I thought they might touch off that tooth of mine, and so they did. Not awfully bad, but I didn't sleep.'

'Oh, well, have it your own way,' Colin said, ignoring the toothache and referring to the arrangement Bobby had suggested. As Bobby turned away, Colin added quite loudly to Mrs Cooper, so loudly that Bobby was sure he was meant to hear: 'Do you think he had toothache really, or is he putting that on?'

Mrs Cooper did not answer and Bobby made no sign of having heard. He went into the house, followed by Cooper, who still went unsteadily and stumbling, almost like a drunken man.

'Pull yourself together,' Bobby told him sharply.

'It's his hair,' Cooper muttered, 'grey hair, all ... all over ... grey hair that's all bloody now.'

'I'm going to ring up to get help,' Bobby said.

In the hall he took down an overcoat from the hatstand and gave it to Cooper, who was shivering violently and seemed very cold.

'You had better put that on,' he said.

They crossed the hall and entered the study. Bobby went across to the door that led into the garden. He did not touch it, but he could see that it was not locked and that the bolts were drawn. Presumably that was how Mr Winterton had left the house. Bobby went to the phone and rang up first the police and then a doctor whose name Cooper gave him.

That done, they went out again to join the other two in their vigil by the body. Mrs Cooper had procured from the garage a motor-rug, with which she had covered the body.

'I couldn't leave the poor gentleman lying there like that,' she said when Bobby rejoined them.

Bobby made no comment. Cooper went back to his seat on the front door steps. Mrs Cooper took her place at the dead man's head and stood there, composed and grave, still with her air of lending a touch of dignity to the crude brutality of the scene. Colin paced restlessly up and down along the gravel path. Bobby occupied himself making a careful examination of the lawn along the path traced by those footsteps in the dew that the sun had made to vanish before his eyes. He found nothing; if any signs existed, they were too slight or hidden for him to distinguish. None of them spoke. Presently a boy arrived with milk from a neighbouring farm. Mrs Cooper told him to leave it at the kitchen door, and, afterwards he ran, wide-eyed and excited, with news that there had been an 'accident' at Fairview. When the doctor arrived, there was already a little crowd clustered at the entrance to the drive where Bobby had told them they must wait. There was nothing the doctor could do except estimate from the appearance of the body that the blow on the head must have been almost instantaneously fatal, that the knife-thrust had been inflicted afterwards, and that death had probably occurred about one or two in the morning.

Soon after that two cars arrived, containing Major Markham and his assistants, and with them, as Bobby saw with some relief, his own chief, Superintendent Mitchell, who had been spending the night at a local hotel and for whom Major Markham had called on his way.

CHAPTER XVI

Mary Raby's Story

THE investigation was soon in full swing. Photographers were busy; finger-print experts busier still; sketches were made; careful measurements taken of everything measurable. The victim's body was subjected to a meticulous examination. Of the lawn, an even more careful and minute examination was made, and a careful search was instituted in the hope of finding the weapon used to inflict the injuries on the head. Bobby's precaution in neither allowing the body to be touched nor in permitting either himself or any of the others to re-enter the house received official approval; and in the house itself a close inspection was organised, inch by inch almost.

But this had not been in force very long before Superintendent Mitchell came out to where were standing the two Coopers with Bobby, who for his part felt his position a little anomalous, not quite sure whether he was to consider himself investigator or investigatee. Mitchell said to them:

'One room seems to be locked on the inside. We can't get the door open; it's the room at the corner there; that last window ought to belong to it.'

'That's Mr Winterton's own room,' Mrs Cooper explained at once. 'The poor gentleman must have locked it behind him when he came out here.'

'It's locked on the inside,' Mitchell repeated.

'I don't see how it could be,' Mrs Cooper said doubtfully. 'Not on the inside.'

'Not unless someone's hiding there,' suggested Colin, who had been pacing restlessly up and down the garden paths but had now come up to join them.

Mrs Cooper looked very startled; her husband looked more like fainting than ever. Mitchell stared at Colin doubtfully.

'What makes you think that?' he asked.

'Well, if the door's locked on the inside ...' Colin replied, and left it at that.

'I helped Mr Winterton to wedge his window securely last night,' Bobby said. 'I heard him lock the door behind him after I said good night. I tried it again this morning, as soon as I saw what had happened when I looked out of my window. His door was still locked.'

Mitchell looked very thoughtful. The locked door evidently puzzled him. Mrs Cooper was looking puzzled, too, and Bobby thought there was some suspicion in the glances she was giving him. Colin repeated obstinately, but not with much conviction:

'Well, if it's right the door's locked on the inside well, then, there must be someone inside.'

Mitchell, still looking thoughtful, went back into the house, and came out again at once with Major Markham and one or two others. They asked for a ladder, and Cooper took them round to the outhouse, where one was kept.

While they were thus engaged, Mary Raby – whose absence Bobby had noticed by now, for, though in the first shock of his discovery he had not thought of her, he had since remarked that she had not yet made her appearance – came to the entrance to the drive. The policeman on duty there, holding back the little, awestruck, curious crowd gathered to stare and chat and whisper together, did not at first want to let her through, but did so when she explained she was one of the household and her position in it. Bobby went to meet her as she hurried up the drive, and she called out quickly:

'Is it true? Is it really true? I've only just heard ... it isn't really ...'

She paused, for she had caught sight of the still form upon the lawn – decently covered now, but of unmistakable significance.

'Oh, how did it happen? Who did it?' she asked, speaking almost to herself in low, stammering tones.

'They're trying to find out,' Bobby answered. 'It's a bad business.'

He wondered how it was she had been so long in hearing of what had happened, but he supposed that he had better leave the question to be put by those in charge.

Major Markham and Superintendent Mitchell came back, with two of their men carrying the ladder they had been for. They put it in position, and Bobby, leaving Miss Raby, went across to Mitchell and told him of his vigil on the threshold of the room the night before; and explained, too, how he had wedged the window. Considerable force had, indeed, to be used to get it open, even to the extent of smashing some of the woodwork. Then the officer who had done this descended again, and Mitchell, with Major Markham following him, climbed up in his place and through into the room.

Those on the lawn waited expectantly, half anticipating the sounds of a struggle to show the criminal had been discovered hiding there. But nothing happened, and the two investigators could be seen moving quietly to and fro inside the room. Colin said:

'There is no one there; not likely there would be; all bunk that the door was locked inside.'

'It can't have been if there was no one there,' Mrs Cooper agreed.

'Well, it was,' Bobby said, with emphasis.

'How can it have been if no one was there?' Miss Raby asked; and again Bobby thought Mrs Cooper looked at him doubtfully and suspiciously.

Some of Major Markham's men came up, and removed Mr Winterton's body to the garage, which had been hastily made ready for its temporary reception, and then a message came that the members of the household were at liberty to return indoors, as the preliminary investigation was now complete. A suggestion Mrs Cooper made that she should prepare breakfast was very favourably received. Mrs Adams and the day-girl, Jane, hitherto held up with the rest of the crowd at the entrance to the drive, were permitted to come through to help Mrs Cooper, now busy in the kitchen. Her husband even yet hardly seemed recovered from the shock of what had happened, and was of little use. Bobby, receiving no instructions, retired to his own room – where he found proof that it had not escaped the swift search made by the investigators – and busied himself writing a full report. Miss Raby, after attempting to enter the study, and finding it had been adopted as police headquarters, went to sit in the drawing-room, where she was presently joined by Colin, who, more from habit than for any other reason, had brought with him his *Ruff's Guide*, and sat by the window with it on his knees, but without opening it.

Presently the finger-print experts appeared to ask if they had any objection to their impressions being taken, and, none of them caring to object, the ceremony was duly gone through, though Colin grumbled that of course all their finger-prints must be all over the house – why not? The finger-print expert explained it was just a formality, and agreed cheerfully when Colin observed that it was a –

qualified – formality. Those of the Coopers, of Bobby, of Mrs Adams, and of the day-girl had been taken, and Miss Raby was about to undergo the same experience when certain savoury smells announced that breakfast was ready.

Mrs Cooper had prepared it on a liberal scale. It was done full justice to, and Mrs Cooper's popularity in official circles became remarkable. Bobby thought he had no appetite, but discovered he had when he put it to the test. Colin, however, contented himself with copious draughts of strong tea he strengthened still further, Bobby noticed, from a private flask, and a little dry toast he left almost untasted on his plate. Miss Raby, too, showed small disposition for food, though she seemed glad of the tea she was offered, and Jane, trying to tempt her with some crisp, fried ham, remarked that Mr Cooper, too, wouldn't touch a thing till Mrs Cooper fair made him, and all the better for it he was, too.

One by one they were summoned into the study, to tell what they knew and to answer the innumerable questions put them. All the time, too, the telephone bell kept ringing, so that one of Major Markham's plain-clothes men was kept almost continually busy answering it. Early in the afternoon there arrived, in a big, fast car, a round little man in horn-rimmed spectacles, who was, Bobby learnt, Mr Waring, the solicitor who had acted both for George Winterton and for his brother, Archibald. He disappeared into the study, and was there a long time, talking to Major Markham. Miss Raby and Bobby were the only two of the household who had not yet been asked for their statements, and, while they were waiting, Miss Raby said to Bobby:

'You know I wasn't at home last night. I suppose I had better say so at once.'

'I wondered why you seemed rather late in coming,' Bobby answered. 'Of course, you mustn't try to hide anything.'

'No,' she agreed. 'The car broke down. Miles had to take the engine nearly to bits.'

'Miles?' Bobby repeated. 'You mean Miles Winterton, Mr Winterton's other nephew?' When she nodded, he said gravely: 'If Mr Miles Winterton was near here last night, you ought to say so at once; he ought to have come along himself. It would make a very bad impression if it was thought he was keeping away on purpose.'

'I don't expect he knows anything about it yet,' she answered quickly, but with a note of hesitation, almost of fear, in her voice, so that Bobby thought he detected in her a hidden apprehension, one of which she herself was perhaps not yet wholly conscious, but that all the same was ready at any moment to leap into full growth.

'Does she know something, or is it just that she's afraid?' he asked himself. 'Is it for herself she's afraid; is it for her reputation, or is it – is it for Miles Winterton, because of what's happened here ... for him, or of him?'

For it was a fact that might be of very strange significance if Miles Winterton had really been in the vicinity of Suffby Cove during the night. There had been, Bobby knew, some bad feeling between uncle and nephew, and now this looked as if identity could be proved – 'identity,' that is, in the sense of identity of time and place between the suspect and the crime.

She saw how he was looking at her, and understood something of what was passing through his mind, though not all. She said quickly:

'I don't want you to misunderstand me. Miles and I have been engaged quite a long time, and some friends I have, who live not very far away on the Ipswich road, know about us. I've met Miles there other times, after Mr Winterton made a fuss about us, and last night we were all there together till quite late. I slept with my friend. They have only two bedrooms; she has one and her mother has the other, and I shared hers.'

'Where did Mr Miles Winterton go?' Bobby could not help asking, though he knew it was not his place to question her.

'He said he would be all right in the car,' she answered,

in a low, uneasy voice. 'It's not his own; he borrows it from a friend; it is very big, with lots of room. It was parked at the bottom of the orchard, and he said it would do ever so nicely. It was a lovely night, quite fine and warm. We were to start early, so as to get back here without anyone knowing.'

'Didn't Mrs Adams know?' Bobby asked.

'Oh, yes, but she promised not to say anything. She said it would be all right. She said it was a shame I couldn't see Miles oftener, and she would do just the same in my place. Only, then, when we were coming back, the car stopped and wouldn't go, and it took Miles ever so long to get it right again. He said it was very old, and nearly worn out.'

The story was probable enough. It might not be difficult to obtain corroboration for it. But accepting it implied that Miles could very well have journeyed hither in the night and done – what had been done, and returned again to the orchard behind the cottage of Mary Raby's friend, and none have known it. Then, too, he knew the house and his uncle's ways, and it might have been possible for him, as it would not have been for a stranger, to entice Mr Winterton out into the garden.

It looked bad enough to Bobby, almost as if the solution lay there. Only there were points unexplained. The theory of Miles Winterton's guilt did not seem as yet to make a coherent whole. But when they knew more—— The small quiet voice of Mary Raby broke upon his thoughts. She had read them clearly, perhaps because of a certain correspondence with her own. She said, with a kind of controlled passion:

'He didn't do it; he never did.'

'Well, tell them everything, but don't tell them that,' Bobby said. 'To declare a man is innocent is as good as saying that you know others think him guilty.'

A policeman opened the study door, and came up to them.

'Major Markham's compliments,' he said, 'and might he have the pleasure of seeing Miss Mary Raby now?'

CHAPTER XVII

Certain Evidence

It was a long time before Miss Raby emerged from the study, and when she did her bearing showed very plainly how trying she had found the ordeal. She said to Bobby as she passed him:

'It's not fair to talk about Miles. I'm sure he doesn't even know yet. Why should he?' She added: 'There's a crossword puzzle I ought to send the *Daily Announcer* to-night, and I can't even think. Shall I send them poor Mr Winterton's instead? That one he was working on, you know.'

Bobby saw that in the reaction of her relief at escaping from the close questioning to which she had been subjected, she was on the point of breaking down and becoming hysterical. He took her into the drawing-room, which was fortunately unoccupied, and made her lie down on the sofa, and then sent Mrs Cooper to her with a cup of strong tea.

'I wonder if this Miles Winterton can be the murderer,' he thought. 'Anyhow, if she doesn't think so herself, it's pretty clear she is afraid we may.'

It was, in fact, a little strange that the young man had not yet made his appearance at Fairview, since by now the news of the murder had probably been published in every evening paper in the country. In fact, Bobby was now called to the front door, where an altercation was taking place with two enterprising reporters who had managed to evade the police cordon outside, and, having got hold of Bobby's name in the village, had asked for him on the pretext of being friends. It was a claim Bobby had to repudiate, as politely as he could, which, however, did not prevent an 'Exclusive Interview with Murdered Man's Guest' appearing next day in one of the London papers.

After that there was another long delay, during which Bobby – who was always learning afresh and with difficulty that patience is a virtue great, and that detectives, like little boys, must learn to wait, and often to wait almost as if for evermore – had nothing to do but sit and muse in the lounge hall. He did, however, manage to obtain from Mrs Cooper, going to and fro, busy with her household duties, a copy of a photograph of Miles Winterton she extracted for him from a collection of family photos.

'The poor lamb in there,' Mrs Cooper told him, nodding towards the drawing-room, as she gave him the photograph, 'has dropped off to sleep, bless her heart. I call it a shame to worry her with a lot of questions. She can't know anything when she wasn't here. And Mr Miles is a real gentleman, and hasn't been near the place for weeks, so what can he know, either?'

'I suppose they've got to question everybody,' Bobby observed, a little surprised by Mrs Cooper's use of the phrase 'poor lamb,' for it was not like her to use such expressions, and they came a little oddly from her, who had more aloofness and reserve than tenderness in her general manner.

He studied, with interest, the photograph she gave him. It was that of a tall, good-looking young man, with a frank open expression, Bobby thought, but then he knew already that looks go for little, and that a man may be a murderer and yet show the world as smiling, frank, and friendly a face as any innocent. For, indeed, murder is the strangest as it is the most terrible of deeds – may discharge itself, as lightning from the clouds, from the most hidden of obscure motives; may be as swift in conception and in execution as it is eternal in result.

By now it was late in the afternoon, and Mrs Cooper appeared with tea – luncheon she had already provided for them all, so consolidating the popularity her breakfasts had won her. She said to Bobby, as she was carrying plates of bread and butter and cake into the dining-room:

'It's a mercy there was plenty in the house, but I don't know how I'm to go on if these gentlemen stay after to-day.. Or what Cooper and me are to do, neither, now the poor master's gone.'

'I believe Mr Winterton's lawyer is here,' Bobby explained. 'I expect he will be able to tell you something.'

'Well, I would like to know,' Mrs Cooper repeated. 'Cooper's worrying a lot. If him and me's to find a new place, we can't set about it too soon. Your face is a little swollen, Mr Owen.'

'It's that tooth of mine,' Bobby explained.

She advised him again to visit the dentist she had spoken of, and returned to her household duties; and soon after that there arrived the summons Bobby had been so long expecting, to present himself in the study.

Major Markham was seated in Mr Winterton's place at the big writing-table. On his left was one of his colleagues, and another was sitting close behind. In Miss Raby's seat was a shorthand writer, taking down everything that was said. There were three of these, taking the work in turn. On the table stood what was already a sufficiently formidable pile of documents referring to the case. A little to the right sat Superintendent Mitchell in his capacity as a helpful observer. He was following everything that passed with the closest attention, though he did not look like it. Close by, Mr Waring occupied an armchair, his hands clasped before him, his round spectacled face puckered up into an expression of extreme distaste, as if he felt this was an affair with which no respectable family solicitor of unblemished reputation and long standing should have been asked to concern himself. Apparently he was already informed of Bobby's identity as an officer of police, detailed here for special duty, for he showed no surprise when Bobby was so addressed, and, indeed, hardly looked up from the pile of manuscript on his knees. Apparently answering some remark Major Markham had just made, he said:

'Oh, it's all exceedingly interesting. Poor Winterton was extraordinarily in earnest about this book of his. In his view, what was necessary for everyone's safety was a store of gold; that meant security, he thought, with things everywhere all topsy-turvy as they are. Quite right, too, in my opinion, and, if his book can be published, it ought to be, I think.'

Mitchell, who, not listening to this, had been looking at Bobby, said:

'What's the matter with your face, Owen?'

'Oh, just a touch of toothache, sir,' Bobby answered.

Major Markham withdrew his attention from the projected book on the gold standard, hardly noticed the reference to Bobby's swollen face, and began to ask a good many questions on Bobby's report, which had been already read.

'You spent the whole night at the door of Mr Winterton's room,' he said, 'and you are sure you heard nothing?'

'Quite sure, sir.'

'Did you sleep?'

'Not very much,' answered Bobby ruefully. 'I dropped off now and again, but only for minutes at a time, and no one could possibly have got in or out without my knowing it – couldn't be done. I thought as I was watching at the door, and the window was fastened up, Mr Winterton was all right. I can't understand it even now. I almost thought I was dreaming, or had gone cracked, when I looked out of my window and saw him lying there on the lawn.'

Major Markham smiled.

'I don't think there's any great mystery about that,' he remarked.

'Never is about anything,' observed Mitchell. 'Not when you know.'

'After you heard Mr Winterton lock his door, and saw his light go out,' the Major continued, 'you went to your own room for a few minutes?'

'I wasn't away for more than five minutes or so,' Bobby answered. 'And when I got back the door was still locked, for I tried it.'

'Five minutes is plenty of time for a man, who most likely hadn't even undressed, to slip out of his room and downstairs again.'

'But the door was locked on the inside,' Bobby protested. 'I am positive of that, for I looked to make sure, and the key was still in the lock inside.'

'It's not difficult to turn a key from the outside by means of a fine pair of pliers,' observed Major Markham. 'In point of fact, there are fresh scratches on the key, and, in a drawer of Mr Winterton's writing-table here, we've found pliers that seem to fit exactly, though that'll have to be confirmed by the experts, Presumably, Mr Winterton came out of his room as soon as he heard you go away, and then turned the key from the outside by means of the pliers we've found, so that you shouldn't know he wasn't there any longer.'

'But why? What for?' protested Bobby, scarcely less bewildered by this explanation than he had been by the thing itself. 'I'm sure he knew he was in danger of some sort. He knew I was there to protect him all I could, and then, and then——'

'Obvious enough,' smiled Major Markham, not displeased by the air of frank bewilderment worn by this smart young Londoner. 'Obviously he preferred the loss of your protection to the risk of your knowing what he was up to. Evidently, therefore, it was something – well, let us say, illegal' – this with a glance at Mr Waring, plainly all ready to defend his late client's memory – 'or, at any rate, something he didn't wish to be known by anyone whose duty it would be to make a report to the authorities. And that plainly links up with the telegram warning him that someone had just been released from gaol. Most likely he underestimated the real danger he was in. Luckily, it shouldn't be difficult to find out who the telegram came from, and who it refers to. We're taking steps to see that every released prisoner for that day or two is accounted for – and, once identity is established, we shall most likely find the whole thing clear itself up. It seems pretty plain that for some reason this released prisoner was able to insist on a secret interview at night with Winterton – and that during the interview the murder occurred, though whether our ex-prisoner was the actual murderer is not quite so certain.'

'Yes, sir,' agreed Bobby doubtfully. 'Only——'

'Only what?'

'Well, sir, if it was like that, who killed the Airedale, and why? That happened before whoever the telegram refers to was released; so it couldn't have been him.'

'I don't see much difficulty in that,' Major Markham said. 'There was certainly already someone here who was concerned in some way – remember that other interview at night you mention in your report with the girl, Laura Shipman. Possibly she had something to do with the getting rid of the dog.'

'Yes, sir. Only I can't see why it was necessary to do that – get rid of the dog, I mean. If Mr Winterton was expecting anyone, he could easily have kept the dog quiet. I'm sure Mr Winterton was very puzzled at the dog's death. I think it frightened him.'

'So far as regards the Laura Shipman girl,' Mitchell observed,' she seems out of what's happened just now. It seems clear that after Owen here saw her, and paid her the reward, she left to visit some friends at Cromer.'

'Ran away,' suggested Major Markham. 'Why? Knew what was coming, perhaps.'

'You'll be able to tell that better after you've heard her story,' Mitchell agreed.

'Probably it'll be a job to get her to speak at all,' Major Markham remarked pessimistically. 'They all know they needn't if they don't want to.' He referred again to Bobby's report. 'You mention in your statement that you saw footprints on the grass of the lawn – leading to the body?'

'Yes, sir, they were quite plain,' Bobby answered. 'They led straight to the body, and then back to the gravel path, just opposite the front door of the house.'

'You didn't measure them?'

'There wasn't time, sir,' Bobby answered, and told again how they had vanished before his eyes – drunk up, as it were, by the suddenly released heat of the sun.

There was a silence for a moment, for his tale, of how the mute evidence of the trail the murderer left had passed away even while Bobby watched, impressed itself oddly upon the imaginations of his listeners. Then Markham, still studying the report, said:

'You are quite clear there were traces of dew on Colin Ross's shoes?'

'Yes, sir.'

'His statement is that he stepped on the grass borders after he came out of the house, and that accounts for it?'

'I am sure that's not true,' Bobby answered. 'I am quite certain he had only just come down from the front-door steps on to the gravel path when I spoke to him.'

'The murder took place, apparently, from the doctor's evidence,' Markham continued, 'somewhere about midnight or a little after. He is quite certain about it; though, in my experience, the more certain a doctor is, the more likely he is to be mistaken. Anyhow, no dew could have fallen by then, and you say yourself, in your report, that the ground under the body seemed dry?'

'Yes, sir,' agreed Bobby again. 'I thought at first – I am afraid I was a bit rattled – but just at first I took it the dew on Mr Ross's shoes proved he was the murderer. Now, I think it only proves that he, not I, was the first to discover the body. Only, why didn't he give an alarm? Unless, of course, he committed the murder earlier and went back later to the body for some reason – either to get something he wanted perhaps, or perhaps to destroy some evidence he was afraid would implicate him.' Bobby paused, and added: 'I've seen the list of articles on the body. There was no mention of a pocket-book I saw Mr Winterton using several times.'

'It was lying on the table here,' explained Markham. 'It has been identified as the one he habitually carried. It had money still in it – about twelve pounds in notes – some letters that don't seem very important, the "released from prison" telegram, and one or two other papers.'

As he spoke he handed to Bobby a careful list of the contents of the pocket-book. Bobby brooded over it for a moment or two in silence. Then he said:

'Mr Winterton was working at a crossword puzzle he seemed very interested in. He wouldn't let anyone see it but he told me once or twice I might find it worth looking at when it was finished. I don't know why he said that, or whether he meant anything. But he used to keep his notes about it in his pocket-book, for I've seen him put them away in it, rather carefully, once or twice. From this list, it seems they weren't in it when it was found.'

'If there had been anything of the kind, it would certainly have been mentioned,' Major Markham agreed. 'But I don't see that it matters, does it? Most likely he got tired of the thing and tore it up. Anyhow, we are here to solve a crime – a murder – not a crossword puzzle.'

'Yes, sir,' agreed Bobby, rebuked, but with something in his tone that made Major Markham ask him sharply:

'You don't suggest that what Colin Ross wanted was to get hold of a crossword puzzle, do you?'

'I don't see my way clearly enough to think anything at all as yet, sir,' Bobby answered frankly. 'Except that I think it strange Mr Winterton talked about it to me once or twice, and that now it's vanished, when I am sure he was very interested in it – for some reason, only heaven knows what!'

'Well, anyhow, there's no trace of it in his papers,' Major Markham observed. 'What's more important is that Mr Waring tells us more than twenty thousand pounds of Mr Winterton's capital seems to have disappeared lately – and putting things together, that and the "released prisoner" telegram, I say, blackmail.'

'It's my own idea,' agreed Mr Waring. 'Only – I can't imagine that a man like Winterton—— Poor fellow, I knew him well – it seems incredible, blackmail. The actual amount is nearly twenty-five thousand pounds, as far as I can make out at present.'

'Twenty-five thousand pounds,' repeated Bobby, staggered at the size of the sum. 'But surely, an amount like that can't have just – vanished.'

'Seems so,' Major Markham told him. 'Mr Waring tells us that late last year the two brothers, Archibald and George, realised securities to somewhere about that amount. The explanation they gave Mr Waring is that they intended exchange speculations – about the quickest way there is just now of making money.'

'Of losing it,' interposed Mr Waring gently. 'Of losing it.'

'After Archibald's still unexplained death,' Major Markham went on, 'George realised another ten or twelve thousand, explaining to Mr Waring that their transactions were incomplete, and that he would take over all liabilities and return his brother's share of the capital employed to his widow. That was done, and Mr Waring knows nothing more, and, so far, there's no trace in Mr Winterton's papers of what became of the money.'

'Went down the drain, most likely,' interposed Mr Waring again; 'that's your exchange speculating all over.'

'Only we don't know,' said Major Markham. 'And we ought to know. What's become of that money may have an intimate bearing on the case. Another thing, our finger-print people have found Colin Ross's finger-prints on the cover of the pocket-book. He accounts for that by saying that his uncle dropped it on the floor last night, and he picked it up and returned it to him. He says no one saw the incident. Miss Raby says no such incident occurred, to the best of her knowledge; and she was in Mr Winterton's company the whole day after lunch. Ross's finger-prints have also been found on the handle of the door leading from this room to the garden. Ross says, last night he went in and out by that door once or twice. Miss Raby says he was never in the room till tea, and she is certain he did not use the door or even go near it. The handle of the knife found in Mr Winterton's body has been examined, and the report has just been phoned to us. It is an ordinary kitchen-knife – such as any number of shops sell, and any number of people use. Colin Ross's finger-prints are on it, too. He says he only remembers touching a knife of the kind once recently – when Mrs Cooper asked him to do some trifling job for her, two or three days ago. Mrs Cooper remembers the incident perfectly, but says she only has two knives like this one, and they are both still in the kitchen. She produced them. The analyst's report says that, while the recent blood on the knife is human, there is dried blood in the crevice between handle and blade that is undoubtedly animal. So that makes it look as if it was the same knife that was used before for getting rid of the dog.'

'I wonder,' observed Bobby thoughtfully, 'if there was any reason, after Mr Winterton's head had been beaten in in the brutal way it was, why a knife should be used as well?'

'To make sure, I suppose,' Major Markham answered. 'Quite natural – you often notice murderers never feel they are sure enough. In that connection, the weapon used for the murder has been found – in the garden, behind some bushes. It's a brick, apparently taken from a heap behind one of the outhouses, left over, I understand, when some repairs were carried out a year or two ago. There is blood on it, and there is no doubt it is what was used. Colin Ross, of course, would have known the bricks were lying there. Also, he acknowledges he has been betting heavily, and that probably means losing heavily – it generally does. If so, he would be pressed for money. But against that is the fact that Mr Waring tells us Mr Winterton has never altered an old will by which all his money goes to his brother and his brother's heirs, so that in fact none of the three nephews benefit. But it is doubtful if Ross knew that. It seems George Winterton had intended to make a will dividing his estate between the nephews; and they would have had a share, too, if he had died intestate. We can't rule out the possibility that Ross expected to inherit a big share of the estate. Only I don't know if that can be proved. There seems no doubt, however, that Winterton had given all his three young men to understand he was intending to alter his will in their favour.'

'One of whom,' put in Mitchell suddenly, 'is known to have been in the neighbourhood last night, and is also said to have been on bad terms with Winterton.'

'Exactly,' agreed Major Markham. 'So, had we better investigate Miles's movements last night, and hear what he has to say first, or is what we know enough to justify us in taking action against Ross? And, in any event, wouldn't it be better to wait till the matter of the "released prisoner" telegram has been cleared up? With such a clear clue in our hands, and such a simple task as discovering to whom the telegram referred, it might be better to wait before taking any overt action – no use risking a blunder when we're pretty sure to know for certain before long. In the meantime we can keep a sharp look-out on Ross. If he's guilty, he may give himself away. They often do.'

'That's to be your job, Owen,' Mitchell explained to Bobby. He added: 'What do you think yourself – that Ross did it?'

'Well, sir, at present it seems there's too much unexplained to make it worth while forming any opinion,' Bobby answered slowly. 'I should like it all to hang together better than it does. We haven't got the visit of that motor-launch explained, and we know no more than we did about Archibald's death – if it was accident, or murder, or, if so, who was responsible?'

'We shall most likely,' Major Markham said, with conviction, 'once we've got to the bottom of that telegram – won't be difficult either, I imagine, when we know it must be someone released so recently.'

'There's so much that wants fitting in,' Bobby went on, half to himself. 'The swilling down of the Greek Temple summer-house in the garden here, for example, and the disappearance of the crossword puzzle. I would give a lot to find that and have a look at it.'

CHAPTER XVIII

Colin Catches Crossword Fever

But of this crossword puzzle it seemed no sign or trace remained in the crowd of papers that filled the drawers of Mr Winterton's writing-table, or, indeed, anywhere else; and, though Major Markham did go so far as to promise that Bobby should be informed if it, or any notes concerning it, were found, very plainly he attached no importance to it.

'Just his way of passing his time,' he commented, dismissing the matter with a gesture. 'It's a perfect craze with some people – crossword puzzles, I mean. Why, I've an uncle who fines himself a shilling for charity for every minute over twenty he takes solving the one in the *Telegraph* each morning, and allows himself sixpence off for every minute he takes less than the twenty. He says he was three and six up last year, and will be more this time most likely. And I expect Winterton was like that, only he was trying his hand at composing instead of solving.'

With this Bobby had to be content; and when presently he was dismissed from the study he found Mrs Cooper in the hall, evidently still worried about her future and that of her husband, and about how the household was to be carried on.

'There's the books,' she said. 'Mr Winterton, poor gentleman, would have given me the money to pay them tomorrow, and now I don't know what I'm to do.'

Bobby promised to speak to Mr Waring, who was, he understood, an executor under the will, and later, Mr Waring himself talked to Mrs Cooper – Cooper himself, still suffering from shock, had retired to bed – and arranged for her and her husband to continue in charge for the present, with authority to meet all necessary expenses.

Colin also, who had said something about finding rooms in London, was asked if he minded staying on at Fairview for the present. It would be convenient, he was told; there were still various matters about which he might be able to give the police useful information, and it might save them much time and trouble if he would remain on the spot for a few days. Somewhat grudgingly, he consented, but Bobby was aware of an odd impression that in reality this arrangement suited Colin very well, and that he had no real intention of quitting Suffby Cove just yet. It might be, of course, that he wished to remain on the spot to watch his interests, for that Colin had a very keen eye for money Bobby was quite convinced. It was understood, further, that Miss Raby was to stay on for the time. Bobby also was to remain ostensibly as a principal witness whose evidence would be required at the inquest; in reality to watch events in general and Colin Ross in particular.

The hour was late before Major Markham and his assistants departed, and even then a sergeant of the county police was left in charge, since much routine work still remained to be done. Both Mitchell and the lawyer had left earlier in the evening, and the remaining inmates of the house, after a day of such great and terrible nervous strain, were anxious enough to seek their beds.

All except Bobby, who sought his room, indeed, but not his bed, and in his room, with his handkerchief to his cheek, paced up and down – up and down, without pause or rest. And the pacing up and down, up and down, of a thirteen-stone man who has neglected to remove a pair of somewhat heavy boots, can be distinctly disturbing, and even trying, to the occupants of adjoining rooms, especially when now and again a stumble over a chair, or a stool kicked from one end of the room to the other, varies the performance.

It was not long before Colin was hammering at the door and begging Bobby, in terms more forcible than polite, to stop that infernal stamping about. Bobby contritely promised compliance, explained that it was that beastly tooth of his, and threw himself on the bed with a crash that shook the house. But in two or three minutes he was up again, once more pacing his room in entire oblivion of Colin's protests. Then came Mrs Cooper, and again Bobby explained that his tooth simply wouldn't let him rest; the only way he could get relief was by keeping in violent movement. He wished to goodness now that he had taken Mrs Cooper's advice and gone to the dentist she had told him about; if there had been a chemist near, he would have knocked him up and got something to relieve the pain – ow-w, it was just like a red-hot needle very slowly boring right up through the middle of his head.

'I know there's nothing you can do,' he told Mrs Cooper; 'no one can.'

Mrs Cooper smiled. To be told there was nothing she could do always put her on her mettle. She came back with a bottle and some cottonwool.

'Try a little of this,' she said.

'Laudanum?' Bobby asked eagerly. 'I say, you are a wonder, Mrs Cooper. But I thought people weren't allowed to buy this stuff now.'

'I had some by me,' she answered. 'I've had it for years. It's nearly finished now,' she added, showing a two-ounce bottle very nearly empty.

Bobby accepted the soaked bit of cottonwool she offered him and put it in his mouth. He drew a long breath of almost instant relief. That was much better, he said, and Mrs Cooper retired, and at last the disturbed household was able to settle down to sleep. Indeed, Bobby's cure was so complete that by morning the swelling had entirely disappeared and he felt sufficiently recovered to go for a swim.

It was a beautifully fine and warm morning, but he had the sea to himself. Few of the fisherfolk of the village indulged in early-morning bathing, and Colin, who was a good swimmer and generally enjoyed an early dip, evidently did not feel up to it to-day. Neither did Miss Raby appear, though she, too, was an excellent swimmer, and generally bathed when the weather was good. While Bobby was drying himself, one of the villagers came up and began to talk, evidently eager for all the latest news about the previous day's tragedy. There were three or four newspaper men, he said, who had passed the night in the village and were offering liberal payment for even the least scrap of fresh information, and Bobby remarked that the police were threatening very severe penalties on anyone who indulged in any gossip, while he himself, for his part, knew simply nothing at all. So, changing the subject, he talked about the bathing, and got confirmation once again of the fact that Archibald Winterton had been a strong and practised swimmer whose death by drowning on a morning as fine and calm and warm as was this one was frankly inexplicable. His brother George, however, had quite frankly preferred a warm bath in the house to all the sea could offer, wherein he had had the sympathy of the fisherfolk, whose own view of the sea was quite simply that it was best kept out of. Few of them could swim a stroke, it seemed, and Miss Raby had been quite distressed by his indifference and ignorance of something so likely to be useful to those living by the sea, both near it and on and from it, and had offered to teach some of the children. She had offered to teach Mrs Cooper, too, and Jane, the day-girl, but had given up when Jane objected to the risk of having her permanent wave ruined and after Mrs Cooper had nearly drowned the two of them by clasping Miss Raby round the neck and upsetting her in deep water.

'Fair lost her head, she did,' said the fisherman, chuckling. 'There's always some as can't abide the sea.'

'Generally she seems such a very capable woman,' Bobby remarked.

'It was the sea did it,' his companion replied. 'If she had the chance she would tell us all when to go to bed and what time to get up, but the sea was too much for her. There was a tale she was to have a job with that gent who wanted to buy up the whole place only Mr Winterton wouldn't let him. Lord, if she had, she would have been a sort of king like round here, and there's some of us would have cleared out.'

Bobby asked a few more questions, but got nothing more than that there had been a general rumour that, if the London man's scheme had gone through, Mrs Cooper was to have had employment under him as compensation for losing her place with Mr Winterton. The defeat of the scheme had undoubtedly been a great relief to some of the villagers, but an equal disappointment to others, who had been dazzled by the thought of all the money that would be brought by it into the district.

'But money's not everything,' said Bobby's companion wisely, 'and as for swimming, I don't hold with it. What's it good for when you've a sound boat under your feet? And if you get swamped – well, swimming only means you drown slow instead of quick.'

Bobby suggested that sometimes ability to swim might mean that you would not drown at all, but his new friend did not agree. You kept out of the water as long as you could, but once it got you – well, it had you, what was the good of prolonging the agony by splashing about?

'Look at Mr Archibald,' he said triumphantly; 'best swimmer ever was, they said, and what did it do for him? Calm, fine morning just like this, but he drowned all the same, all along of swimming.'

'Perhaps it wasn't all along of swimming,' Bobby suggested, and stored this talk away in his mind, for there was some of it, he thought, that might, if only he knew how, be woven into the pattern which he felt, once he could complete it, would make a picture coherent and complete of all these tragic happenings.

He went back to the house, where all day long there was a constant coming and going on matters connected with the investigation. But Mitchell did not appear, and for Bobby there was nothing to do but to watch and wait and think, think perpetually without respite or pause.

The special task he had been allotted of watching Colin was not one that occupied him much, for Colin never stirred from the house. With his inevitable companion, *Ruff's Guide*, before him, and a sheaf of papers on which he was apparently making those elaborate calculations of weights and ages he was always so careful to let no one else get a glimpse of, destroying them utterly to the last fragment so that no one else should have any idea of the conclusions he had arrived at.

For Miss Raby's movements Bobby was not specially responsible, but she, too, spent the whole day in the house, occupying herself with the morning's correspondence and afterwards with the typing of a fair copy of the chapter of his book on which Mr Winterton had been at work. Bobby, finding her thus occupied, introduced the question of the crossword puzzle Mr Winterton had been amusing himself with composing.

'He never let you see it, did he?' Bobby asked. 'I think I

remember he said he wanted to finish it alone, all by himself.'

'He was rather funny about that,' she answered. 'He seemed quite anxious to keep it away from everyone – I can't think why.'

'You've no idea what it was?' Bobby asked again. 'I should like awfully to have a look at it, but it seems to be missing somehow.'

'Perhaps he got tired and tore it up,' she suggested. 'I made a copy of it once – the first version, I mean.'

'You did,' Bobby exclaimed, controlling his excitement. 'Have you got it still?'

'I don't think so,' she answered. 'I made it one afternoon before I realised he was so keen on finishing it by himself. It seemed rather silly, but, of course, if he wanted to complete it himself, all alone, I didn't mind. I copied it with the idea of helping, but if he didn't want to be helped it wasn't any good.'

'Don't you think you might have it by you still?' Bobby insisted, with an anxiety he could not quite conceal, for somehow he had grown in his thoughts to attach an odd kind of importance to this crossword puzzle, and Mr Winterton's insistence on keeping it from the sight of other people.

But Miss Raby shook her head.

'I've looked,' she said. 'I remember taking it home to work at it, but I can't remember anything else about it. I expect it got destroyed with my rough tries – when you are making up a puzzle you have to make all sorts of tries. I always have a big pile to burn after I've got one finished, and I expect the copy of Mr Winterton's got torn up with some of them. Anyhow, I'm sure I've not got it now, because they asked me about it yesterday, and I looked very carefully and there's not a trace of it anywhere. It can't be anything important, can it?'

'No one can say, if it can't be found,' Bobby answered moodily.

Miss Raby, dismissing the question as one that at any rate had little interest for her, went on with her typing.

'Though I don't suppose the book will ever be published now,' she said regretfully to Bobby, still glooming over the loss of the crossword, 'and it's such a pity; it's awfully clever, poor Mr Winterton was so wrapped up in it – he really thought he had a message to give the world: that there was no safety except in gold; real money that's always real, and not paper you can burn or mice can chew or anything.'

'I suppose that's what his book was about,' Bobby remarked, rousing himself from his crossword meditative gloom, and asked if he might look at it.

Miss Raby saw no objection, and Bobby took the typed sheets and found himself plunged into a highly technical discussion of currency theory of which he could understand very little. He was still struggling with it all when there arrived a tall, good-looking young man in a quaint, old-fashioned car that must have been quite four or five years old and that looked antediluvian, so that garage hands crowded round it as round some prehistoric relic. He was Miles Winterton, the murdered man's second nephew, and Miss Raby gave him a greeting that was by itself enough to show on what terms they were. She introduced him rather shyly to Bobby, and Mrs Cooper, previously warned that he was coming, appeared to say she had got ready for him a room just across the passage from the one Bobby occupied. She had before suggested to Bobby that he ought to go to the dentist, and now she suggested it again, evidently fearing another disturbed night. But he protested her cure had been so complete there was no fear of that.

'I haven't had a twinge since you gave me that stuff of yours,' he assured her. 'You know, I don't believe it was really toothache at all; it was just the result of all that excitement and worry, if you know what I mean. I suppose a girl would have fainted; I got the toothache instead. Girls always know what's best. It's made Mr Cooper quite ill, too, hasn't it?' he added sympathetically.

Cooper, indeed, was plainly still in a highly nervous condition, going about his work with a deathly white face and hands that shook and trembled, but getting little sympathy from his almost openly contemptuous wife.

But, indeed, none of them felt quite normal yet, unless it was Mrs Cooper, who seemed her usual quiet, dignified, efficient self. Even Colin, though he hardly spoke and kept his nose close to his *Ruff's Guide* and his calculations he was so careful to let no one else see – precautions he had redoubled recently, covering his notes with his hand or his book the moment anyone drew near – was obviously in almost as nervous and wrought-up a condition as was Cooper. Miss Raby held herself in better control, but Miles was very restless and agitated and made no attempt to conceal the fact that he felt himself under suspicion.

'The first I knew of it was when they came to root me out at old Aunt Aggie's I had asked to put me up for the night,' he told them more than once. 'They wouldn't believe at first I knew nothing about it. I hadn't seen the paper. I did notice something on a placard about "Seaside Murder," but how was I to know that meant poor old uncle? At me for hours, they were, asking all sorts of fool questions, and now, just when I thought I was sure of a job in South Africa – big public works contract; seven years' safe at least – they've given it to another johnny and I'm on the street again, just as Mary and I were fixing it up to get married whether uncle liked it or didn't.'

'You're all right now,' Colin grumbled, without looking up. 'Aunt Archy comes in for the money, apparently, and she'll hand out a good whack to you – she was always pally with you, and thought it was so sweet and romantic about you and Mary. Jimmy will get something, too. I shan't. She thinks I'm a lost soul. I shan't get a penny, unless I——' He paused. 'Uncle George meant us to have it all between us, but Aunt Archy won't mind that. No sportsman; a woman never is.' He paused again. 'I'll do the sporting thing,' he said. 'If I make good my claim to what he meant us to have, I'll go straight whacks with you and Jimmy.'

'What on earth are you talking about?' Miles demanded. 'Haven't got another will up your sleeve, have you?'

'Perhaps,' retorted Colin. 'Why not? Uncle George always said he meant to make one.' He added: 'With a few more thousands I could start a stable that would have the rest of 'em beat standing. Anyhow, you've nothing to worry about; you're all right either way.'

'Well, I don't see why that should make the police johnnies look down their noses at me,' Miles complained. 'The worst of it is, I can't prove I spent the night tucked up in the car. I did, but I suppose I could have got over here all right enough and done in poor old uncle and got back again without anyone knowing.'

Mrs Cooper had come into the room on some trifling household errand or another, just in time to hear this remark. She looked at the two young men somewhat queerly and then went out again.

'Oh, Miles,' Mary Raby protested, 'don't talk like that. Mrs Cooper heard you, and didn't you see how she looked?'

'Well, it's what everyone's thinking,' Miles grumbled, 'police especially.'

'They think just the same of me,' Colin pointed out; 'perhaps they think now we did it together.'

'Oh, lor',' exclaimed Miles, and then no more was said, and Bobby, sitting near, was silent, too, thinking more and more of that lost crossword puzzle he could not help believing, if only he could find it, would throw some light upon the mystery.

Then he got up suddenly to leave the room, and, as he did so, passing behind Colin, was just in time to see him push his open *Ruff's Guide* over scraps of papers that seemed covered not so much with figures as with scribbled letters, incomplete words, and other jotted notes that looked very much as if what Colin were working at was no turf calculation of weights and ages and so on, but rather some crossword puzzle. Bobby stopped and said:

'Hullo, you've got the crossword fever, too?'

'It's the one in the *Announcer* this morning I was trying,' Colin muttered, crumpling all his notes together in his hand. 'That's all.'

CHAPTER XIX

Blank Walls

Two or three days passed with no apparent change in the situation so far as Bobby was aware, though journalists still haunted the neighbourhood in the hope of picking up stray crumbs of 'exclusive' information, and though officers of the county police still bustled to and fro on mysterious errands.

At Fairview, life had fallen back into an accustomed household routine under the firm and competent direction of Mrs Cooper. Cooper himself, apparently quite recovered from the danger of the breakdown with which the shock of recent events had seemed at one time to threaten him, was now going again, as usual, about his ordinary duties, and was displaying, too, a somewhat unexpected dexterity in dealing with the eager newspaper men. He provided them with a stream of quite unimportant information, made opportunities for them to take innocuous photographs, and generally went out of his way to give them all the help he could, yet without ever saying or doing anything indiscreet. It was from him, however, that the *Announcer* special correspondent got the first hint of the theory he elaborated at some length in his paper that the murder was the work of unknown burglars, and that Mr Winterton, hearing someone moving about outside the house, had ventured forth to see what was happening, and then had been attacked and murdered by those he had interrupted.

'The use of the weapon employed – a brick apparently picked up at random from a heap behind the house – suggests very strongly that the crime was entirely unpremeditated,' declared the *Announcer*, quoting Cooper almost textually, and quoting also his testimony to the popularity Mr Winterton enjoyed with all who knew him; for, indeed, both the Coopers were stout upholders of the complete innocence of Colin Ross, as of that of the entire household.

'Asking questions the way they do, you would think the police suspected us all,' Cooper grumbled to almost everyone who came near him. 'Me and my missus and all, and young Mr Bobby Owen, too, though he has only been here a day or two and never met the master before, and, Lord knows, the missus and me, we've nothing to gain by losing a good place. Why, Mrs C. used to say it was almost like having your own house, with no one to interfere with you or the work or nothing – and there's not so many places you can say that of. And if it was anyone in the house, how did they manage to get the poor gentleman out there on the lawn?'

All this duly appeared in the *Announcer*, where Bobby read it and mused upon it in the long hours he spent going over and over in his mind every detail of the deaths of the two unfortunate brothers, and trying, but in vain, to fit into one coherent whole the story of these two crimes that he was now well persuaded were so closely connected. Then at last a message came that he was to report at once to Mitchell in London, and, glad of the prospect of action to relieve the intolerable strain of his ceaseless consideration and re-consideration of a problem that seemed insoluble, Bobby got out his motor-cycle and covered the distance to town at a rate that would have fully justified the immediate reimposition of the speed limit.

Arrived at headquarters, he was sent up at once to Mitchell's room, where he found the Superintendent expecting him.

'Anything new to report?' Mitchell greeted him.

'No, sir,' Bobby answered.

'What have you been doing with yourself?' demanded Mitchell next.

'Just thinking,' Bobby explained.

'Ah, then, you've been busy,' Mitchell said, and the influence of Bobby's public school training was so strong on him still that at first he thought this comment was sarcastic and implied a rebuke, for, indeed, England is the only country in the world in which the stammering excuse of a junior, beginning 'I thought,' is at once cut short by a severe and crushing: 'You aren't paid to think.'

However, a second glance told Bobby that Mitchell was quite serious, and really considered time spent in thinking to be time well spent.

'The hardest part of my job,' Mitchell added with a faint sigh, 'is to get men to think; tell a man he's to start for the Hebrides by the next train and he's all bright and alert; tell him to go and think it over, and he crawls off looking like a Channel passenger after a rough December crossing. Thinking get you anywhere?'

'No, sir. But I noticed Colin Ross working at a crossword puzzle, and it seems now he cuts the one out of the *Announcer* every morning.'

'Interesting,' muttered Mitchell. 'I suppose the one you say Mr Winterton was trying to compose hasn't made its appearance anywhere?'

'No, sir. Miss Raby told me she made a copy of it once with the idea of helping, but when she found Mr Winterton wanted to work it out alone she put it aside and now she can't find it. She thinks it was most likely destroyed with her "try-outs"; she always has a lot to burn after completing a puzzle. She says she is quite certain she hasn't got it now, and she can't remember much about it, except that "gold" was one of the words used."

'Pretty sure to be,' commented Mitchell; 'the poor chap had gold on the brain all right. It's a pity we can't get hold of it, but if it's been lost or destroyed, there's no chance. Anyhow, I can't quite see why Colin Ross should be taking a sudden interest in the *Announcer* puzzles, unless it's just to pass the time. I take it he knows he is very likely to have to stand his trial?'

'He says he is ready to face arrest,' Bobby answered gravely. 'He says no one can prove anything against an innocent man.'

'He would have had to face it already but for one thing,' Mitchell remarked grimly. 'Major Markham would have proceeded to arrest before this only for that wire – the "released prisoner" wire. We've tracked, questioned, traced, examined, every single soul, man, woman, or child, released from gaol about that date, and we've proved pretty conclusively that it is simply not possible for there to be any connection between any of them and this affair. It seemed the most certain, promising clue a poor worried detective could be supplied with, and it's simply gone out – like that.' Mitchell, as he spoke, blew out a match he had used to light a cigarette. 'Markham was very let down – so was I, for that matter. I believe he's been trying the asylums, but the wire said quite plainly "gaol." The only thing I can think of is that it must have been a code telegram, meaning something quite different from what it said.'

'Yes, sir,' said Bobby, very doubtfully; 'but it seems an odd phrase to use in code.'

'I know,' agreed Mitchell, 'but there it is – we've checked up on every living creature released about that date and it seems clear the telegram simply can't refer to any one of them. Unluckily, it's had a bad effect on the investigation. Markham was so sure he held the clue to the whole thing in his hands that other lines of inquiry have been rather neglected, I'm afraid. I daresay I should have done much the same. If you see a broad, straight road leading direct where you want to go, it's natural to follow it. Unluckily, this time it's led straight to a blank wall, and now Markham has got to go back and start fresh from the very beginning, after losing valuable time – and losing time in an investigation of this sort is often fatal.'

'The telegram must have meant something,' Bobby persisted; 'someone must have sent it for some reason.'

'That's what counsel for the defence will say if Markham decides to arrest Colin Ross,' Mitchell observed; 'someone sent it; it wasn't Ross; it was the murderer; therefore Ross is innocent, and where's your chance of getting a verdict? That's what Markham sees, and, if you ask me, it's making him shirk the responsibility of arresting Ross. My own idea is that he means to use the inquest as a kind of "try-out," and then, if the jury returns a verdict of "wilful murder," he can act on it, and the responsibility will be theirs, not his. You see, he's an Army man, and the one thing you learn in the Army is to obey orders, which means leaving the responsibility to someone else.'

'Yes, sir,' agreed Bobby. 'I suppose the sender of the telegram can't be traced?'

Mitchell consulted a paper on his desk.

'It was sent by someone who gave an address at the Brilliant, a small hotel off the Strand. The name given is illegible, but looks like Miller or something of that kind. The name in the hotel register is the same kind of illegible scribble, but looks like Miller, too – the hotel people had turned it into Mutton, which seems unlikely. He didn't say where he was going when he left, and he registered as coming from Dover. We've asked the Dover people to inquire as far as possible, but they've had no luck; couldn't expect it, with nothing more to go on.'

'No, sir,' agreed Bobby, and added somewhat dispiritedly: 'This case seems all blank walls – lost crossword puzzles; footsteps in the dew that vanish while you're watching them; telegrams that don't mean what they say; deserted summer-houses with freshly swilled floors; strong swimmers that get themselves drowned in perfectly calm weather; dogs that don't bark and yet have their heads knocked in to prevent their barking.'

'Cases generally are like that,' Mitchell reminded him, 'till you get the one right line to follow. By the way, how's your toothache? Face looks better.'

'Oh, quite gone now, sir, thank you,' Bobby answered. 'I'm afraid one night it was so bad I disturbed the whole house walking up and down, but Mrs Cooper had some laudanum by her and gave me some, and after that I had no more trouble.'

Mitchell drummed with his fingers up and down the table, and it was a long time before he spoke. At last he said:

'Yes, I see what you mean, but I don't see that it helps us much so far.'

'No, sir, not so far,' agreed Bobby.

'Well, carry on, carry on – till you come to another dead end like Markham with the telegram. Now he's trying to make up for lost time – a thing you never do – by following up other lines very energetically. He has tackled Laura Shipman. She sticks to it that she found the watch where and when she says; says that if it was lost at another place and time, then someone else must have picked it up and put it where she found it. A lie, of course, but the dickens to prove. She may decide to tell the truth after a time; they do occasionally. But it's quite clear that whatever she knows, if she knows anything, she had nothing to do directly with George Winterton's murder. There's no doubt when that happened she really was where she says. Jennings has been questioned, too, and owns up he bought the classy wireless receiving set he's got with two five-pound notes he received through the post anonymously. His story is that a lady driving a motor-car as nearly as possible killed him a little before – car skidded and missed him by inches. He says he was badly scared, and threatened to summons her, but afterwards thought perhaps it hadn't been her fault, and, as no harm had been done, didn't even report it. When the two five-pound notes came, he thought they came from her as compensation for the fright she had given him.'

'I wonder if that story's true,' Bobby remarked, half to himself. 'I had an idea myself he had had some sort of windfall and that it might have been by way of a kind of compensation.'

'Only your idea was it might be to make up for the attack on him when he was tied up to a tree the morning the motor-launch visited Suffby Cove?' observed Mitchell. 'Well, I can tell you this. Markham has had the two notes traced – luckily the wireless people Jennings bought the set from kept the numbers. Both notes were issued to Mr George Winterton; and what do you make of that?'

'That the coming of the launch had something to do with him,' Bobby answered promptly, 'and that he had something to do with the assault on Jennings, or knew about it, and tried to make up for it by sending him money.'

'Exactly,' agreed Mitchell. 'And how much further does that take us? Another blank wall, it seems to me. You remember a City man named Shorton you saw at Fairview, and heard uttering threats against Winterton?'

'Yes, sir.'

'Well, Markham, who has his own hands pretty well full following up lines he didn't want to bother with while he was relying on that unlucky telegram, wants me to interview Shorton, and I want you to come along, so you can make a full report to Markham when you get back. Seems Shorton is rather a dab at swimming.'

'I understand he had a good try at swimming the Channel one year,' Bobby remarked; 'didn't quite manage it, but did well enough to win one or two bets.'

'Also,' observed Mitchell, 'it seems as if there's some scheme of his for developing the coast along there that Winterton was holding up and that may go through now. Well, well, come along, and we'll run our heads hard against another blank wall.'

CHAPTER XX

A Big Idea

MR SHORTON'S offices were in one of the big buildings recently erected on the Thames Embankment, and when Mitchell and Bobby were shown into his private room they found him bending over a table, drawn up before the window, and covered with maps and plans and other papers.

As they entered, he looked up at them, but with a somewhat abstracted expression, and with one hand still upon the plan he had been examining.

'You're from Scotland Yard?' he said. 'About poor Winterton, I suppose. Dreadful affair; but I'm glad to see you. Fact is, I was thinking of coming round to have a talk with you people myself.' He paused, and said slowly and impressively: 'You know, the man who is behind all this, he's big – a big man – brains.' With another gesture Shorton passed his hand above the mass of papers on the table. 'A big man,' he repeated. 'A genius, almost.'

It was an observation so unexpected, and at the same time fitting in so well with their own thoughts, that both Mitchell and Bobby were a little startled, and could not help exchanging quick glances as if to ask each other what each thought of that. Recovering himself instantly, Mitchell said:

'Indeed. Who is he?'

'I only wish I knew,' Shorton answered. 'I would give quite a lot to know.'

And here again Mitchell and Bobby exchanged quick glances, for once more Shorton seemed to be expressing exactly their own thoughts.

As if he had almost forgotten his visitors, Shorton fell again to examining his maps and plans and papers in a kind of ecstasy of admiration. He had a note-book in his hand, and now and then he jotted down a figure or a word in it. Looking at them again, he said:

'You know, it's big, that's what it is. Big. That's the trouble with half the men you meet nowadays. No vision; no guts; won't go all out. And you must go all out if you mean to do anything. Look at Rugby. Can you play Rugby at a jog-trot? Of course you can't. And you can't play the business game at a jog-trot either; no, nor life itself at a jog-trot. You've got to go all out, and that's what I like about this. It goes the limit; it's big, virile, aggressive. None of the gentle jog-trot that gets you nowhere. Tackle your man and go straight for your goal – that's the way to win, whether it's Twickenham or business. I tell you again, there's a Man behind this.'

'I think so, too,' agreed Mitchell, who, during this harangue, had been looking at the papers spread out on the table. 'That's a plan of the Suffby Cove district, isn't it?' he remarked.

'Yes,' Shorton agreed. 'Do you smoke? Have a cigarette?' He offered some first to Mitchell and then to Bobby. 'Every detail thought out,' he continued. 'Every possible contingency provided for. A masterpiece of foresight and organisation. I'm a business man myself, and I've had some experience, but I take off my hat to the man who's worked all this out.'

'But surely,' Mitchell suggested, 'you have some idea who it is?'

'Not the foggiest,' answered Shorton. 'What's more, except for just a few of the leading men in the City, I can't think of anyone with a big enough brain to carry it through. There are touches that make me think of——.' He named an extremely well known City magnate – one whose name was just then very prominently before the public. 'There are touches of brilliance in the working out – real brilliance, flashes of it – that made me think of him at once. But there are – well, almost philanthropic touches about it, too, that aren't like him at all.'

'Philanthropic touches?' Mitchell repeated. 'In what way?'

'Well, what I mean is, there's a sort of consideration shown for other people. Everyone's been thought of in a way not at all necessary from the strictly business point of view. Mr Winterton's servants are provided for; arrangements are made for the Suffby Cove villagers, the farmers near are to be encouraged to provide the fruit and vegetables and meat we shall want, and so on – everything thought of, so as to work out for the best for everyone. It's colossal. Upon my soul, it's wonderful to think of a man able to plan big like this, and at the same time grasp and think of every minute detail – it's like planning a world-wide campaign, and at the same time every single detail for to-morrow's meals, from the mustard at breakfast to the nightcap before you go to bed.'

Again Mitchell and Bobby exchanged swift glances. At this last sentence the same idea had flashed upon them both, and the quick look they exchanged told them each that this was so, and confirmed them in it. Mitchell said:

'Very interesting. It all sounds a little like what we are looking for – clever's no word for him, either. But you said you were thinking of coming round to see us?'

'Yes,' Shorton answered. 'You see, what the scheme really is – well, the idea is to make an English Monte Carlo. Monte Carlo began as a sea-bathing establishment, you know – they still call themselves "Sea Baths, Limited," or something like that. Well, we'll go in for all kinds of sea sports – bathing, boating, fishing, and so on – but the real attraction will be roulette and baccarat.'

'What about the gambling laws?' asked Mitchell mildly.

'That's where the cleverness of the thing comes in,' Mr Shorton explained enthusiastically. 'Genius, almost. Look at the map there, and you'll see Suffby Cove is a splendid natural harbour in shape, protected on every side, but it's shallow water. The idea is to have two or three flat-bottomed vessels, rather like the houseboats you see up the Thames, only larger and more strongly built, and, of course, fitted up in style. We shall have small powerful motor-boats to act as tugs, and every evening the house-boats will be tugged out to sea beyond the three-mile limit. Then play will begin. Most likely we shall have music and dancing on the top deck; and meals will be served, and drinks of course – rather jolly to have a dinner and dance well out at sea on a calm summer night. But the real thing will be the play inside – available for those who like it. Others can enjoy themselves on deck, but there'll be baccarat and roulette going on inside. Some time about midnight, or later, the motor-boats will tow the house-boats back, and play will stop the moment the three-mile limit is reached. Anything illegal in that?'

'Hardly for me to say,' Mitchell answered cautiously. 'Question for the law officers of the Crown to decide, I suppose. No doubt they'll consider it. Was that what you were coming round to the Yard about?'

'That's right,' Shorton said.

'What about bad weather?' Mitchell asked. 'I can't imagine a sea-sick gambler myself.'

'Oh, that's been thought of,' Shorton answered. 'Everything's been thought of. The house-boats will only go out in calm weather. If it's at all rough, they'll stay in, and there'll be bridge – poker, perhaps, for club members. Of course, it'll have to be run on club lines, but there's no difficulty about that.'

'There never is,' agreed Mitchell. 'Call yourself a club, and there's not much you can't do. I suppose the house-boats will be anchored in the Cove – will they?'

'Yes, we'll build a wharf there for them to tie up to, but we shall generally use Fairview when the weather's bad. Fairview will be the club-house.'

'Oh, Fairview comes into it, does it?'

'Everything comes into it,' Shorton answered enthusiastically. 'Our idea at first was a kind of middle-class Gleneagles, run on slightly less expensive lines. We shall provide all sea sports. We shall have our own golf-links – the lay-out for golf-links is ideal. There'll be a little rough shooting, too, as well as all the other usual attractions. Our own cinema, perhaps. All that will be for the hotel we shall put up on the Suffby promontory itself, on the east side of the Cove – a wonderful position, close to the ruins of the old lighthouse that was done away with years ago. But in addition there'll be the Fairview club across the Cove, with bridge and poker on land, and roulette and baccarat when the weather's good enough for the house-boats to be tugged out. Of course, those will be the profitable evenings. We shan't make so much out of the contract and poker evenings. Except,' he added with a gentle smile, 'for selling champagne and sandwiches at an – er – adequate price.'

'Very interesting idea,' Mitchell admitted. 'A kind of night-club by the sea, and, once beyond the three-mile limit, you snap your fingers at the law.'

'That's right,' agreed Shorton. 'Only, of course, everything most respectable, because there'll be money in it – big money – and that means being jolly careful everything's just as it ought to be.'

'Mr Shorton,' said Mitchell gravely, 'you are tempting me to think you are something of a cynic.'

'What do you mean?' asked Shorton indignantly. 'What's there cynical about that? It's just sense.'

'Often the same thing,' Mitchell observed. 'But it certainly seems a very original idea.'

'Genius,' Shorton repeated. 'Every detail thought out, down to the names of the fishermen to be offered permanent jobs to provide sport for visitors fond of fishing and boating – that'll all be free, of course; at least, we shall call it free, but it'll come into the bills all right – tremendous attraction if you provide something free; people don't mind then how much they pay for it through the nose. Even Winterton's old servants thought of: the steward and stewardess at Fairview are to be his old butler and wife – their name's Cooper, I think. Their local knowledge should be useful. You know, that appeals to me in this scheme. Such care taken to see that no one is injured – everybody concerned has been thought of. Then there are plans for enlarging Fairview; a motor-coach service of our own, free, of course, for taking people to and from the railway. We shall be a bit dependent on the weather, but then that's always the case in England, and, as the memorandum suggests, that may help us in a way by emphasising the gamble. "Try Your Luck at Suffby Cove: First the Weather, Then Roulette" – an advert like that ought to go over big. But what'll really fetch the well-to-do respectable class we're aiming to get is the way we'll be dodging the law. It's the flavour of illegality will do it. Respectable, suburban churchgoers, whose idea of reckless gambling is risking half a crown at contract, will troop along so as to be able to tell their friends they've been to the British Monte Carlo, and hint at the dreadful orgies taking place there – and a good lot of them will want to come along and see for themselves, and try their own luck. We shall run the hotel on very strict lines indeed, but, just across the Cove, there'll be Fairview, standing for all that's wicked and romantic and bold and reckless, and all our really respectable guests will be equally shocked and tempted – wickedness is so attractive to the highly respectable who've never dared before, and now they'll see a chance.'

'Is that in the Memo?' Mitchell asked.

'Word for word,' Shorton answered.

'Bit of a psychologist, your man.'

'Bit of a genius,' returned Shorton gravely. 'Take it from me, this is going to be one of the biggest things of the century. A visit to Suffby Cove is going to be the great adventure in the lives of every really respectable family in the suburbs and provinces of the land – once we've got into working order. Patriotic, too. "Keep British Money at Home" – that'll be another of our slogans. Why, sir, in a year or two, I hope every British citizen will blush to admit he intends to go and lose his money at Monte Carlo when he can get rid of it just as easily at Suffby Cove – "British Baccarat for British gamblers." '

'Jolly good,' approved Mitchell. 'Only I'm afraid you won't be able to provide the sunshine of the south of France.'

'Certainly we shall. Most certainly,' declared Shorton, with some indignation. He turned to his papers again. 'There's an estimate here,' he said. 'Yes. A score of high-power lamps – artificial sunshine twenty-four hours a day all the year round; more than Nature manages. "On Suffby Cove Beach, Perpetual Sunshine Day and Night" – that'll be another slogan. Take it from me,' he repeated, almost with awe, 'everyone connected with this scheme will be a millionaire in ten years or less – and all that money now wasted in France all kept in the country. The Government won't be able to touch us; and they ought to be willing to help, in the public interest. It's disgusting to think of all the good British money that's poured out on the Monte Carlo tables. But there won't be any need for that, once we've got into working order. Look at the money greyhound-racing makes – that's just animated roulette. We shall be seafaring roulette, and we shall do better still. One side of Suffby Cove – respectable, law-abiding; the other side – wicked, law-breaking. The combination – irresistible. That's the Memo. again.'

'I should like to read it,' Mitchell admitted. 'It sounds as racy and cynical as a Somerset Maugham play. But I agree there are first-class brains behind it; and it's someone with first-class brains we are trying to get in touch with, too. You say you don't know who this Memo. comes from?'

'Haven't the foggiest,' declared Shorton. 'But I take off my hat to him, whoever he is.'

'I take it the thing didn't drop on you out of the sky?'

'Oh, no. Dreg & Sons sent it me – they're solicitors. Office in West Street – between the Mansion House and the Bank. In a small way, I'm told; but quite good reputation. They may know who they are acting for, I suppose; but, when I rang them up to ask, they said they didn't.'

'Have you done business with them before?'

'Never heard of them till this came along.'

'You aren't prepared to go on without knowing who it is you're dealing with, are you?'

'I know it's someone capable of drawing up a scheme like this, and that's good enough for me. I don't care who it is – he's the man I want. First-class brains like his aren't so common as all that. Besides, there's an option they've got. Only a little while ago I had written the Suffby Cove idea off as a complete wash-out – dead as a bottle of whisky after a Scots ship's engineer has had a go at it. Then I got an offer to take an option, on the right to come in as a fifty-fifty partner, providing pound for pound on the capital already spent. It seemed like found money. I had no idea then that Winterton was changing his attitude.'

'Was he?' Mitchell asked sharply. 'Have you any proof of that?'

'There's a note by him, that came with the Memo. It expresses willingness to negotiate, and names a figure – rather a high figure, but we should have been willing to pay if we had had to. Now, of course, that the poor fellow's gone, we shall have to start negotiating again, but I don't anticipate any difficulty – both Mrs Archibald Winterton, the other brother's widow, you know, and the bank, who are joint executors, are quite ready to be reasonable.'

'May I see the note you speak of?' Mitchell asked.

Shorton found it, and Mitchell took it to the light, and studied it with care. It consisted only of a few typewritten lines, not addressed to any one person by name, but expressing a general willingness to consider any offer made. The signature was written, and over it Mitchell pored so long that Shorton grew impatient.

'It's of no value now,' he pointed out. 'Now the poor fellow's gone.'

'Have you any objection to my keeping it for a time?'

'The letter? Why? What for?'

'For examination,' Mitchell answered placidly. 'The signature looks stiff to me – almost as if it had been traced. I should like expert opinion on it.'

'You mean it's forged?' Shorton cried. 'But that's absurd; quite absurd. What would be the good? It's only an expression of willingness to consider offers; nothing binding about it. What would be the good of forging a thing like that?'

'First-class brains might see some good,' Mitchell retorted. 'And I quite agree with you there are first-class brains in this affair somewhere – the question is, Where? How was the money for the option paid?'

'By solicitor's cheque.'

'Has it occurred to you that Mr George Winterton's death has occurred somewhat opportunely for the success of this scheme of yours?'

'Why, no. Certainly not,' Shorton answered quickly; though for the first time looking a little disturbed. 'There's his letter, for one thing, and, besides, he couldn't have reasonably held out against renewed offers. My difficulty before was raising capital, and I admit my scheme wasn't a patch on this. With such a magnificent idea to work on, and a promise of fresh capital, I didn't value Winterton's opposition a row of beans. If he had really turned stupid – and that's quite inconceivable – then we would have gone on without him, till he got tired of holding us up.'

'Yet I believe you had a somewhat violent interview with him on your last visit to Suffby Cove?'

'Oh, yes. I told him just what I thought of him. He had done the dirty, he and his brother; double-crossed me, Archibald did. But I saw no chance of raising fresh capital then – now, of course, it's there.' He made a gesture with his hand towards the papers on the table. 'Before that I did feel pretty sick. I thought I had lost my time and money, too, just because the Wintertons were playing the dog in the manger – didn't want to exploit the possibilities of the place themselves, and didn't want anyone else to.'

'But now they're both dead ... ?' Mitchell mused.

'I don't deny I'm not sorry Archibald is out of the way,' Shorton admitted. 'He might have turned obstinate. For him to go and get himself drowned seems almost – well, providential,' said Shorton reverently. 'But, as I've just told you, George Winterton, poor fellow, was coming round, as that letter of his shows. He was never so set against it as his brother was, and, anyhow, with the fresh capital promised, we could have gone ahead all right. He would have come in sooner or later – sooner rather than later, too.'

'Then you don't admit that Mr George Winterton's death helps your plans in any way?'

'Certainly not. Complicates matters a bit, that's all. But not in any way serious.'

'Except,' suggested Mitchell drily, 'for Mr Winterton himself.'

He went on to ask a series of further questions, some of them quite unimportant, but others leading up to the admission that, on the night of the murder, Shorton had been alone in the flat he and his wife occupied – his wife being away on a visit, and the daily maid they employed having left at five, as usual. He had spent the whole evening alone, busy with some work he had brought from the office, and had made his dinner off some sandwiches and some fruit he had brought in with him. The upshot was that no independent evidence existed to prove he had spent the night at the flat at all, though, also, there was nothing to show that he had not. He was beginning to grow perturbed – though not seriously so to all appearance – under so much questioning, but quite willingly signed the statement Bobby prepared. And, in answer to a casual question, he admitted that he was an excellent swimmer, referring with pride to his attempt on the Channel.

'Archibald Winterton was a good swimmer, too, I'm told,' Mitchell remarked. 'It seems curious he should get drowned on such a fine morning.'

'Very curious,' Shorton admitted. 'I could hardly believe it. I had been for a swim myself early that morning. I was staying at a little place just along the coast there at the time, trying to see if I could find another site to carry on with, as I had been double-crossed over the Suffby Cove plan. And I can't say I was altogether knocked up with grief and sorrow when I heard what had happened. As for the other poor fellow, that was different altogether.'

'Quite so,' murmured Mitchell, but, when he and Bobby were outside, he said musingly: 'But I wonder if it was so different, after all? Just at present it seems as if the Winterton brothers have a way of dying just a little too conveniently for Mr Shorton's business interests.'

'Yes, sir,' agreed Bobby dutifully. 'And yet I think he is right in saying George Winterton would hardly have held out for long against a really good offer; and Shorton told us himself, at once, he had been in the vicinity when Archibald was drowned. He would hardly have said that if he had had anything to do with it.'

'He might have reckoned we were bound to find out,' Mitchell pointed out.

'It leaves so much unaccounted for – the motor-launch, and the attack on Jennings; the lost crossword; the telegram; the swilled summer-house floor,' Bobby urged.

'Oh, we haven't got the whole story yet by any means,' Mitchell agreed. 'One thing that is certain, though, is that Shorton is right when he says there are first-class brains in the business somewhere. And I think it's just possible they belong to Mr Shorton himself. But that's only a guess as yet, but one we can't neglect any more than we can your theories. Perhaps Messrs Dreg & Sons will be able to tell us something more.'

CHAPTER XXI

The Illegible Signature

BUT Messrs Dreg & Sons had no information to give. They recognised, of course, that it was their duty, as themselves, in some sort, officers of the law, to give every assistance in their power, but none the less the fact remained that they had no knowledge of the identity of the person by whom they had been instructed in the matter of the proposed 'Suffby Cove Sea Sports Development Co. Ltd.,' to give the project the full title provisionally bestowed upon it.

Nor would they admit that it was in any way irregular or unusual to act for a client of whose identity they were unaware. They pointed out that in many business transactions secrecy was essential. Very often a premature disclosure of a plan might mean its complete wreckage; and once it became known that such or such a person was interested, to guess the end in view became, in many cases, comparatively easy.

'Suppose, for example,' Mr Dreg explained tolerantly, 'that a firm of national, or even international, repute – well, for example, like the house of Rothschild – is backing some new enterprise, and that fact gets known. Half the City's on the track at once. Every speculator wants to take a hand. If it's a question of securing control of some company, everyone rushes to buy shares till the price is forced to a point where all chance of profit vanishes, or it grows so difficult to buy, and there is so much delay, that the whole thing is held up, and a promising scheme ruined. Or it may be a question of negotiating for the purchase of some property or some new patent. Let it be known that any firm of standing is interested, and speculators are after it immediately, hoping to make the firm interested pay through the nose. I've seen deals that promised big things ruined like that, and I daresay every City man would tell you the same.'

Messrs. Dreg also made it perfectly, though tactfully, clear that they did not believe for one moment that these inquiries Mitchell was making had any real or substantial connection with the unfortunate murder at Suffby Cove, of which they had read, they vaguely remembered, various confused and uninteresting details in the paper. They quite understood, they intimated politely, that the authorities were merely making use of the coincidence of a crime having been committed in that neighbourhood to camouflage their interest in the 'Suffby Cove Sea Sports Development Co. Ltd.'

'A project, which in our considered opinion,' declared Mr Dreg, with great emphasis, 'is not only entirely legal, but one deserving the support of every patriotic and right-thinking citizen. In our view the Government would do wisely in giving it a certain amount of public recognition, by allowing, perhaps, a Minister of Cabinet rank to lay the foundation-stone of the proposed hotel, or something of that sort. It would be much appreciated, and would do much to help our efforts to stop the notorious scandal of the constant stream of British money that pours into Continental resorts and into the Irish sweepstakes. Surely British money should be kept at home. Surely we are all agreed there. Then look, too, how much will be done to relieve unemployment.'

'Patriotic, and philanthropic, and profitable, too,' murmured Mitchell. 'That is your view?'

'Exactly,' said Mr Dreg, much pleased. 'It could not be better expressed.'

Mitchell made another effort to get hold of any detail that would in any way suggest the identity of Messrs Dreg's client, but once more entirely failed. It seemed they really knew nothing. They could not even give the exact date of the first telephone message received, where it had come from, or, indeed, anything at all about it. It had apparently not been taken very seriously at first. In its first form it had merely been a request to know if Messrs Dreg would be prepared to act in a certain matter for a Mr John Smith, who had reasons for not wishing to appear in it personally. A cautious, non-committal reply had been made, and no more thought of the matter, or importance attached to it, till there had arrived a messenger, bringing a parcel containing a sum of five hundred pounds in one-pound notes, and full instructions.

'And I don't mind saying,' Mr Dreg went on, 'that it was when I read those instructions, and realised their extraordinary clearness, vision, insight; their breadth of view combined with a minute attention to detail; their grasp of the present, and their provision for future developments; their understanding both of finance and of psychology, combined with the novelty of the proposal itself, that I grew really interested. I was, in fact, greatly impressed. I never remember being so much impressed. You seem surprised that I am willing to act for a client of whom I know nothing. I say, I know this, that he is a most remarkable man, a man of unusual powers and profound experience, a man in short of the highest ability.'

'Do you think it could be Mr Shorton himself?' Mitchell asked.

Mr Dreg started, and looked slightly taken aback.

'Well, I had considered the possibility,' he admitted. 'Of course, it's possible. I don't know that Mr Shorton quite impresses me as being quite – well, big enough. But it's difficult to judge. You have to be associated with a man some time before you can form a real opinion of his powers. Yes, possibly it is Mr Shorton. But that is purely guess-work. The only thing that isn't guess-work, but fact, is the enormous possibilities of the idea. Think of the national benefit to be derived from keeping in the country all this money that's going abroad – Ireland, France, anywhere. Consider the employment we shall provide. It's a scheme I'm proud to be associated with, and I think I am safe in saying that my clients, as an act of grace, but actuated by those public-spirited motives which lie, *pari passu*,' said Mr Dreg impressively, 'with our more purely commercial aims, would be perfectly willing to pay to the revenue any reasonable tax on their turnover that might be mutually agreed on.'

'Worth their while, no doubt,' Mitchell commented drily. 'to get, what would look like Government patronage, official approval – like the efforts of the greyhound-racing people to get an official board of control appointed. But at present all that is no business of ours at the Yard. Very interesting scheme, of course, and very kind of you to explain it to us so fully, but simply nothing to do with us at present – not a police matter at all. It may become so later on, for all I know, but not at present. Our business is at the moment to find out who murdered George Winterton.'

'Very sad affair,' commented Mr Dreg; 'but I can't see there's the slightest connection. Certainly none that I know of, or can even imagine. Mr Winterton's opposition to the scheme had been withdrawn, as shown by his letter, now in Mr Shorton's hands, expressing willingness to negotiate – and I think one may make a safe guess that the opposition he had expressed merely meant he was holding out for the best possible terms. I have seen that so often.'

'Perhaps,' agreed Mitchell, rising to go. 'Then all I can do is to ask you to communicate to us any new fact that comes to your knowledge, and especially to inform your client, Mr John Smith, that we are extremely anxious to get in touch with him, that our inquiries have nothing whatever to do with the legality or illegality of the very remarkable and interesting scheme he has in hand, but that we should take a very grave view of any reluctance he might conceivably display to coming forward – not that we anticipate that for one moment. But, if he fails to get in touch with us as promptly as possible, he must not be surprised at any action we may think it necessary to take.'

'I shall certainly deliver your message as soon as the opportunity occurs,' Mr Dreg answered stiffly. 'And, on your side, I am sure you will understand that I consider it my duty to protect my clients' interest, to the best of my poor ability, consistently with my professional obligations.'

'Oh, quite so,' said Mitchell; and, when they were outside, he added to Bobby: 'All of which means that Dreg smells money in this sea-gambling stunt, and means to have his share if he can – if the thing does get going and isn't interfered with, I daresay it'll mean a lot to be appointed solicitor to the company. What do you think?'

'Looks to me,' said Bobby slowly, 'that it's just another blank wall we're up against – and I think we shall get no more assistance from Mr Dreg than he can help.'

'Think it really is Shorton behind it all?'

'I don't think I'm thinking at all just at present, sir,' Bobby answered frankly. 'I'm just bewildered.'

'Good,' declared Mitchell, 'being bewildered is the first step to getting understanding.'

'Well, then, sir,' Bobby observed thoughtfully, 'I've taken a pretty big first step towards getting understanding if I may measure by the extent of my present bewilderment. And all the same, though I can't see how on earth it can be fitted in, I've noticed a copy of Shakespeare in the Fairview library, and I'm going to have a look at it to-night.'

'I daresay I could guess which play,' Mitchell commented; 'but all that's only the psychology of the thing; what we want is evidence. Treasury counsel would have quite a lot to say if we offered them the one for the other. Well, you had better get back to Suffby Cove and report to Major Markham. I'll write to him to-night, and you can give him any further details he wants – but whether it's Shorton behind the "Suffby Cove Sea Sports Development" scheme, or whether it's someone else, I'm no more sure than I was before.'

'No, sir,' agreed Bobby. 'Though I can't help thinking the whole business, from the appearance of the launch in the cove the morning Jennings was tied up, right to the handing in of his instructions to Mr Dreg the other day all makes one complete whole, if only we could see how. And I was wondering, sir, if I might slip round to the Brilliant Hotel and have a drink there, and see if I could get a look at the register, or the chance of being able to make something out of the signature of the man who sent that telegram. It must have meant something,' he added almost despairingly.

Mitchell looked at him sadly.

'Young man,' he said, 'official life is telling on you – the usual deterioration is setting in. A year or two ago, you would have gone there first and asked permission after.'

'Oh, no, sir,' Bobby protested, quite hurt. 'I always asked permission, unless there wasn't time, or I thought I mightn't get it.'

'Your instructions,' said Mitchell severely, 'are to get on your motor-cycle as quick as you can, and proceed at full speed to Suffby Cove, so as to put yourself at the disposition of Major Markham at the earliest possible moment.'

'Very good, sir,' answered Bobby; and added: 'I ought to explain, sir, that I had some engine trouble coming up I asked them at the garage to see to. I'm not sure the bike will be ready for another half hour or so.'

'I don't know,' sighed Mitchell, 'what discipline's coming to. Now when I joined the force – but perhaps I've told you about that before. Anyhow, lose no time in reporting to Markham. My own idea is, he is only waiting to hear from us to decide whether to have the ports watched in case Shorton tries to bolt.'

'There's hardly evidence enough against him to make him want to do that, is there?' Bobby asked, surprised.

'Oh, no,' Mitchell agreed. 'Only when a man is guilty, he never knows what the evidence is against him and the more he doesn't know, the more likely he is to lose his head and bolt.'

With that Mitchell nodded and departed, and Bobby made his way to the Brilliant Hotel, a small establishment near the Strand, its dingy outer appearance harmonising little with its name. But, inside, it seemed comfortable enough. The drink supplied was of excellent quality, and when Bobby introduced himself no difficulty was made about allowing him to examine the register.

The name entered there was, as Mitchell had described it, a mere illegible scribble, of which the hotel interpretation, 'Mutton,' seemed as good as any other. But 'Mutton' as a name seemed to Bobby lacking in verisimilitude, and, besides, he could not find any trace of anything like any crossing of the two supposed 't's.' The more he pored over it, the less he could make of it, and then he adopted the expedient he had heard of some time or another of going over the writing with a dry pen. But that did not seem to help much, except to confirm him in his belief that the two centre letters were not 't's'. But, if they were not 't's,' two 'l's' seemed the most likely suggestion for them he could think of, and that, again, suggested the name might be really 'Miller.' Another experiment with the dry pen persuaded him that there were two strokes to the letter between the undoubted 'M' with which the name began, and the two tall letters in the middle of it. But, then, that would make it a 'u,' and transform the name into 'Muller,' and for a long time Bobby remained brooding and intent, every sense he possessed concentrated as it were upon the open page before him.

At last he closed the book, and spoke to the hotel clerk, who had been regarding him with some amusement. It was information about 'Mutton,' 'Miller,' or 'Muller' that he wanted, but apparently the passage of that gentleman had left little trace. No one seemed to know much about him, or remember anything of interest. He had not struck any one as being a foreigner, and, disappointed at having failed to learn anything more, Bobby asked permission to use the hotel phone, and rang up to report to Mitchell.

The official who answered his call said, however, that the superintendent had not yet returned, so Bobby had to be content with leaving a message that he thought it just possible the name was 'Muller' and, if so, that perhaps Mr Muller might be a German.

'Motor-launch from oversea somewhere; sack from

Holland; the telegram; and now someone who may be a German,' Bobby said to himself as he hung up the receiver and turned thoughtfully away. 'I suppose I needn't emphasise all that to Mitchell – he'll see it sharp enough – but I had better turn in a memo as well. For it does look as if the wheel had come full circle again.'

CHAPTER XXII

Shakespeare

FOR one or two reasons of no special importance – a clean handkerchief was one of them – Bobby thought he would call at Fairview for a moment or two on his way to the county police headquarters, where his instructions directed him to report to Major Markham the details of the interview with Mr Shorton.

During his wanderings about the neighbourhood before the tragedy of Mr Winterton's death he had noticed a path that ran from behind the house, through the garden, and past the Greek temple summer-house, to join the main road half a mile or so further on, thus saving travellers to or from the south some considerable distance. The path was only a foot track, but quite practicable for cyclists who did not mind pushing their machines most of the distance or lifting them over one or two low stiles, and now Bobby thought to save a few minutes by following it.

A gate in bad repair, fastened only by a latch, led into the Fairview garden, and, after Bobby had passed through this, he came almost at once to the summer-house. Remembering the odd incident of the recently swilled floor that had so bothered him with its apparent lack of purpose, he leaned his motor-cycle against a convenient tree and went across to see if any further attempt at cleaning out the place had been made. But what he saw was something different, for there was plain evidence, in freshly turned earth and clay and in the recently disturbed stone flooring, that someone had been digging there.

Of the fact itself there could be no doubt. The flooring had been replaced in position and efforts had been made to clear up, but the traces of what had been done were plain enough. Someone, for some purpose, had been digging there, and the conclusion seemed plain that something either was or had been hidden there.

But what that something could be, though he asked himself the question, he made no effort to determine. If whatever had been hidden there was still there, why, then it would be better to have witnesses for the discovery, and for his seniors to be in charge of the necessary operations. And if whatever had been concealed had been removed, then, too, plainly it would be for his seniors to decide what steps to take.

But he was a little pale as he came out again from the gloom and shadows of the half-ruinous summer-house into the fresh air and the sunshine, and he was a little glad, too, that the trees and shrubs growing near hid the place well enough to make it unlikely that there had been any witness of his visit.

He went on slowly towards the house, thinking that, after all, people do not dig up the floors of deserted summer-houses without good reason; and that here was another puzzling item, that might or might not be important, to fit into the general bewilderment and maze it was his business to make straight.

Leaving his cycle in the drive, he entered the house, and as he did so Miss Raby came out quickly from the study.

'Oh,' she said, looking a little disappointed as she saw Bobby, 'I thought it was Mr Ross. You haven't seen him, have you?'

'No, why? Isn't he in the house somewhere?' Bobby asked in his turn.

'No. He must have gone out late last night after we thought he had gone to bed. He went upstairs very early. He didn't say anything about going out, but his bed hasn't been slept in, Mrs Cooper says, and there's someone on the phone keeps ringing up and wants to speak to him, and says it's important.'

'Oh. Who is it?'

'I don't know. It's a man's voice, but he won't give his name or leave any message. It's something about money or racing, I think, but he won't say.'

'Well, if he rings up again, have another shot at getting him to say who he is,' Bobby told her. He added slowly: 'If Ross's bed hasn't been slept in, he must have been out all night.'

'I suppose so.'

'And no one's seen anything of him all day?'

'No one at all,' Miss Raby said. She added with an uneasy, somewhat tremulous laugh: 'Of course, it's silly to be nervous, but how can you help it, after what's happened?'

Bobby did not answer, nor did he join in her laughter. He was thinking of the disturbed floor of the summer-house. Absurd, of course, but ... He broke off his thoughts abruptly. Anyhow, he was a man under orders, and his business was to obey them, not to start a fresh investigation on his own responsibility. That Colin Ross seemed to have disappeared, and that digging had recently taken place in a deserted summer-house where it might reasonably have been supposed no one would poke an inquisitive nose for months to come, were two facts that very likely stood in no kind of relation to each other – if, indeed, there were any two facts in the whole of this complicated business that were not more or less intimately related. At any rate, all he could do was to report them to his superiors, for such action to be taken as they might think proper.

Miss Raby said in a detached sort of tone, much as if she were making some remark upon the weather:

'I shan't be able to stand it much longer. I expect I shall go mad or hysterical or something.'

'Well, that wouldn't do any good,' was all Bobby could think of to say.

'You don't expect it to, do you? That isn't why it happens; it's because you just can't stand any more – then you crash,' she said moodily. 'I know quite well you think it may be Miles.'

'I don't know what to think, if you ask me,' he retorted. 'Besides, what does it matter what I think?'

'Well, the police think,' she answered more quietly, 'and you're police, aren't you?'

He was too disconcerted to reply at first. He did manage to stammer something incoherent, but that was all, for that his identity was known to this girl had never even occurred to him. But he felt he had done badly in letting her see so plainly that she had hit upon the truth, though he felt also quite sure that it would only have been foolish to attempt to deny what apparently she was well convinced of. At last he said:

'How do you know? Who told you?'

She turned away with an impatient gesture, as much as to say that that did not matter and in any case she was not going to tell, and then Mrs Cooper came into the hall from the back part of the house.

'I heard someone talking,' she explained. 'I thought perhaps Mr Ross had come back.'

'He didn't sleep here last night?' Bobby asked.

'His bed hasn't been touched,' she answered cautiously. 'I can't see his hat and raincoat anywhere. It looks as if he went out instead of going to bed last night; but, if he did, he didn't say anything. Perhaps he meant to come back and then he changed his mind.'

'It seems funny,' Bobby commented. 'I wonder what can have become of him?'

Mrs Cooper smiled gently and tolerantly.

'Cooper says there's a big race-meeting to-day,' she observed dispassionately.

'He didn't say anything about it?' Bobby asked.

'Oh, no,' she answered, 'nothing – he hasn't mentioned racing or horses or anything of the sort since that dreadful night. But things wear off, don't they? Racing was the one thing Mr Colin seemed to care about, and I thought perhaps it might have come over him again – in a sudden way, perhaps, all the stronger for its having been held back. I don't know, of course; it's only an idea. The young lady's nervous,' she added, looking at Mary Raby, still with her tolerant, half-amused smile, 'but that's only because of what's happened before.'

'It's all getting too much,' Miss Raby said, and turned abruptly and went back into the study, where she was supposed to be busy with the letters that were still arriving for Mr Winterton and with clearing up work in connection with his projected book.

'I'll make her a good strong cup of tea,' Mrs Cooper observed, 'and take it her. She's eating hardly anything – nerves, it is, and you can't wonder, either.'

She disappeared towards the kitchen, and almost immediately Miss Raby came out of the study again. She seemed calmer now, as if the momentary withdrawal in the quiet of the study had restored her composure. She said:

'Oh, you remember that crossword puzzle Mr Winterton was trying to compose and you said you wanted to look at.'

'Have you found it?' he asked eagerly.

'Well, not found it exactly,' she answered. 'I knew I hadn't got it myself because I looked everywhere, just as I knew there wouldn't be a copy here, because Mr Winterton was always so careful to tear up all the attempts he made. I thought then it was because he was afraid of being laughed at. But what's happened is that I must have got the copy I made mixed up with those I did for the *Announcer*, because they've sent back some they don't want and that's with them. The *Announcer* man is quite cross about it, and says he doesn't know why I wanted to send them such a feeble effort. He says one or two of the others aren't bad, but that particular one is like a child's work. I suppose I had better write and tell him it was included by mistake.'

'I don't quite understand,' Bobby said though with some excitement, for it was still in his mind that in some way he had not very clearly defined to himself this crossword puzzle

Mr Winterton had spent the last days of his life in working at might hold the solution of all these happenings and tragic mysteries. 'You mean the copy you made of Winterton's crossword, and thought you must have destroyed, you had really sent to the *Announcer*, and now it has come back from them?'

'Yes,' she said, and went back into the study, returning in a few moments with a large sheet of paper ruled in squares, some of them blacked out in the ordinary orthodox cross-word puzzle fashion. 'It's all there,' she said, 'clues and all, but it doesn't seem quite finished.'

'Have you worked it out?' he asked.

'No, I haven't tried,' she answered. 'It doesn't look very difficult though.' She indicated a pencilled note scribbled across one corner, and signed with some indecipherable initials. The note ran: 'Very poor, childish, much below standard.' She said: 'That's what the *Announcer* man thought of it. I must tell them it was sent in by mistake. I must have picked it up with the others.

'Some of the clues seem rather far-fetched,' Bobby remarked.

'Oh, they are,' she agreed.

'Have you told anyone anything about it?'

'No,' she answered, shaking her head.

'Then please don't,' he said, putting the paper carefully away as he spoke. 'I ask that for your own sake first, perhaps even for your own safety. And, if I did belong to the police, I should ask it with all the authority the police possess – whatever that may be.'

'Very well,' she said soberly.

'I know I can trust you,' he said, and had no time for more as once more Mrs Cooper came back into the hall. To her he said: 'Miss Raby is really anxious about Mr Ross. I don't suppose there's any need. Where is Mr Miles Winterton?'

'He said he was going down to the village to ask if they knew anything of Mr Ross there,' Mrs Cooper answered. 'He ought to be back by now.'

'Oh, nothing can have happened to him,' Miss Raby exclaimed.

'Of course not,' Bobby told her sharply. 'You must pull yourself together. Giving way to ideas won't do any good.'

'It's all been a big strain,' Mrs Cooper interposed mildly. 'You can't wonder; I feel it myself.'

Indeed, for a moment the mask of her composure seemed to drop, and for that instant, just that one passing instant, both the others seemed to have one glimpse of a soul tormented, driven indeed by terrors that were only held in control by the utmost effort of the will. Then, in another instant, she was her usual calm, strong self again, and, as if to excuse herself, she repeated:

'It's all been a big strain. No one knows who hasn't been through it. And Miss Raby's young. I'm older – and then I've Cooper, too. I'm not alone. You mustn't wonder, sir, if Miss Raby shows she feels it.'

She moved away then towards her own part of the house, as if she felt she had said too much. The other two looked after her, and Miss Raby said gratefully:

'She's been rather nice – since it happened, I mean. But I thought she didn't feel it much: she never showed she did, not till now.'

'It's hard to tell what other people are feeling – or thinking,' Bobby remarked. 'Remember, please, not to say a word to anyone about that crossword having turned up.'

He was going to say more when once again Mrs Cooper returned, this time with a cup of tea she had said before she was going to make.

'You drink this, miss,' she said; 'it'll do you all the good in the world; you'll feel all the better for it.'

'Well, I'll be off now,' Bobby said to her. 'And don't worry about me if I'm a bit late. There's someone I want to see, but I shall be back to-night, so, if anyone asks, you can tell them I'm not running away.'

'I don't suppose any of us are thinking of running away,' Mrs Cooper answered with her slow smile. 'I'm sure Mr Ross isn't! It's only he couldn't keep away from the racing any longer. And Mr Miles won't be long now, and as for me and Cooper, if a letter we had to-night means anything, we may be staying on here permanently.'

'Oh, how's that?' Bobby asked.

'Well, sir,' Mrs Cooper explained, 'it seems there's some idea of turning this place into a kind of country seaside club, as I understand it. There was talk of that before, and the letter is from a lawyer gentleman in London, a Mr Dreg, asking if we would like to stay on in charge, and, if so, to send him our references, and wages required. Cooper thinks it might suit us very well, and so do I, and it would be a relief not to have to look for a new place that might turn out very different from what you thought. Sometimes ladies are very different when they're engaging you from what they are when you are working for them.'

'I can quite believe it,' agreed Bobby. 'Oh, by the way, I've borrowed a copy of Shakespeare from the bookcase in the study near the door. If anyone notices it's missing, you might say I've got it. I suppose that'll be all right, won't it?'

'I suppose so, sir,' Mrs Cooper answered. 'Anyhow, I don't know who there is to object, the way things are. Has your tooth been troubling you again?'

'Since you gave me that stuff of yours,' Bobby declared enthusiastically, 'I've forgotten I had a tooth in my head except at meal times. And,' he added, forestalling the question he saw was coming, 'I'm not going to the dentist now, not unless it starts again, and I don't believe it will, either.' He had the copy of Shakespeare he had spoken of in his hands, and as he spoke he turned over the pages idly. 'I remember,' he observed thoughtfully, 'a year or two ago something I was mixed up in made me awfully interested in one of Shakespeare's plays – *Hamlet*, it was. Now there's another I'm working up an interest in.'

'Indeed, sir,' said Mrs Cooper placidly. 'Which is that, sir?'

But Bobby did not answer. Instead, looking at his watch, he exclaimed at the hour, protested he would be late for his appointment, and hurried off. With rather a puzzled air,

Mrs Cooper watched him go, and then turned back into the study, where Miss Raby was busy once more with her typewriter.

'I don't wonder at you being nervy like, miss,' she remarked. 'I am, too, though I try not to show it, and, if you ask me, so is Cooper, though he would sooner die than admit it. A man won't if he can help.'

'I thought he was looking awfully ill and white,' the girl remarked.

'He doesn't seem as if he can digest his food,' Mrs Cooper said. 'It's his nerves, though he won't admit it. I tell him we want something to take it off our minds.' She was running her finger along a line of books on a shelf near. 'Something quiet, not too exciting, rather dull and slow,' she explained. Her searching finger paused. 'Shakespeare,' she said; 'that ought to be just it, and I expect that's why Mr Owen's taken the other copy.'

CHAPTER XXIII

Various Theories

WHEN, however, Bobby reached, a little late, the county police headquarters, it was to be told that Major Markham had been called away on an urgent summons, and might not be back for some time. So Bobby, after visiting the canteen to get something to eat, found a corner to wait in, and there busied himself with the crossword puzzle returned to Miss Raby from the *Announcer* Office.

It was headed, as Bobby remembered it had been, when he had seen what was probably the earlier version Mr Winterton had shown him: 'A Crossword Mystery: by George Winterton. Key word: "Gold" '; and Bobby noticed, too, that a number of the clues still had a small cross placed against them, with the reference underneath: 'Clues marked with a cross require further consideration, as being either too obvious or not obvious enough'; and Bobby made the same reflection that he remembered had entered his mind before, that the happy medium was probably as difficult to construct in crossword clues as in everything else.

Then he set to work on the puzzle. He did not find it very difficult, and was not much surprised that the *Announcer* crossword editor had dismissed it in so summary a manner. One or two of the clues bothered him; several seemed rather far-fetched; occasionally, one or another made him smile. But, in proportion as he got nearer and nearer to finishing the thing, so he grew more and more disappointed. What he had expected from it he hardly knew, but certainly, in a vague kind of way, he had expected that it would throw light upon recent happenings.

That however, so far as he could see at present, it did not seem to do, and he was still working at it, still trying to hit on the meaning of some of the clues, still hoping against hope to find in it somewhere some hidden significance, still racking his brain in especial over an effort to attach any sense to one clue that ran: 'Mr J. Ball wanted very much to know who was the gentleman when Adam did this: use present tense and modern form,' when one of the local men, a sergeant, strolled up, and asked what was making him look so pale and worried.

'It's this crossword puzzle. I can't make head or tail of one of the clues,' Bobby answered, showing it.

The sergeant read it over slowly and thoughtfully. As it happened – and that, indeed, was the reason why he had spoken to Bobby when he saw what was occupying him – the sergeant made crossword puzzles something of a hobby, and, indeed, prided himself not a little on his ability to solve them. Not only had he once won a prize offered by a London paper for the first correct solution received of a somewhat complicated example, but on the analogy of the legend of the Hindu student who, when applying for employment, recommended himself as 'Failed B.A.,' he was even entitled to write, 'Failed, Torquemada,' after his name, for, indeed, it is not everyone who dare essay that dreadful maze. So now it was with the air of an expert that he turned his attention to puzzle and clue.

'Who is Mr. J. Ball?' he demanded.

Bobby hadn't the least idea.

'Most likely someone in Dickens,' the sergeant opined. 'They generally are.'

Bobby thought it very likely, but could not see where the connection with Adam could come in.

'There's a book called *Adam Bede*, isn't there?' asked the sergeant, 'only, not Dickens.'

Bobby agreed that there was such a book, and further agreed that it was not by Dickens.

'Three letters,' mused the sergeant. 'It's generally either "emu" or "ape," when it's three letters, but they don't seem, either of them, to fit in here.'

'No they don't, do they?' observed Bobby.

Then they were interrupted by a message to the effect that though Major Markham had not yet returned and might be some time yet, as what he was engaged on seemed likely to turn out of great importance, he had rung up to give some instructions, and had also directed that Bobby was to hand in his report to Inspector Wake, the senior officer present.

So Bobby gave a full report to the officer in question, who proved an elderly man, on the verge of retirement, but still very keen, and very interested both in the report itself and in the answers Bobby gave to the questions put to him on it.

'I've been a bit out of this affair,' he confided to Bobby. 'Not so young as I was, and I had to put in for sick leave – only reported back yesterday. But I've put in a lot of time reading up the reports and statements taken – Lord knows, there's enough of 'em; there's been some work put in on this case.'

'I'm sure there has,' Bobby agreed.

'If you ask me,' the inspector continued, 'it's that telegram put us off – seemed like the key to the whole affair, and then a complete wash-out when we proved it couldn't possibly refer to anyone recently released from gaol here. Just a code message, if you ask me, meaning something quite different. Very likely came from your man himself; Shorton, I mean, and, if you ask me, Shorton is our man. I thought so from the first, and now, if you ask me, your report makes it certain.'

'That would mean,' observed Bobby meditatively, 'that it is Shorton himself who drew up the scheme Dreg received, and that it was he himself, again, who instructed Dreg to submit it to himself.'

'Exactly. Covering his traces very cleverly, if you ask me,' answered the inspector. 'Who else is there? Who else knows enough about it, or has studied the idea enough to draw up an elaborate scheme like that? It's a sound rule, isn't it? If there's no one else – why, then it must be the man you've got in mind. Another sound rule is to notice who gets the benefit. Look at the facts. Just at the bare facts – undisputed facts – I mean. Shorton has a big business deal on – real big business – with a pile of money at stake. Archibald Winterton holds the whole thing up; perhaps for private reasons, perhaps because he wants a bigger finger in the pie. Anyhow, he holds it up. Next thing is, he dies – mysteriously drowned. All we can say for certain is that, if it was murder, the murderer must have been an expert swimmer too, and that he must have been a friend. Only his being a friend could account for the silence of the dog. Archibald quietened it when he saw it was a friend coming. If you ask me, what happened was that the friend said he had come along special for a big business talk, but how about a dip first? That suited Archibald all right, and in they went; and, when they were a good way out, the friend catches Archibald a whack on the head, stuns him, sees him drown, and the current taking the body out to sea, so that he knows it's a sure thing, before the body's recovered, there'll be nothing left to show of the blow on the head. The friend himself swims quietly back to shore. The dog recognises him again, and takes no notice. The friend dresses and gets away without anyone seeing him, and there you are.'

'It certainly seems it might have happened like that,' Bobby agreed.

'And then,' continued the inspector, 'he finds he has his work to do all over again when George Winterton turns awkward just the way his brother did. But, when you've gone as far as what Shorton had, you don't want to turn back without getting what you've risked your neck for, and it's a fact, isn't it, you yourself heard Shorton using threats to George Winterton.'

'Yes, that's true enough,' Bobby agreed again.

'Well, then,' Wake continued, 'the next thing is to get rid of George, or else what was done to Archibald would all be wasted. Only there's the dog in the way; so its head is smashed in, and the body dropped in the sea. Next thing is to get Mr Winterton alone somewhere; and, if you ask me, I shouldn't wonder if that wasn't what the telegram was for – a code message, meaning; "Meet me outside your house late to-night".'

'Funny sort of code,' Bobby objected. 'Funny appointment to make, too. Why should Mr Winterton keep it?'

'Promised big things; curiosity excited,' the inspector answered promptly. 'As for it's being a funny sort of code, all codes are funny till you know what they mean, and a code that seems to have a plain meaning on the face of it, but really means something quite different, is always the safest sort. Well, he keeps the appointment, and he's done in. Shorton gets away again without being seen, and there you are; and, if you ask me, that's why there seems to be a sort of anxiety to keep the Coopers here. Perhaps they know nothing, and most likely they don't, or suspect anything either, but, anyhow, what they do know is they've got a chance of a good job if they go on not knowing or suspecting anything. It's only a straw, of course, but, when you find a straw being blown along the road you're following, it's often a sign it's the right road you're on. And don't forget another straw is that Shorton happens to be a first-class swimmer.'

'It's a possible theory, of course,' Bobby said slowly. 'But isn't there rather a lot left out? There's all that business with the motor-launch the whole thing began with, and there's the interview with the Shipman girl, and other things – the summer-house floor, for instance, someone swilled, and that, now, someone has been digging up.'

'Most likely the motor-launch has nothing to do with the case. Why should it? That was quite a time before Archibald's death. As for the Shipman young woman, well, she's a good-looking baggage, and most likely there had been some sort of flirtation going on. And the thing's complicated enough without our worrying about the gardener at Fairview trying to clean up a summer-house – which I expect is what happened – or doing a bit of repairs inside.'

'Mr Winterton sent money to Jennings, which looks as if he were interested,' Bobby pointed out. 'And digging up a floor is hardly doing a bit of repairing, is it?'

'There's no proof the notes came from Mr Winterton at all,' Wake pointed out, in his turn. 'We know they were issued to him, but they may have passed from him to someone else, who sent them to Jennings. As for the summer-house floor, what can that have to do with Mr Winterton's murder, when it happened days after it? You don't suppose his body's been dug up on the quiet, and buried there again, do you?'

'No. But I would like to know what's been happening there,' Bobby persisted doggedly. 'Then there's this crossword I've got here, that Mr Winterton was working at, and that Colin Ross seemed so interested in.'

'What on earth,' demanded the inspector, looking quite bewildered, 'can that have to do with the case? Holy Moses, half the people you meet have got a craze for the things – why, at home, they're always fiddling about with them, and expecting thousand-pound prizes that never come!'

Bobby had to admit that undoubtedly crosswords were a passion with many people, and then another inspector came in, and Wake, pleased with his statement of his theory of the guilt of Mr Shorton, and confident no flaw could be found in it, repeated it all over again in even greater detail.

But the newcomer seemed quite unconvinced.

'They don't murder you in the City,' he said with decision. 'Only skin you alive, and when they've got all you have, why should they murder you as well? What they do is, turn you loose to grow some more wool for them to clip. Most City men ought to be murdered themselves, if there were any real justice in the world, but they don't commit murders. No need. You can take it from me, Miles Winterton is the man we want. It's a good sound old rule: look out for who benefits. Pick up the motive, and there's the murderer as well. Look at the facts. I mean the real facts there's no getting away from. This Miles young man is known to have had a row with his uncle – got caught flirting with the pretty secretary, and was kicked out. They want to marry but can't; the young man being out of a job, and uncle having turned nasty. But, once uncle's out of the way, there's no one to object to their marrying, and even if they don't come in for a share of his money, as very likely they thought they would, Mrs Archibald Winterton is on their side, and would be pretty sure to help them. You can take it from me, that's the way it was. The first thing was to get rid of the dog.

'Next, Miss Raby makes up some excuse for getting uncle out of the house late at night – very likely lets him suspect she and Miles are to meet and he'll catch them if he goes to look. Anyhow, they get him outside on some pretext like that, and finish him off. You can take it from me, it's good enough for an arrest, and I know the Guv'nor thinks so, too.'

The 'Guv'nor' was Major Markham, but both Bobby and the other inspector looked doubtful, and Bobby said:

'If it was like that, what about Archibald's death?'

'Oh, that was just an accident – nothing in that,' retorted the other. 'Take it from me, never look for murder till you're obliged.'

'What about – well, about all the other things that have happened?' Bobby still objected. 'The Laura Shipman girl, for instance. Where does she come in?'

'She doesn't,' answered the other promptly. 'Her story's true. The woman you saw talking to George Winterton that night wasn't her at all. Ten to one it was Miss Raby – you can take it from me, the whole thing you watched was just a dress-rehearsal of the murder, and Laura Shipman's tale is true. It was the Raby girl picked up your watch, and went off with it, but afterwards she got nervy, or smelt a rat, and got rid of it where Laura Shipman found it. A very smart idea of yours,' he added consolingly to Bobby, who was looking a trifle crestfallen at the thought that this idea, which had never occurred to him before but which seemed all the same possible enough, might be the truth of the matter, 'and I don't say it wasn't; very smart indeed; but you can take it from me, the smarter an idea is, the less likely it is to be practical. A detective officer doesn't want to be too clever, it doesn't – do.'

'He's worried,' explained Wake, with a nod towards Bobby. 'He wants to work everything into the case, including why there was fried potatoes for lunch yesterday and only boiled the day before. Now there's a crossword puzzle he's got on his mind.'

'Worrying things, crossword puzzles,' his colleague agreed; 'but what have they got to do with the case?'

'Search me,' answered Wake, with classic simplicity.

'Shall I tell you what put me on to it?' the other asked Bobby. 'I'll tell you. You young fellows don't always appreciate the importance of the merest trifles, and it was quite a trifle that lighted up this whole affair for me – and one I got from you yourself, though I don't think you saw anything in it. I was reading up the case, just to refresh my mind on some points, when I came on one of your reports that said the Raby girl let on she had come back from London one day by the evening train. But the station-master told you she had really arrived by the afternoon train. Now, you can take it from me, when you notice a discrepancy in the evidence, you want to go for it.'

'I think that, too,' agreed Bobby. 'It's often important.'

The other looked severe. In his view, Bobby was there to receive instruction, not to express agreement.

'Lots of men don't know one when they see it,' he said,

plainly implying that in his opinion Bobby was in that class. 'But a discrepancy, if and when you see it, is always the starting-point you want. Now, there's proof Miles Winterton was in the neighbourhood and keeping quiet about it. Most likely they met that afternoon and laid their plans. In point of fact there's a bit of evidence two people answering their description were seen walking together by the cliff. And, on the night of the murder itself, we know – he admits it – that Miles slept in a car not so far away. He could easily have got to Suffby in it, left it at a little distance, proceeded on foot, most likely by a field-path you won't know about, that runs from the main road to the village; past the Fairview garden, without anyone seeing or hearing him. Equally easy to get back the same way.'

Another officer had come into the room, and had listened to all this with great attention.

'Wasn't there a third nephew?' he asked. 'A James Matthews, or some name like that? No one ever seems to have thought of him.'

'He doesn't appear in the case at all,' Wake remarked.

'Just as well to make sure of that,' observed the newcomer. 'The more you're in a thing like this, the more you would want to look as if you weren't. It seems he's a painter, and lives in Paris, and though, of course, that isn't anything against him, in my humble opinion, he ought to be looked up.'

'We don't know he was ever near the place,' Wake objected.

'Do we know he wasn't?' retorted the other. 'In my humble opinion, it's the most unlikely person you want to think the most about. It's not a bad rule: look round, fix on the most unlikely, and make sure about him, one way or the other, first of all.' He added thoughtfully: 'In my humble opinion, it was that telegram put the whole investigation wrong. Seemed like a snip, and turned into a wash-out instead.'

The others all evidently agreed with this observation, and, encouraged by the general approval, the speaker repeated:

'Pick on the most unlikely first, and then the next least likely, and work through 'em like that till there's only one left, and then you have your man. At least, that's my humble opinion.'

'If you ask me——' began Wake.

'You can take it from me——' began his second colleague; and just then the door opened, and there came in, breezily, Superintendent Andrews, Major Markham's principal lieutenant.

'Hello, boys,' he said cheerfully. 'You can all look forward to a rest cure now. I'm telling you for sure – the Suffby Cove mystery's as good as cleared up, and now it's only a question of arresting the murderer as soon as we can lay hands on him.'

'Who is it? What's happened? Is it Colin Ross – Mr Shorton – Miles Winterton – the third nephew, Matthews?' they all asked in chorus, and Andrews smiled on them genially:

'I'm telling you for sure,' he said again. 'It's Colin Ross all right. The Laura Shipman girl's come through at last, and we're proceeding to arrest right away.'

CHAPTER XXIV

Explaining an Infallible System

It was an announcement that reduced instantly to silence the astonished exponents of the different theories that had just been advanced. Not that they were convinced, not that they believed or accepted for one moment this rival proposition, for no man worthy of the name, or unworthy of it either for that matter, ever gives up his own belief so easily as that. But it was a superintendent who spoke, and, therefore, they, as befitted men under discipline, remained silent, and kept to themselves all the overwhelming objections and difficulties that at once occurred to them.

All, that is, except Bobby, and perhaps that was because his own special private theory – the one he hoped and believed Mitchell shared with him, though they had never discussed it openly – had not yet been relieved by expression, and was in consequence still eager to give itself form and substance in speech. Anyhow, while the others still clung in silence to their own beliefs, and still kept silence over the innumerable flaws they perceived in the superintendent's, Bobby burst out:

'Colin Ross? Do you mean ... a confession ...?'

The superintendent surveyed the young man smilingly. Rather cheek for a young fellow, not yet even a sergeant, to start questioning his seniors like that. Still, he seemed keen, and the superintendent liked keenness; and then, too, about this young man there hung a flavour of the prestige the Yard bestows upon even its most junior members. So the superintendent decided to explain.

'Well, yes, in a way,' he said. 'Enough to clear it all up now Miss Shipman's found her tongue. They often do if you give them time to think it over after a talk, and then take them over the same ground again. That' – said the superintendent reflectively unheeding the impatience of his auditors – 'that is where these third-degree merchants go wrong. They badger the subject till he gets so fed up he tells any lie that comes handy, because he simply don't know where he is any longer – and then you don't know where you are either. While if you only treat 'em as if you loved 'em, as likely as not, after a time, they'll start telling the truth. Less strain on the memory, for one thing.'

The others had listened to this little homily on the art of extracting confessions with an impatience that, in the case of Bobby, was mingled with a certain discreet amusement, for he had recognised that the superintendent was repeating, almost textually, remarks made to him by Bobby's own chief, Mitchell. Inspector Wake, letting his impatience master him, burst out:

'Beg pardon, sir. Do you mean Laura Shipman's owned up she and Colin Ross did it?'

'Not quite that,' the superintendent answered; 'but with what she has told us, and the evidence we had already – well, it's good enough. We know he's been plunging pretty heavily on the gee-gees, and most likely he's badly dipped, like all the other racing men you come across, and that reminds me – anyone been here yet from Dugdale & Co.?'

'I don't think so, sir – the big bookmakers?' Wake said.

'Yes. We've got a sure line now that Ross ran five different accounts with them, under different names – that means he's been hit in five different places, most likely. Dug's been wired to let us have full particulars of the different accounts. Well, there's your motive – badly hit under five different names, and a rich old uncle in the background. Then, of course, we know he was on the spot at the time. There's identity established. We've the evidence of Owen here that he behaved in a most suspicious manner; and then there're the finger-prints, though a jury always looks a bit sideways at finger-prints. And now we've got what the Laura Shipman girl has told us as well.'

Wake turned to Bobby.

'Didn't you say Ross had disappeared?' he asked quickly.

'They told me, at Fairview, they hadn't seen him since last night, and didn't know where he was,' Bobby answered. 'Mrs Cooper, the housekeeper, seemed to think most likely he had gone off to some race-meeting.'

'Not him,' declared the superintendent cheerfully. 'He's bolted. So much the better; clinches it, that does. You want a water-tight case to satisfy a jury now-a-days, and when a man bolts that clears the road for you by putting the ace of trumps up your sleeve. Good sound reasoning that, when a man runs, there's a reason. But he won't get far. All the ports and air-ports were warned some time ago.'

Wake jerked a thumb at Bobby; with a deep and subtle cunning, using Bobby to express the dissatisfaction he himself felt with the superintendent's confident pronouncements.

'I'll bet that young man's not convinced,' he said. 'He wants the whole thing complete – every item covered – from what Archibald Winterton was going to have for breakfast the day he got drowned, to why the gardener's been swilling the floor of the Fairview summer-house.'

'Not swilling it, digging it up,' Bobby protested meekly. 'Of course, I don't know yet what Miss Shipman's said.'

'Oh, there's no secret about that,' the superintendent admitted. 'She's made a statement, and signed it all right. Seems there was a pretty hot flirtation between her and, first of all, Archibald himself, the wicked old sinner, and then the nephew, young Ross. Seems, according to her, George Winterton had tumbled to it one of his nephews was carrying on with some girl in the village, but he didn't know which of the two, and he didn't know which girl. But he was wrathy and upset about it, and that's why he rather boiled over when he found Miles was doing a bit of the same sort of thing with his secretary girl. He seems to have jumped to the conclusion it was Miles who was mixed up with the other girl in the village as well, and he went right in off the deep end and cleared Miles out. But apparently, Archibald was a wary old bird, and George had no idea his brother had been fooling with the same village girl – of course she swears black and blue there was nothing to it but a bit of kissing, and now and again meeting each other in Yarmouth or somewhere, and doing a dinner and the pictures. She had some letters from him, though, and Colin Ross tumbled to what was going on, and was mad jealous, she says. Notice that – the jealousy, I mean?'

'Means' – cried with some excitement the last of the three men listening to him – 'means ten to one it was Ross did in Archibald, too. That explains why the dog never barked; it would know him, of course.'

'Most likely it was like that,' agreed the superintendent, 'only it's lucky we haven't got to prove it against a smart defending K.C. Proof' – he added thoughtfully – 'proof is the very devil.'

And this remark was greeted with a sympathetic murmur from all his three colleagues, for so thought all of them, and so thought Bobby, too, though he considered it more in accordance with the discipline he always respected when he remembered not to join audibly in the murmured approval of his seniors.

'That don't matter, though,' the superintendent went on, 'because, if we land Ross for one murder, the other doesn't matter, seeing you can't hang the same man twice. Miss Shipman, after Archibald's death, didn't quite know what to do with his letters. She wanted to get rid of them, and at first she thought of burning them, she says, but she seems a thrifty young woman, and don't like waste, so she hit on the idea of selling them to his brother. She wrote an anonymous letter, offering them him, and hinting otherwise they might be sent to Mrs Archibald. Well, George Winterton naturally didn't want that to happen, so he offered her a tenner for them, and she agreed; and what you saw,' added the superintendent to Bobby, 'was her handing them over, and collecting her ten pounds.'

'Why in the middle of the night?' Bobby asked.

'She didn't want to be recognised, either by him or by anyone else, and she didn't want her old grandmother she lived with to know anything about it, either. Ten pounds was big money to her, and she didn't mean to share it. So she says she thought the safest way would be to slip out late one night, and then, very likely, she knew well enough it was mighty near blackmail, and she wanted to be sure none of us were waiting for her. She says, too, it was her Owen saw the same night, earlier on, when he noticed someone slipping off in the dark. That was her warning Mr Winterton he was to look out for her later on the same night, and to have the money ready. And, if she hadn't given herself away over that watch business, no one would ever have known anything about it, for I reckon Winterton burnt the letters as soon as he got them. And all that put together – jealousy established; racing losses; hard up most likely; Owen's evidence; the finger-prints – make up as sound a case as ever I hope to take into court.'

A constable made his appearance, with a message. A Mr Castle, the emissary from Messrs Dugdale, the well-known firm of bookmakers – 'turf agents' they preferred to call themselves – had arrived, and the superintendent welcomed him warmly.

'Glad to see you, sir,' he said. 'It's important for us to know fairly accurately just how much Mr Colin Ross's losses amount to.'

Mr Castle looked very gloomy indeed.

'Our clients mostly lose,' he admitted. 'Got to – or where should we be? But this Ross bird – he knows the game all right. Two years ago we closed his account – found it getting too hot for our liking. And then the dirty tyke opens five more accounts with us under different names – ought to be illegal, that ought, but he done it. They were trying to call him from the office this morning, shutting down on all five. Why he's won steady on four of 'em and not dropped so much on the other, neither.'

'Won? Won what?' asked the superintendent, quite taken aback.'

'Winnings,' answered Mr Castle seriously. 'That's what he won – winnings. Before we heard from you, we had been going into it already, because, of course, if a client goes and wins right along, we know there's dirty work somewhere. Why, if they all done that, we should have to shut up shop, and then,' said Mr Castle menacingly, 'there'd be some more on the dole for you.' He paused and shook his head severely in profound moral reprobation of a client who so forgot what was right, and proper, and customary – especially the last of the three – as to win instead of losing. 'But, though we went into it careful,' he continued, 'we couldn't trace how the trick was done – mostly it's monkeying with late wires, or altering postmarks or something of that sort. Plain enough how one account was worked – it was run on the infallible system. So that was all right.'

'Infallible system? What's that?' asked Wake eagerly – as eagerly as all the others waited for a reply; that is, very eagerly indeed, and yet with a subtle, certain, subconscious knowledge that there would be a catch somewhere.

Mr Castle hesitated a moment.

'Well,' he conceded finally, 'I suppose there's no harm telling you, seeing lots know it, and you could easy find out. It's backing the favourite, in every race that's run, for a pound, or whatever unit you fix on. If the favourite wins, you pocket your winnings and start fresh. If it loses, you back the favourite in the next race for your unit, and enough in addition to cover what you've lost. And so on, always starting fresh each time you win. Bound to come off in the long run, because always, sooner or later, there is a favourite that does win. But we don't mind a client working that scheme, because, sooner or later he always has a go, and then we get back all we've lost, and more, too. Besides, it needs a lot of patience, and attending every racemeeting, and capital, as well, against a special run of favourites falling down. But this account was run straight on those lines, and made a steady win all along, though nothing to hurt. The other accounts are different. Putting them together, you can see they're run by someone who knows the game better than we do ourselves – every horse chosen on inside knowledge; every one of 'em weighed up; every turn of the odds taken advantage of. It's a lovely thing,' declared Mr Castle, a gleam of enthusiasm breaking through the gloomy resentment of his manner, 'to work out how them accounts has been handled. A senior wrangler what was pally with every single jockey and trainer in the game couldn't have done no better. After our bosses had looked at 'em a bit, they held a meeting to decide whether to close down the accounts and do no more business with a bloke like him, or invite him to come in and be a partner. Only I reckon they calculated, if they made him a partner, it wouldn't be long before they weren't.'

'But then, do you mean' – asked the superintendent, who was feeling slightly bewildered by this long explanation – 'do you mean Ross hasn't lost any money betting?'

'Done us down,' said Mr Castle resentfully, 'for nigh on five thou. in the last two years. Thank God,' he added piously, 'there's never been a client like him before, and I hope there'll never be another. Why, if blokes all go and win, what's to become of us? Never thought of that, most likely – killing the golden goose what lays the good old eggs, if you ask me.'

The superintendent did not answer. He looked very worried. He felt things were not turning out as they had been expected to do, and he didn't like it. He roused himself and looked at Bobby.

'You had better get back to Fairview,' he said; 'and let us know if Ross turns up there, or if you get any word of him. Oh, about that summer-house – you say the floor looks as if digging has been going on there, floor taken up, and so on?'

'Yes, sir,' said Bobby. 'Quite recently,' he added.

'All right, carry on,' the superintendent said. 'I'll send a sergeant and two or three men along after you, and you can dig up the floor again. I don't suppose there's anything there,' he added, 'but it'll be just as well to make sure.'

'Yes, sir,' said Bobby, and he left a heavy silence behind him in the room as he quitted it to fulfil his instructions.

KEY WORD: 'GOLD'

DIE NORTH GAS OFT
IS AH P I S
G SALONA SUPERNAL
ARUM TIE AREA I
MENAI MORMON G
S PEAR ADA TILT H
ORA SPINE N ALT
U NETTLES LEECH
TO A Y H V A
H GRIT CAPONS H
KO N IT ON V ENO
F BALE E R SAPE U
E LEAVEN NAN IDES
E ERNI BE USR E
T TODDLE RAGES A
O EM I M NO
IF BEWARE RUINED

CHAPTER XXV

Secret of the Crossword

When, on his return journey, Bobby drew near Suffby Cove, instead of going straight on through the village to Fairview, he waited by the roadside for the appearance of the police car the superintendent had promised should follow him. It would be better, he thought, to carry out the intended search as quietly as possible, and, when the car appeared, he proposed to its occupants, a sergeant and two constables, that they should avoid the excitement their passing through the village would probably cause by making a somewhat long detour that would bring them out on the main road again a little distance south of their objective.

This was agreed to, and at the point where the footpath Bobby had used once before left the road, they parked their car and the motor-cycle in a convenient field and followed the path to the Fairview garden gate, through which they passed to reach the summer-house. The little building was well hidden from the house by surrounding trees and shrubs, and, indeed, was subject to observation only on one side, where a long vista opened on the distant sea. On that side they set up the protection of a tarpaulin sheet they had brought with them to act as a screen, and then, hoping they had secured themselves from interruption, they set to work.

That the stone flooring had recently been lifted and replaced, that the earth underneath had been disturbed to some depth, was sufficiently plain. But for what purpose did not appear, for though, taking it in turns – since only two men could work conveniently at a time in that limited space – they dug over every inch, going always deep enough to reach plainly untouched subsoil, they found nothing.

'Nothing here,' said the sergeant finally. 'Except a mare's nest,' he added with a side-look at Bobby.

And Bobby had nothing to say, for it seemed clear that

once more the investigation had come full stop against a blank wall.

One of the two constables was inclined to grumble at so much hard and useless work, but the other, an older man, said:

'Someone's been before us, that's what; someone's been first and got it, whatever it was. Got it and took it or moved it somewhere else.'

'Well, what was it, anyway?' retorted the other, without either expecting or receiving a reply.

Bobby remarked thoughtfully:

'I think it explains what had really happened when I thought the floor had been swilled down, and couldn't imagine why anyone should want to wash-out a tumble-down old place like this. Most likely the idea was to throw water down to see where it soaked in quickest, as a guide to where to begin digging. And that means two entirely different sets of people are concerned – those who hid in the first place, and those who came to seek later.'

'Yes, but what was it?' the sergeant repeated, though also without either expecting or receiving a reply.

They all grew busy again, replacing the earth they had dug up, putting back in position the stone flags of the flooring, removing as far as possible all traces of their night's work. Then they all went back to where they had left car and motor-cycle. The sergeant and his two men departed, and Bobby, disappointed and troubled, too disturbed in mind to think of bed or sleep, even though every muscle ached and his back gave him the impression of having cracked right across, took his motor-cycle and wheeled it back along the foot-path and then on to the extremity of West Point that formed on this southern side the other of the two projecting points guarding the entrance to the Cove.

There he sat down on a bank covered with short sweet-smelling grass. It was so late now that it had grown early again, and already the sky was light in the east with the glow of the coming dawn. Bobby had cigarettes with him, and as he smoked one after another, and watched the light of the new day spread over sea and land, he tried yet again to solve the problem this tangled case presented. But it seemed hopeless. He could not even keep his mind steady. Round and round his thoughts went, forming ever new patterns, but never one that seemed to correspond with that reality had woven.

There were all those theories he had listened to the previous evening, for instance. All of them seemed to have at first and in their own degree that whole and complete relation with the fact he sought for, and yet thereafter to vary from it entirely. It was like a crossword puzzle, of which you got one small corner right but all the rest baffled you entirely, most likely because one of the words you had got hold of and thought right was really completely wrong.

'Something was certainly hidden under the floor in the summer-house,' he told himself, 'but who hid it?' Who's got it? What was it?'

But, though he said this out loud, he, like the sergeant and the constable before him, neither expected nor received any answer.

His mind went back to the very beginning of it all – the mysterious launch that had appeared and vanished on the morning of the attack on Constable Jennings. Was what had been once hidden under the summer-house floor something landed from that launch? It seemed likely. But, then, that meant smuggling, and what smugglers leave their contraband goods so long hidden so near the place of landing? One does not smuggle goods simply to bury them and leave them. Besides, there was the difficulty of supposing that two well-off, retired business men would engage in large-scale smuggling operations, and the further difficulty of the complete lack of any evidence that any smuggling of any sort had been going on.

Smuggling, in the ordinary sense of the word, Bobby felt must be ruled out.

Could it be, he wondered, that someone landed from the launch had been suffering from some illness or injury, had died on reaching shore, and, to avoid publicity, the body had been buried in the summer-house and then removed elsewhere?

A fantastic, almost ridiculously improbable conjecture, Bobby decided, and yet, in his tired state, let his mind play with the notion. One difficulty seemed to be that apparently two sets of people were concerned – those who had hidden in the first place, those who had come later and sought and, one supposed, found as well.

His thought went back to the 'released from prison' telegram, and dwelt upon it almost with pleasure, for at any rate it was a fact, a solid fact, in this shifting sea of chaos and conjecture. He thought it almost certain Mitchell would be following up the important clue stumbled upon in the register of the Brilliant Hotel when Bobby found that the name entered there was quite possibly 'Muller.' Because, of course, a Muller, coming from Dover, suggested the Continent in parts whereof at present gaols seem somewhat unusually full. That Mitchell's mind and his own had been working on the same lines he was quite convinced, even though they had said so little to each other. But, then, that was almost always Mitchell's way; he liked to know which way your mind was working. If he thought it the right direction, he would give you encouragement; if he thought you were on the wrong track, he would point out the obstacles in your path and expect you to say how you intended to surmount them. But what he always wished for more than anything was the impact of a fresh mind upon facts considered entirely independently. For that reason he favoured but little the kind of general conferences most of his colleagues put so much trust in, for he said that several different minds, considering the same facts all together at the same time and place, were as likely to influence each other in the wrong direction as in the right – especially when half those present were subconsciously almost as keen on pleasing and flattering their seniors by supporting them as on putting forward fresh and independent points of view. Whereas, Mitchell held, if two people, working separately and independently on the same set of facts, saw them pointing in the same direction it was very likely indeed that that direction was the right one.

Only the difficulty was always the old one. Intuitions and beliefs may be very convincing, but are no good at all to show a jury. Only solid evidence counts, and of that, in spite of the deep yet vague belief in Bobby's mind, he had almost none. Perhaps Mitchell, following the clue of the hotel register, might find some, but it was only a chance, and a poor one at that.

It was very quiet and peaceful there as the sun climbed ever higher in the sky and spread his light and warmth over the earth beneath. Against the glowing eastern sky the other headland across the opening to the Cove showed clearly, with every detail on it in sharp outline. Bobby could even distinguish the path leading down from the now deserted house Archibald Winterton had occupied to the beach beneath. He must have followed it when going for the swim from which he was fated not to return alive, and Bobby found himself wondering whether that mystery would ever be cleared up; whether, indeed, there was any mystery there at all.

In his rather depressed mood he was inclined to tell himself there was small chance of any really satisfactory answer being found to these questions.

A blank wall everywhere. That was what it seemed like. Even that crossword puzzle from which – he no longer knew why – he had been inclined to hope so much, appeared totally devoid of all interest. Certainly it contained some curious features, but none to which any real significance seemed to attach. While waiting at the county police headquarters he had nearly completed it, and now he took it out again to have another look at it. His eyes caught the heading to which before he had not paid much attention: 'Key word: Gold.' So far as Bobby could see, there was no reference to gold, either in the words to be discovered, or in the rather far-fetched clues to them. Besides, crossword puzzles have no need for key words. It is ciphers key words belong to, not crossword puzzles; and this was no cipher, but only a beginner's first attempt at constructing a crossword puzzle – that, and nothing more.

Bobby was as nearly as possible throwing the thing away without bothering about it any more.

Only somehow that expression 'Key word: Gold' stuck curiously in his mind, haunting it, so to say, with vague and shadowy suggestions. He found himself wondering whether that first idea of his had been correct, and whether this that looked like a crossword was in fact a cipher.

Only he could not for the life see how that could be, or how the word 'gold' could be the key to it, when apparently neither that word itself nor the letters composing it had even the most remote connection with anything else in the puzzle?

Looking at it yet again, he noticed that the first word was 'Dig.' That, Bobby reflected, was what they had spent a good share of the night in doing to no purpose, and if the crossword had no other meaning or message than that, it wasn't going to be very interesting. But still there did seem to be a vague connection there between the puzzle and actual fact.

But then again there was nothing in the crossword about a 'summer-house.' The word 'house' appeared, it was true, and with a sufficiently obvious clue. Oddly enough, it was one of the clues that had a star affixed, with the reference to the note beneath suggesting that clues so marked were either too obvious or not obvious enough and needed 'attention,' this last word 'attention' being twice repeated, as if for emphasis.

Certainly nothing could be much more obvious for 'house' than the clue, 'A snail carries his on his back,' but several others equally obvious were unmarked. Indeed, the whole puzzle seemed quite elementary. Bobby had found little difficulty in completing it. He wondered if the position of the crosses with which some of the clues seemed so unnecessarily marked bore any hidden meaning – any relation, for instance, to what was described as the key word, 'gold.' But he could trace none, though he did notice that the clues so marked seemed often to be grouped together in twos or threes, as if they were obscurely connected in some way.

A little odd, too, he thought, that this word or warning, 'attention,' twice repeated in the appended note, was the expression, as Bobby well remembered, Winterton had used in speaking of the puzzle to Bobby. More than once he had repeated that it might, in certain undefined circumstances, repay 'attention.'

Had he meant anything, Bobby wondered, or had it merely been the expression of an author's proud belief that his own special creation was something quite out of the way?

Once again Bobby read over the words with which he had filled in the blank spaces; once again he pored over each clue in turn, trying in vain to make the words yield some meaning, trying to discover some significance hidden in the phrasing of the clues.

He could see nothing. He could not even imagine how to begin. There was nothing to take hold of, no imaginable starting-point; it was like grasping at the vacant air in the hope of finding there a secure handle to hold by.

As for the clues that were starred, with the suggestion that they required 'attention,' for the life of him he could not see that they were either easier or more difficult than the others, or what attention they could require. 'A snail carries his on his back' could only mean 'house,' and had a star. But that other one about 'Sam' and a 'pan' and a 'boat' was equally obvious, and yet had no star. Then the one for 'dig' was rather difficult perhaps. It ran: 'Mr J. Ball wanted very much to know who was the gentleman when Adam did this: use modern form and present tense.' Not everyone would recognise 'John Ball,' the mediæval rebel, under the description 'Mr J. Ball,' or remember his catchword – slogan it would be called to-day – 'When Adam delved and Eve span, who was then the gentleman?' That was starred, too. The clues to the words 'beware' and 'ides' were both elementary, and yet one was starred and one was not. In fact, Bobby could see no order or reason in the way in which the stars were assigned to some clues and not to others.

Only – with a sudden leaping excitement he asked himself if possibly it was not the clues themselves, but the words to which they referred, that needed attention, that bore perhaps some meaning, and would, as Mr Winterton had said, repay attention.

Bobby wrote down the words to which the starred clues referred, taking those across first and then those down. He got the result:

'Dig. North. Gas. Beware. Ruined. South. Feet. Of. Ten. Corner. And. Light. House.'

Incoherent enough. A mere medley, apparently making no sense. Yet, as he sat and pored over them, it seemed to him that from these words a kind of faint aroma of a meaning distilled itself. It hovered over the words, danced like a flickering light that vanished before he could seize it, came, and was gone again. He tried to put them together, to see which of them would make a consecutive meaning. 'Beware' and 'ruined,' for example, were words that might go together. But 'beware' is of the present or the future, 'ruined' is of the past, so that would not do. What else was there that would fit in with 'beware'? 'Gas,' perhaps; yes, that would certainly do. 'Beware gas' made sense all right, and then there was an 'and,' and 'and' is a conjunction, suggesting that the sentence, if one really existed, was in two parts. The end of the sought sentence then might be 'and beware gas.' But how to arrange the other words in any satisfactory order? There was 'ruined,' for one, to start with. It made him think of the ruined summer-house where he and the others had worked so hard during the night. But there was no reference to a 'summer-house,' ruined or not, in the puzzle. There was the word 'house,' certainly, and the word 'light,' which might go with 'house' perhaps. 'Ruined lighthouse' would make sense, but there was no lighthouse, ruined or otherwise, that Bobby knew of anywhere near. But he was growing excited now, and he saw that, of the words that were left, several – 'ten,' feet,' 'north,' 'south,' 'corner' – might refer to measurements, perhaps to directions where to 'dig.'

His hand was trembling a little as he wrote down the message now in this form:

'Dig ten feet north (south) of south (north) corner ruined lighthouse and beware gas.'

That at least made sense – a sort of sense. But was it a sense that stood in any relation to actual facts?

It was comparatively late now and, in the village, signs of life had been apparent for some time. Bobby got his motor-cycle and began to wheel it over the turf towards the rough path that ran by the edge of the cliffs between Suffby village and its nearest neighbour along the coast. He saw a man going early to work, walking along the path towards him, and recognised him as one with whom he had at times exchanged a word or two. The newcomer looked astonished to see Bobby standing there with his motor-cycle, and said something about an early ride, and Bobby, ignoring this, asked him if there was any ruined lighthouse in the neighbourhood. He answered, a little as if he doubted Bobby's sanity, that he had never heard of one. But Bobby was in no mood to take 'No' for an answer. Circumstance had said 'No' to him too long, and, now that at last he had seemed to extract some hint of a 'Yes,' he was not going to be put off with another 'No,' if he could help it. He took two half-crowns from his pocket and jingled them together.

'Quite sure?' he said. 'Quite sure there's nothing in the shape or way of a ruined lighthouse anywhere near here?'

The other looked longingly at those two half-crowns reposing in Bobby's open palm. Not often did a chance to earn five shillings so easily come his way. Why, five shillings would mean a joint of pork for a slap-up dinner for the whole family the coming Sunday, such a dinner as they would remember and talk about for months to come.

But he shook his head.

'There ain't nothing of that sort round here, guv'nor,' he answered emphatically, 'not since poor Mr Archibald, the gent that got drownded, pulled down almost all what was left of it and made the rest into his garage next his house.'

The next moment he stood still and bewildered, gasping alternately at the five shillings thrust into his hand and at the flying figure on the motor-cycle vanishing at breakneck speed along that rough path by the cliff side.

CHAPTER XXVI

Colin's Last Words

ALONG the rough, uneven cliff path Bobby's machine bumped and roared, while in its rider's head seemed to echo and re-echo that phrase with which the crossword puzzle had been headed: 'Key word: Gold.'

For that injunction, 'Dig,' it seemed to him might well be in close relationship thereto; and 'Gold' prove indeed the key, not only to the puzzle, but to other things as well, as so often in human history 'Gold' has been the key and cause of so many other tragic happenings since man first chose to link his fate so closely to this bright, yellow metal. Two deaths already, Bobby reminded himself, had their places in the tragic tale, and there might well be, he knew, a third to add to the count if he arrived too late.

He slackened speed a little as the village drew near. He noticed a wisp of smoke coming from the Fairview chimneys. Probably Mrs Cooper was getting ready for the day's work, for, though in the summer most of the cooking was done on a small electric stove, she often made use as well of the big, old-fashioned kitchen range which also heated the water for the baths and other household purposes.

In the village, too, most of the inhabitants were up and about. Some of them came out of their cottages to see what stray motorist was passing so early in the morning, and Bobby felt he had started conjecture and curiosity that would be hard to satisfy. It was too late to bother about that, however, and, besides, as Mary Raby apparently knew his business, very possibly others did as well. For the tiniest hole in a secret is like the tiniest hole in the bottom of the biggest of tanks – very soon it's all out.

He found himself wondering if Mrs Cooper were one of those who knew; if perhaps she had been the first to guess. He tried to remember anything he might have said or done that could have given her a hint of the truth, but could think of nothing.

He left the village behind, rounded the Cove, followed the track – smoothed and levelled and made into a tolerable road by Archibald Winterton when he first came to live here – that led to the house Archibald had occupied at the end of the headland. The gate leading to the grounds round the house Bobby found padlocked when he came to it, but when he dismounted, to look more closely, he had little difficulty in assuring himself that it had been opened and re-fastened only recently.

He did not bother to lift his cycle over, but left it standing against the hedge, and, climbing the gate, he went on towards the house.

It was closely shuttered, and had, even in the bright morning sunshine, that deserted and melancholy air empty houses so soon acquire, as if they knew somehow that thus they lacked all significance or use. The garden looked wild and neglected, too, for, though one of the men from the village had been engaged to come and tidy it up every week, he was paid less than he thought fair, and so neglected his work and often did not come at all.

Though Bobby had explored the promontory pretty thoroughly one morning shortly before the tragedy of George Winterton's death, he had not given the house itself, or the grounds surrounding it, much attention. His chief interest then had been in the little half-private beach below, whence Archibald Winterton had started for his last swim.

The house was a long, low building, facing due south. At the east end – that is, nearest the sea – was the garage, attached to the house, and much older and much more solid in construction than the rest of the building. Evidently it had been largely reconstructed, but a good part of the original walls remained. The space in front of the door had been flagged, and advantage had been taken of the great thickness and strength of the walls to support, above the garage proper, an enormous tank, into which, when it was working, an oil engine pumped water for the household from an adjacent spring. It was a tank that looked big enough, Bobby thought, to supply not only one household, but a whole village, and must hold, he supposed, a good many tons of water.

The garage door was secured by a strong padlock. Bobby examined it carefully. New, he told himself; too new, indeed, in his opinion to have been there long, exposed to sea air and weather. To him it had very much the air of having been in position only a very short time. Bobby had no key. Nor had he any authority to force an entrance; but, after all, breaking into an empty garage is not quite the same as breaking into a house, and, without his knowing why, he was aware of a strange belief that for some reason there was no time to lose.

He examined the padlock closely, and was able to recognise it as one of a well-known make he would not find it easy to open. It had not even the disadvantage of the high hasp so many padlocks are made with, so that there is no difficulty about inserting a lever and twisting till the padlock breaks. The door was strong, too; and then he thought of examining the 'peak' or 'peg' let into the wood of the doorpost. That looked, in fact, very much as if it had merely been let in without any precaution taken to twist or spread the ends, so as to give them any real hold. In addition, the wood looked worn and ragged, as if another hole had been made there before in the same place. Taking hold of the padlock, and using it itself as a lever, he was able, by exerting all his force, to drag out the peg, when, of course, the padlock ceased to secure anything. Bobby looked at the disengaged padlock as it lay in his hand.

'Whoever put that on, meant it to stay on,' he mused, 'only they forgot a padlock is only as strong as the peg that holds it. But why should anyone be so keen on making an empty garage so secure as all that?'

He opened the door, and at once was assailed by a strong, rather sweet, overpowering odour that set him coughing and retching, and his eyes watering so much that he could not for the moment see very clearly. But, when he could, it was to make out huddled in a corner, in shadow, where the strong bright rays of the morning sunshine that streamed in by the open door did not reach, the prostrate figure of a man.

'Ah, my God, a third!' he said below his breath, and ran across, nor was he surprised when he recognised Colin Ross.

The sweet, pure sea air had already done much to overcome the poisonous vapours that had affected him at the opening of the door, and he remembered rather grimly that warning at the end of the sentence he had constructed: 'Beware gas.' Evidently, he had not erred in putting those two words together. But now, looking closer, he saw it was not only the poison of the gas that had affected Colin, but that he had been bleeding from deep wounds in the chest, where he had been stabbed twice over. The bleeding did not seem to have been serious, however, perhaps having been arrested through the action of the gas in slowing down the circulation.

Looking more closely, Bobby thought it was not certain that death had yet occurred. He could not feel the heart beating; he could not distinguish even the faintest sign of breathing; and yet somehow it seemed to him that some traces of vitality still lingered, however precariously; that as yet the physical habitation was not utterly emptied of that strange essence, power, principle, that bears the name of life.

Bobby had, like other members of the police force, for whom the training is obligatory, some knowledge of first aid, but this he felt was far outside his capacity to help. And he had committed a grave blunder, he recognised now, in coming alone. He should have brought with him someone he could send for help. As it was, he would have to go for help himself, he supposed, and that would mean leaving Ross alone, and leaving also, unwatched and unguarded, a place that might well repay a close and prompt examination. Anything might happen while he was away, but there was no help for it; and then, getting to his feet and looking round, he saw that in one spot digging had been going on. He could not help going across to look. The floor was paved, but here a flag had been lifted, and, underneath, a small hole had been made in the solid foundation of the old lighthouse. Close by lay an open box, very strongly made and metal lined. It was quite empty, and considerable violence had evidently been used in breaking it open, for it was badly smashed, while near by, lying on its back, was a book Bobby saw was a volume of Coleridge's poems, open at *The Ancient Mariner*. But what struck Bobby most was the small size, both of the hole that had been hollowed out in the foundation of the building, and of the box itself. The hole could have held nothing much larger than the box; the box could not have held any great quantity of whatever had been its contents; the book alone, if that had been inside, must have nearly half filled it.

'If it was gold the box held – "Key word: Gold",' Bobby thought, with a touch of disappointment, 'there can't have been more than a few pounds' worth – a hundred or two at the outside.'

And that seemed to him a very poor, inadequate explanation to put forward for so grim a sequence of tragedy.

Then he rebuked himself for wasting time on fresh speculation while a dying fellow-creature needed aid, but, all the same, he could not help picking up the broken box and sniffing at it, with the result that once more he had to go coughing and staggering to the doorway to get there the relief of the pure and strong sea air, so dazed, indeed, that for the moment he could only cling to the doorpost and wait till the nausea and faintness passed.

He remembered having noticed a flight of stone steps at the back of the garage, and it struck him that very likely they led to the huge water-tank above. A drink of water would help to revive him, he thought, and take away the feeling of nausea he was suffering from.

He crossed quickly to them, accordingly, and, ascending them, found his conjecture was correct. The steps led to a huge chamber wherein the water-tank was situated, and a ladder gave access to the tank itself. Climbing the ladder, Bobby was able to fill a tin dipper he had found, and the drink of water he took refreshed him greatly and relieved both the burning sensation he was experiencing in the throat and stomach and the dizzy and giddy feeling in his head that had before seemed to be growing steadily worse. Finding himself much better, he descended to the garage again, giving this time the empty box a wide berth. But he had an impulse to look at the book, and, as he had expected, he found it bore Mr George Winterton's book-plate, so that it had plainly come from Fairview. He noticed, too, that the poem of *The Ancient Mariner*, at which it lay open, had a blue pencil-mark placed against the line:

Water, water everywhere, nor any drop to drink.

He noticed, too, that the word 'drop' had been crossed out, so that the line now read: 'Water, water everywhere, nor any to drink.'

At the moment it did not occur to him to attach any importance to these alterations; the one thing he had to do was to get help for Colin Ross, even though he knew well enough that it was far too late for any help to be effective.

He supposed vaguely that the scribble in the book was the work of someone trying to re-hash the old joke about water being far too valuable and useful for it to be wasted as a mere drink.

In the tin dipper he had found he had brought some water down with him, and he took it across to the still unconscious Colin. He did know enough, thanks to his first-aid studies, not to try to pour a liquid down the throat of an unconscious man, with the possible result of choking him, but used it instead to bathe the sufferer's lips and temples and his forehead, in the hope of giving him a little relief. And, though he was not sure, he thought he was able to detect some slight sign of returning life, as if the fresh sea breeze, blowing into every corner through the open door and chasing away the still lingering poison of the released gas, was acting as a restorative.

It was only later that he remembered how the candle near its end will flare up for one uncertain second before it goes out for ever.

An eyelid fluttered, or he thought it did. Again he moistened Colin's lips and temples, and now the dying man moved slightly, as if in an effort to rise, and seemed to be about to try to speak. Bobby leaned nearer, thought he saw a gleam of recognition in the other's eyes.

'Do you know me?' he asked.

This time Colin spoke quite clearly.

'Yes, of course,' he said, but the name he uttered was not one that Bobby knew. He added, still speaking quite clearly: 'Why are you all here? All of you? Why? ... How? ...'

'There is no one but me,' Bobby said. He stooped nearer still. 'Can you tell me what happened?' he asked.

But Colin's eyes were already closing, the animation passing from his expression. He had evidently understood, and was trying to answer, but his words came brokenly, often dying away into an indistinguishable murmur. There was something about '... always a sportsman ... uncle meant ... would have whacked up with Miles and Jimmy ... worked it out at last ... they followed me, the two of them ... did me in, the gas first'; and then finally, in a louder voice: 'Water! water!'

Thinking he was thirsty and wanted to drink, Bobby put the dipper to his lips, but with a violent and apparently angry effort, his last, Colin pushed it aside.

'No, no,' he muttered; and then, very loudly and clearly: 'You've no guts! Give me the knife.'

A long shiver passed through his body. It was finished, and Colin Ross's life on earth was over. Bobby rose to his feet. He was a little pale himself now, a little shaken,

for those last words had seemed to make all clear at last.
'Plain enough now,' he said to himself. 'That ought to be proof good enough for anyone.'

CHAPTER XXVII

Herr Nabersberg's Story

THERE was nothing now that could be done for this last victim of the tragic sequence that was so slowly wearing itself out, of which even now Bobby did not feel that the end had yet arrived. For a moment or two he stood still, brooding over the body. Then, remembering that there was work to be done, a task to be achieved, he covered the dead face decently with his handkerchief and turned towards the door, meaning to go for help.

But as he left the garage he heard the sound of approaching motors, and he wondered, a little doubtfully, who it might be, for the idea flashed into his mind that in certain circumstances it might well be that his own name would figure as the fourth upon the list of victims.

But, when he turned the corner of the house and came in sight of the drive that led up to it, he recognised, leading the little group of men who, having left their cars at the entrance-gate, were now walking towards the house, his own chief, Superintendent Mitchell. By his side was a stranger, a small round man, round of body, round of head, with broad, flat features and a small dark moustache. His cheeks were sunken, his dark, small eyes bright and feverish; he had altogether something of the air of an invalid, of a man just recovering from some severe illness or experience. Behind them came Major Markham with two of his assistants, Superintendent Andrews and Inspector Wake. Mitchell nodded a greeting to Bobby.

'They told us in the village they had seen you pelting up here full tilt, and so we thought we had better see what the hurry was,' he remarked. 'Found something, eh? You look as if you had.'

'Yes, sir,' Bobby answered. 'Colin Ross is there, in the garage. He's dead – murdered, I think.'

'Murdered?' Mitchell repeated gravely. 'I was half afraid ——' He turned to Major Markham. 'Then that ends the question of arresting him,' he said.

'Are you sure it is murder and not suicide?' Major Markham asked Bobby. 'Ross must have known we were looking for him.'

'It can hardly have been suicide, sir,' Bobby asserted. 'I could see no weapon, and the garage was locked on the outside.'

'Nothing to show how it happened? Who did it?' Mitchell asked.

'He was still alive when I found him,' Bobby said. 'I don't know how he had lived so long. He had been stabbed in the chest, and poison gas has been released in the place, it reeks with it. I think perhaps the effect of the gas slowed down the bleeding, and the effect of the bleeding was to weaken the breathing and prevent so much gas being inhaled. He was quite unconscious, but after fresh air got into the place, and after I had bathed his face and mouth with some water, he seemed to revive a little. I asked him if he recognised me, and he said, "Yes," but I don't think he did. Then I asked him what had happened, and he tried to tell me, but I couldn't make out much of what he was saying – it was too indistinct, until just the very last. I think, at the end, he was repeating the last thing he had heard before he lost consciousness, something he had heard someone say. It was, quite plainly: "You've no guts! Give me the knife".'

The others only stared, not understanding, but Mitchell put up a hand with a gesture of amazement, almost of fear.

'He said that. He said that,' he repeated, twice over, but more to himself than to his companions. He turned to Major Markham: 'That makes it plain enough, I think,' he said slowly.

'I don't see how,' retorted the Major, not too good-temperedly.

'It confirms what I was saying, doesn't it?' Mitchell asked. 'You remember I was talking about Shakespeare's *Macbeth.* There's a quotation that comes in *Macbeth*, I think: "Infirm of purpose! Give me the dagger." Now, we've the same thing in modern idiom: "You've no guts! Give me the knife." I was telling you how once, some time ago, we had a case the papers got to calling at the trial: "Hamlet in Modern Dress." Well, what I think we've been watching is "Macbeth in To-day's Setting".'

'It doesn't seem credible,' Major Markham said slowly. 'I don't say you're wrong, but it's hardly credible. A bit far-fetched, too, isn't it?'

'The more circumstances and environment change,' Mitchell answered, 'the more human nature remains the same. Ambition, the will to the end with no care for the means, a determination so fixed it considers nothing else – and in the end the result may add up to much the same total even though the background's different.'

They were inside the garage now. Bobby had warned them to be careful in entering, but the fresh, strong sea air, penetrating to every chink and crevice, had by now dispelled nearly every trace of the poison that had lingered there so long. Except for a certain watering of the eyes, and a tendency to cough, the new-comers experienced no inconvenience. They clustered round the dead man, but there was nothing they could do, except strengthen their resolve that his murderers should be brought to justice. They examined carefully, too, the cavity hollowed out under the garage floor, and the broken box that had apparently been hidden there. Wake, sniffing it too closely, got so strong a whiff of the gas with which the wood was still impregnated that he had to go outside to recover himself. Mitchell said:

'Well, it's pretty certain the gas was inside that box all right. As I see it, Ross found the box, opened it, the gas knocked him out. Then someone else came along, ran a knife into him to make sure, as they thought, and made sure, too, I suppose, of whatever was inside the box – which can't have been much. What about that book?'

'I think it must have been in the box, too, sir. I can't think why,' Bobby said. 'It smells of the gas so strongly, it must have been soaked in it for some time.'

Mitchell picked it up, and held it cautiously at arm's length.

'*The Ancient Mariner*,' he remarked. 'Nightmarish sort of thing; nightmares enough in our line without reading about 'em. Someone's been marking it.' He read aloud the line as it had been altered: ' "Water, water everywhere, nor any to drink." Hum,' he commented. 'I suppose that means a whisky and soda would be preferred. Quite so, quite so! but curious, very curious.'

'Hardly affects us just now, does it?' Major Markham asked with a touch of impatience.

'That's just it,' agreed Mitchell, 'but it's odd, very odd.'

'What strikes me, sir,' Bobby ventured to interpolate, 'is that it's such a small box – there can't have been anything much in it.'

'Except gas,' commented Mitchell. 'Quite a lot of gas, if you ask me – gas, and a book of poetry. Curious. You haven't told us yet what brought you along here, by the way? You don't seem to have made any report?'

'No, sir,' Bobby answered. 'I only got the idea after our night's work in the Fairview summer-house turned out such a wash-out. I went off then, by myself, to try to think things out, and I had another shot at that crossword puzzle Mr Winterton was making up, and that we thought had been lost, and somehow all at once I seemed to see there might be a message hidden in it. It was only just a chance, but I had a feeling if it was right, there wasn't much time to lose. So I came along as fast as I could, but I was too late by twelve hours, or more perhaps.'

He produced the crossword puzzle, and showed how he had managed at last to extract from it that message which had brought him here hotfoot, but too late.

'I suppose,' he said finally, 'that poor Mr Ross had worked

out the same message and acted upon it. I think he had been watched, and was followed. But I must say I never thought such a small sum was in question. That box can't have held more than two or three hundred pounds' worth of gold at the outside.'

There was a very obvious disappointment in his tone as he said this, for, indeed, a sum so comparatively paltry seemed to him a trivial cause for three murders – he felt that so rich a harvest of death should have had a richer, more plenteous seed. But Mitchell turned to the sickly-looking stranger, who so far had not spoken.

'Herr Nabersberg,' he said, 'how much did you say was involved?'

'The amount of gold I purchased on behalf of the Winterton brothers and on my own, acting as joint partners, and indented to them at Fairview, Suffby Cove,' Herr Nabersberg answered precisely, 'was to the value of thirty thousand pounds at par. It was contained in ten iron-bound boxes, each weighing somewhere about fifty pounds. The gold itself was nearly all in English sovereigns – minted in 1915 and 1916. I was told it was part of money sent out by the English Government during the war to facilitate their operations in the East. There were a few American gold "eagles," as they call them, as well, but only a few. That box' – he pointed to the one lying on the floor – 'was not one of ours, and that hole is not big enough to have held even one of them.'

He had spoken in an English well enough phrased, but marked by a very strong German accent. A little gasp went up from his listeners as he mentioned the amount of the gold concerned, and Wake, who had come back to join them, said, half aloud:

'Thirty thousand in solid gold. No wonder there's been some dirty work going on.'

'It seems we aren't at the end of the story yet,' Mitchell remarked, 'for there's nothing here to show what has become of the gold. That Ross had worried out the message of the crossword, seems pretty sure, but that message certainly didn't mean the gold was hidden there. Perhaps what was hidden, what Ross found, what his murderers killed him for and escaped with, was just the secret of where it is really hidden.' He turned to Nabersberg: 'You can't give us any idea?' he asked.

'Only that the first plan was to bury it in an old summer-house,' the German answered, 'but then it was thought that was not very safe, and it was moved somewhere else, but where, I do not know, for I only had word that it was to be moved just an hour before I was arrested and put in prison. After that, of course, I heard nothing.'

'Herr Nabersberg,' Mitchell explained to Bobby, seeing how bewildered the young man looked, 'has only recently been released from prison in Germany.'

'I was a political prisoner,' Nabersberg explained. 'Of course, that made it much more serious – meant much severer treatment.'

'Pretty slow of us not to think of that,' observed Mitchell. 'The whole lot of us ought to go to the bottom of the class. Every man jack of the lot of us took it for granted an English prison was referred to. But there are lots of prisons on the Continent, and, by all accounts, some of them are pretty full just now.'

'Full?' repeated Nabersberg with a gesture of two lifted hands. 'They are – stuffed. That is the right English word, is it not? Why, where I was sent, they were furious; they said they had no room at all; even in the Governor's bath-room there was a prisoner, they said. Oh, they made a great fuss, but they had to take me in all the same.'

'Simple enough when you've been told,' Mitchell observed; 'but I kicked myself pretty hard for not having thought of it before, especially when you remember about that launch coming from abroad, and the sack, made in Holland, used for wrapping Jennings's head in. I suppose,' he added to Bobby, 'from the phone message you turned in after your visit to the Brilliant Hotel, you thought it might be something like that?'

'I just thought,' Bobby answered, 'that a man with a

name that might be German, who registered as coming from Dover, did rather suggest a foreigner.'

'It did,' agreed Mitchell, 'and when we tumbled to your hint, and had inquiries made of every alien we could trace, if any of them knew anything of the Wintertons, or of anyone doing business with them, it wasn't long before we found Herr Nabersberg.'

'I landed at Dover in the afternoon,' Nabersberg remarked, 'and by ten o'clock in the evening I was in your police bureau, answering your questions, and then, before sunlight this morning, you had me from my bed again. But for my illness I should have been here in your country before. As soon as I was released I procured a friend who was travelling to England to send a message for me, without mentioning my name, to Mr Winterton, that I would be with him soon.'

'It was that precipitated the murder, I expect,' Mitchell observed. 'I think the receipt of that message got known, and it was felt there was no time to lose – that the gold must be secured, and Winterton removed, before your arrival.'

'It is very likely,' Nabersberg agreed. 'It is a pity I was delayed, but though I was well in prison, for, indeed, there I did not dare to be ill, as soon as I was released – as soon as I got to Paris and knew that there I was safe – then I was very ill indeed. I should be there still in my bed, but that I was anxious about the gold consignment, and how it was to be handled. For long years I have had business relations with the Wintertons; it is inexpressibly a shock to know that such a fate has been theirs. In England, they should have been safe. One does not expect such things in England. Of course, in Germany to-day——' He broke off with a shrug. 'That is,' he said, 'provided you are not of those who are in power there. But our gold, the ten boxes, surely it should not be difficult to find them?'

'Looks to me,' observed Major Markham, 'as if someone else had found them first.' He added: 'I suppose it's this gold that was smuggled in by that motor-launch Jennings reported in the spring?'

'Was it smuggling?' Nabersberg asked. 'I do not know the English law, but both Mr George and Mr Archibald Winterton told me it was not smuggling, and could not be, for you have here no duty on gold, no prohibition on its import. But that the affair should be kept secret was necessary for me, for if the German Government had heard of it, and known that I was implicated – well, I should not have found it so easy to get released from prison, or so comfortable while I was there.'

'Was it gold that was bought in Germany and smuggled out, do you mean?' Major Markham asked.

'It is what one might have been accused of,' Nabersberg replied. 'Actually it was shipped from Holland. For me, it would have been very serious if our transaction had become known – there are so many of what used to be ordinary business deals that to-day one is subject to sharp punishment for attempting. The two Mr Wintertons, too, they wished for absolute secrecy. Mr George Winterton believed that in gold alone – in the possession of gold itself – is there safety to-day. Paper anyone can print, or forge, or copy, but God alone makes gold. And he had a fear that your Government – like the Bolshevik Government, or in America, too – would take away their gold from those known to possess it – impound it, confiscate it, take it over, buy it at a fixed price, the Governments use different names but at the end it is the Government that has the gold and not you. That, George Winterton thought, might happen here, too, and he did not mean that it should happen at his expense. For gold means power, safety, security: who has gold, has the mastery, but not if others know and can come and take it from him.'

'I don't know so much about power and safety,' Mitchell observed. 'There's no safety anywhere in this world, so far as I've ever noticed. And power lies with circumstance.'

'Who has gold, has the mastery,' Nabersberg repeated obstinately. 'So they believed, so I believe. If you have gold, you have all. But, apart from their own feelings, they promised me to take no action till I had been able to leave

Germany. You see, gentlemen,' he explained with a slight hesitation, 'my position there had grown serious. I knew I was in grave danger.'

'Working against the new Government?' Major Markham asked.

'Oh, no. I never interested myself in politics,' Nabersberg answered quickly. 'I wished only from any Government that it should leave me alone. No, it was discovered' – he hesitated; he braced himself for a disclosure; it came out at last, with an obvious effort, with a certain dread of the effect – 'it was discovered that my maternal grandmother was a Jewess.'

He paused. As there were no exclamations of horror; no outward manifestation of terror or abhorrence; as, indeed, his hearers only looked puzzled, he went on:

'I had no idea that was so. I had never dreamed of such a thing. If I had been asked, I should have said I was Nordic – Nordic of the purest type. But someone discovered the truth, and whether out of malice, or because they felt it their plain duty, I was denounced in a letter to the authorities.'

'What happened?' asked Major Markham.

'I was, of course, immediately arrested and interrogated,' Nabersberg answered simply; 'but you can see how serious it would have been for me, if anything had become known of my gold purchasing transactions with the Wintertons. It is unfortunate that the Hitler Government does not feel it can fully depend on the zeal and the loyalty and devotion of Germans of Jewish descent. For me, of course, I denied that I was Jewish, but the truth was proved beyond doubt, and then it looked bad for me, because I had tried to claim I was pure Nordic. That was considered to make my case very grave, even though I pleaded that I had not known of my poor grandmother's unhappy birth – it seems even that her father was a Rabbi, though her family cast her off entirely after her marriage with a Christian. My business, of course, was ruined. My friends forgot even my existence. I do not blame them. If any had tried to communicate with me, they might easily have been thrashed to death by the Storm Troopers, or perhaps sent to a concentration camp. Fortunately there were extenuating circumstances I was able to bring forward. It was proved that when I saw a number of high-spirited young Storm Troopers kicking an aged Jew into a canal, and then pulling him out to kick him in again, I gave the Nazi salute as I passed. Also, when the son of a friend of mine was baptised, I had sent, as a christening gift for the baby, one of the new youth dagger-knives with "Blood and Honour" engraved on the blade; and to another child, for a present at Christmas, I had sent a box of tin soldiers, and two toy cannon. That weighed very much in my favour, and finally I was released on promising to hand over my business – I am an analytical chemist – to a real Nordic, a young Nazi who had distinguished himself greatly by his zeal against Jews, but who afterwards had the misfortune to blow up himself and my laboratory, through a misapprehension of chemical quantities – chemicals caring, apparently, very little whether you are Jew or Nordic, if you do not mix them in the right proportions. Another condition was that I should leave my country for its good, since only the pure Nordic may take part in the building up of the new pure Nordic State. I regretted it, for I should have liked to take my share in building up the magnificent new Germany, where all learning, all art, all science, will be purely Nordic, but I recognised that was impossible. It was the heavy strain of all these events that, when I reached Paris, made me collapse altogether. I had asked a man I met in prison – he had been arrested for having attended a Communist meeting some years before – to let the Wintertons know of my release, but without mentioning my name, for I was still nervous. There are some relatives of mine still in Germany – cousins on my father's side, so that they are free from the Jewish taint there is in my blood – and they would probably suffer severely if this transaction of mine became known. There was danger of that, for one of the men we engaged to help navigate the launch suspected the contents of the boxes we landed, and

Mr Winterton had information that he might attempt to get help, and perhaps raid Fairview and try to seize the gold. That was why it was decided to remove it to a safer place. And when Archibald Winterton was drowned, in a way hard to understand, his brother suspected that the first step had been taken. He was inclined to believe that an attempt had been made to kidnap Archibald. He thought some boat had been lying off the coast, waiting for a chance, but that it had miscarried so far as the kidnapping was concerned, though, perhaps in trying to escape, Archibald had been drowned. I did not think it very likely myself. I thought more probably it was an accident – the drowning, I mean – but he wrote to me in a very nervous strain; and he said, also, that he thought he would be wise to apply for police protection, though he promised that he would not say more than he could help, or betray my share in the business, or even let his possession of the gold be known. Indeed, I knew he was anxious himself to keep that a secret, if it was at all possible.'

Major Markham had been listening to all this with close attention, and with great excitement. Now he burst out:

'Can that be the truth of what happened to the elder Winterton?'

But Mitchell was turning over and over in his hands the book of Coleridge's poems, and now he said:

'What's become of the gold?' We must find that out – ten boxes, iron bound, are not so easily hid.' He paused and looked at Bobby: 'I don't know if I'm dreaming, but I should have thought this book made it plain enough. Don't you think so, Owen?'

CHAPTER XXVIII

Completed Evidence

Bobby could only look puzzled. For the life of him he could not see how Coleridge's *Ancient Mariner*, even when marked with a blue pencil, gave any clue to the hiding-place of the vanished gold. He held his tongue, therefore, and Herr Nabersberg broke out excitedly:

'You know where it is? You know where it is hidden? Ah, that is a relief. For one-eighth is mine,' he explained. 'One half belonged to George Winterton, and three-eighths was his brother's; but the one-eighth is mine – and all I have in the world now I am no longer true German, true Nordic.'

The poor little, round little, flat-faced, dark-skinned man sighed heavily as he said this. It was evident that even the prospect of recovering his money hardly cheered a spirit so depressed by the loss of its proud claim to be a 'true Nordic of the purest type,' torn from him by the discovery of his Hebraic maternal grandmother. Probably he would willingly have given up the whole of his share of the gold to have the right to call himself once again 'pure Nordic.' But none of the others quite understood his grief, or even took much interest in it. Major Markham had the volume of Coleridge in his hand, and was vaguely turning over the leaves.

'You mean there's some message, plan – something here that shows where the gold is hidden?' he asked. 'I don't see anything.'

'Well, I may be wrong,' Mitchell admitted, 'only I don't think that box was put there just for fun. I don't suppose, either, that the book was put inside it for no reason, any more than the gas was.' He turned sharply upon Nabersberg. 'You say you are a chemist. Did you provide the gas?' he demanded.

'It was my suggestion,' the German admitted. 'The box itself could be opened safely, but it was divided into two chambers, and, if you removed the partition between, the gas was released. It was not dangerous,' he added, 'except to the stomach and the eyes – no one should have died of it, though consciousness might be lost. You would be very sick, very dizzy for a very long time. But you should not die.'

Mitchell looked at him a little oddly.

'We have a law in this country,' he remarked, 'forbidding

the use of man-traps. But I take it, then, there were two compartments – one holding gas, and an upper one in which was this book? I take it there was a reason for that book being there. The crossword was headed "Key word: Gold," But there's nothing about gold in the puzzle itself, so I take it, again, what that means is that gold is somehow the reason for the puzzle's existing at all. The message the crossword hid tells how to find the box. But there's no gold in it, only gas, and a book of poems. The gas is for protective purposes. The book is there – why? I take it, because it tells where the gold is really hidden. At least, that's how it strikes me.'

'Yes, but' – said Markham, still feverishly turning the pages – 'I don't see anything. You mean, hidden writing?' he asked. 'Invisible ink, letters pricked out – what do you suggest looking for?'

Mitchell glanced at Bobby, as if inviting him to reply. But Bobby could only continue to look puzzled, and Nabersberg, with growing excitement, took the book from Markham.

'There is something here,' he cried, 'you have seen. What have you seen?'

'Only what you've all seen,' Mitchell answered. 'A very well-known quotation, marked with blue pencil, altered so as to read: "Water, water everywhere, nor any to drink." Looks to me like a pretty broad hint, quite in the line of the man who made up that crossword, with its meaning hidden with such careful carelessness you would never guess there was any meaning there at all.'

' "Water, water everywhere",' Bobby burst out. 'Why, that might mean the big tank overhead.' He added: 'Ross said something, just before he died, about water. I thought he wanted to drink, but he didn't.'

'Plenty of water up there in the tank,' agreed Mitchell, 'but not to drink.'

'To hide, then,' Bobby cried. 'To hide the lost gold.'

'Anyhow, the bottom of the tank would make a good hiding-place, and one likely to occur to the Wintertons,'

Mitchell said. 'Drive your car into the garage with the boxes of gold on board, dump them into the tank, the work of a few minutes, lock up the garage, and walk off, and who was to guess anything out of the way had happened? Burying them under the garage floor, or anywhere else, would have been a much longer, much more troublesome job. You couldn't be sure of not being seen, or of not leaving some traces behind someone about the place – servants or someone – mightn't notice.'

'We'll have a look,' Major Markham cried, and Andrews, who had been listening very intently, said:

'There's a tap somewhere, you can empty the tank by it quite easily. Perhaps that's why it was put in. The builder who had the job told me about it. Of course, the tank can be emptied by cutting off the supply from the spring and opening all the taps in the house. When he had the tap put in, Mr Winterton said he wanted a quicker way of emptying the tank when it had to be cleaned, but perhaps it was the gold he wanted to be able to get at in a hurry, if he had to.'

'It might be that,' Mitchell agreed.

The tap in question was soon found, and by the aid of tools, brought from the motor-car tool-boxes, it was easily opened. Watching the water running away by the channel provided, Major Markham remarked:

'We may be too late. It may not be there now.'

'You mean, perhaps we aren't the first to guess the riddle of the blue pencil correction of *The Ancient Mariner?*' Mitchell remarked. 'No. But it would be a long, awkward job to fish up all those ten boxes. They had to be found, hoisted to the edge of the tank, carried away. And there's not been too much time, for it can't be many hours since Ross was attacked. I doubt if there's been more than one night to remove the gold in. And they would hardly dare to bring a car right up to the house, any more than they would dare empty the tank the way we are doing – even if they knew about the tap. They had to work in silence. They would never dare risk the noise and commotion of all that water running off. Most likely they left their car on the main road, and carried each box of gold to it in turn as each box was retrieved.'

Andrews, who had been up above, watching the lowering of the level of the water, came to the head of the steps.

'There's something showing, sir,' he called, with excitement in his voice. 'Looks like boxes.'

They all joined him. Someone had an electric torch, and was flashing its light into the interior of the tank. The retreating, gurgling water showed the tops of five boxes. Mitchell said:

'Looks like they got away with just half of them. To-night, I expect, the other half would have gone.'

They waited a little longer, till all the water had run off, save for a few puddles and trickles that remained in the cracks of the cemented floor. Andrews, followed by Bobby, dropped over the edge of the tank. Mitchell, who had the torch in his hand now, and was flashing its beam to and fro, called out:

'What's that just by your foot, Owen?'

Bobby stooped to pick it up. It was a leather pocket-book soaked through and through by its immersion. Bobby got it carefully on his folded handkerchief, and then passed it up to Mitchell, who retreated with it to the garage below, where he busied himself with it while the rest of them occupied themselves with the five remaining boxes.

That task accomplished, and the boxes safely deposited on the floor of the garage, Major Markham crossed to where Mitchell was still busy with the pocket-book and its soaked contents.

'Found anything useful?' he asked.

'It has Cooper's name and address on it,' Mitchell answered. 'Quite useful when criminals leave their name and address behind. I suppose it fell out of his pocket while he and his wife were busy hauling up the five boxes they got away with. They were a bit over-excited, most likely, and forgot to be as careful as usual. At last they had the gold in their possession that they had been working for so long, and a detail like a dropped pocket-book got overlooked. Like those two in Chicago who planned a perfect murder and then left a spectacle-case belonging to one of them on the scene of the crime. And it would be their excitement and hurry recovering the gold prevented them from making sure Ross was really dead.'

'That was why they left his body here, instead of trying to hide it, I suppose,' Major Markham remarked.

'Well, as for that,' Mitchell answered slowly, 'they may have thought this was as good a hiding-place for the body as anywhere else for the time being. It couldn't have been removed without a good deal of risk, and they had their hands full – working out where the gold was, and then getting hold of it. Later on, I expect they would have come round in a boat and sunk the body far out to sea, well weighted. If they had done that, and the gold and Ross were both missing, what with that, and the evidence already against him, no one would have felt much doubt of his guilt, and we should have been looking for him all over the world, while all the time his body was lying quietly a few miles out there at the bottom of the North Sea. This is interesting, too,' he went on, and showed, among other papers – some of them had been packed tightly round it, and had largely protected it from the action of the water – the original of the crossword puzzle, carefully written out in George Winterton's handwriting, with his signature, and a note of the date, two days before his death, when it had been completed. But the puzzle had all its blanks filled in in a different writing, and the words from which Bobby had constructed the hidden message were scribbled in the same writing all over the margin. Then in one place they were written in the order in which Bobby also had placed them, and were followed by the initials: 'C.R.'

'That's Ross's writing, and his initials, too,' Bobby said.

'Evidently he worked the thing out the same way as you did,' Mitchell agreed. 'Then he came along here, and the Coopers followed him. I expect they had been watching him. Perhaps they had guessed that the crossword held the secret of the gold. They watched and followed. They saw him overcome by the gas released. They took their precautions, before they entered the garage after him. They found he was still breathing, and used a knife on him to make sure, as they thought, and afterwards forgot everything else in their eagerness to discover where the boxes of gold were hidden. Possibly, too, the gas had affected them to some extent. Perhaps Mrs Cooper's head was not as clear as usual. We could wait for them here, if we liked, for I take it they are sure to return to-night. But I don't think there's any need. It seems to me our evidence is complete.'

He looked at Major Markham, who answered slowly:

'They will be at Fairview, I suppose. Yes, I think we can go and find them there.'

CHAPTER XXIX

Some Explanations

It was decided that one of the constables of the county police, who had been acting as chauffeur for Major Markham, should remain on the spot until arrangements could be made for the removal of the body of the unfortunate Colin Ross. Meanwhile the five remaining boxes of gold, all in sovereigns minted in 1915–16, were removed from the bottom of the tank, and packed safely in the waiting cars – an operation taking up some time. While it was being carried out, Major Markham, in the company of Mitchell, went through the rest of the soaked papers in the pocketbook they had discovered. There seemed to be nothing more of much interest, and Major Markham observed thoughtfully:

'Anyhow, there's enough to prove the thing is Cooper's property, and that's all we want. Yet, apart from that, I doubt if even now we have enough foolproof evidence to convince a jury, after a clever counsel has been suggesting doubts and picking holes in it for an hour or two. And I don't see we have much except pure assumption to put forward to identify the two Coopers with the murder of George Winterton.'

'Luckily that doesn't matter,' Mitchell remarked. 'Even for three murders, one hanging is quite satisfactory. All the same, it makes a fully coherent story.'

'Even now,' Major Markham said, 'I don't quite understand how they managed to carry out the first murder – that of Archibald Winterton, assuming they did, that is.'

'It was the first step in Mrs Cooper's planned scheme to get possession of the gold she knew the Winterton brothers were importing secretly,' Mitchell answered. 'It was the secrecy that gave her her chance. They wanted secrecy so as to be secure against official interference, and all the general upset and confusion of the outside world. A poor sort of security it proved that led to both their deaths. In this world, the more you seek security, the more you invite danger.'

'You suspected the Coopers from the first?' Major Markham asked.

'Only one suspicion among a host of others,' answered Mitchell. 'Suspicion's easy; it's proof that's difficult. The start was the certainty that something of value had been landed from that motor-launch, and that in consequence George Winterton was afraid of something. The difficulty was to find out what the something of value actually was, and to understand why a man apparently engaged in secret, and therefore probably illegal, activities of some sort or another, should himself invite police protection. One can understand that, now one knows what he was doing was importing boxes of English gold sovereigns. There is nothing illegal or immoral, I suppose, about bringing into a country its own gold coinage, even in these days when all kinds of what used to be ordinary business transactions have become criminal. Yet one can understand, too, that Winterton, with his ideas, his fanatical belief in gold, his conviction that in gold alone lay real actual value, and that only if you held actual gold did you hold actual value, was anxious to keep secret his possession of a store of it. He felt safe then – the old story of seeking security, and so creating a greater peril. Of course, in his case, there was the additional factor that, until his associate and partner, Herr Nabersberg, was released, any hint of their transactions that had got public, and reached the German Government's ears, might have been very serious for Nabersberg – sort of "shot at dawn" for him. Only the other day I read in the papers about some poor devil in Berlin getting a stiff sentence for paying his own money from a Swiss bank to a Hungarian one, and already in Russia and the United States it's a criminal offence to have gold in your possession. Apparently, too, Winterton was more than half afraid of an attack by the men who had been on the launch in which the gold was brought over. He seems to have thought they might make a night landing and try to secure it by force, and apparently he suspected it was they who were responsible for Archibald Winterton's death. If he had only known it, his real danger lay in his own household. But I suppose he never thought of quiet Mrs Cooper, going about her household duties, or ever realised how she felt her managing and organising abilities were cramped and stifled, or how she saw a chance in his gold to give them a wider field where they could grow and expand as she knew they could.'

'And the first step was to get rid of the elder brother,' commented Major Markham. 'But how was it done? There was no sign of any struggle – nothing. I remember you were talking about a cat as we came along, but I didn't know what you were referring to.'

'One of the first things I noticed,' Mitchell explained, 'was that Mrs Cooper was very keen in proving an alibi for George Winterton. There was no real suspicion against him; it wasn't at all likely he had had any hand in murdering his brother. But Mrs Cooper seemed oddly anxious to prove an alibi for him. That might have been pure devotion towards her employer. It might have been simply that she wanted to bring her name into the case. People are like that sometimes. It might have been that, in proving an alibi for her employer, she incidentally proved one for herself and her husband as well. Anyhow it was quite clever. Normally a guilty person tries to throw suspicion on others. Mrs Cooper is a better psychologist than that. She knew that when you insist on other people's innocence, at the same time you suggest your own. Besides, with her intelligence, she probably realised there was no real case against her master. But to prove the alibi, she told a story of a black cat on his window-sill, and how, in chasing it away for fear it might disturb him, she and her husband had seen George Winterton, through the open window of his room, sound asleep in bed. That was all very well, but young Bobby Owen happened to overhear a chance remark to the effect that, at the exact moment when the Coopers declared the only black cat in the village was on their master's window-sill, one of the fishermen of the village was chasing it away from his boat, because he thought it brought bad luck. That meant there was a discrepancy somewhere – a mistake or a lie somewhere. It wasn't much to go on; it might have been a quite unintentional, unimportant confusion of dates. If it was a lie, it might merely have been that of a loyal servant protecting her master against an accusation she knew to be false. But it did suggest Mrs Cooper was worth watching, and last night another little bit of useful information came in.'

'What was that?' Markham asked quickly.

'We had been getting a line on her past life, you know,' Mitchell answered, 'and now we've found that she acted as swimming instructress at one time at a small seaside resort on the south coast. You'll get a note of the details by the first post this morning, I expect. But here, at Suffby Cove, she had always let it be understood she couldn't swim. She had even staged some little performance to give people here that impression. One point that had seemed difficult was to understand how the Coopers, either one or both of them, supposing they had a hand in the murder of Archibald, had managed to escape observation. It was certain they were back at Fairview quite early. But if they had come back by land, they must have been seen, and there was no record of a boat, which also, for that matter, would most likely have been seen. But an expert swimmer could easily swim across the opening of the Cove, from one headland to the other, would almost certainly have escaped notice at that hour in the morning, and could easily have towed a non-swimming companion across as well, especially one furnished with some sort of air-bladder or another for additional support. As we know now, Mrs Cooper was a good swimmer, that is most likely how she or they returned to their own side of the Cove. They carried out the murder without much difficulty. One or other of them – I imagine Mrs Cooper; I think she carried it out alone – hid during the night near the beach from which the elder Winterton used to start for his swims. After he had swum out some distance, Mrs Cooper appeared from her hiding-place, and the Airedale, knowing her quite well, gave no alarm. Mr Winterton was in the habit of taking a thermos flask of hot coffee with him, to drink after coming out of the water. Owen noticed as soon as he arrived at Fairview that thermos flasks were always put ready with hot drinks for any before-breakfast bather. It struck him that it would not be difficult to tamper with Archibald Winterton's flask, or even to substitute for it another that had been already drugged. So he complained of toothache, and Mrs Cooper, who always wanted to manage everything for everyone, and to tell everyone what to do, gave him the name of a dentist to consult, and meanwhile provided him with laudanum to relieve his – er – pain. Laudanum is not easy to get hold of under the new regulations, but she seemed to have a good supply of it; and it was at least possible that when Archibald Winterton came out of the water he took a drink of coffee that had been dosed with laudanum, and then, in his resulting dazed, half-conscious condition, was taken back into the water, so that the tide should carry him out till he was caught in the current that sets in along this coast with the movement of the tide, and was swept out to sea. Defending counsel might make out that was all pure conjecture, but to my mind it gives a clear, coherent picture, and I feel pretty sure that's what happened, and that it was the first blow in Mrs Cooper's campaign to obtain possession of the gold. She meant it to open for her the wider life she believed her powers had a right to, just as poor young Ross wanted it to start his ideal racing stable – she had her ideal too; sometimes ideals can lead you wrong as well as right, I think, unless you remember still to be careful about your means. Well, after that there remained the other brother to dispose of. The first step was to get rid of the Airedale. A much inferior intelligence to that of Mrs Cooper would have seen that, if another death occurred without the dog giving an alarm, suspicion would at once be directed to the people the dog knew. So it was killed. Mrs Cooper probably knew the gold had been originally hidden in the summer-house, but did not know that subsequently it had been moved. By testing the floor with water, they made sure digging had taken place there, and the exact spot. Then came the "released from prison" telegram to warn her they had no time to lose. I imagine they kept a close watch on their employer's correspondence, and knew exactly how things were going. Most likely Mrs Cooper saw at once that the telegram would be very apt to throw any investigation all wrong – as it did, too. How she managed to induce Winterton to dodge the watch Owen was keeping, and to get him out on the lawn that night, I don't suppose we shall ever know for certain, unless she tells us, but it wouldn't have been difficult to fake a 'phone call, or some other message, purporting to come from Nabersberg, and making an appointment outside the house in the dark, on some pretext of being watched or followed, and being afraid to come in the day-time. Then, of course, Colin Ross helped them a lot by drawing suspicion on himself. It's pretty certain he knew something about the purchase of the gold, and I fancy his uncle was a little scared of him, and afraid he might ferret out the secret, and perhaps betray it. Somehow he had guessed that the secret of its hiding-place was hidden in the crossword puzzle. When Ross saw his uncle lying dead on the lawn that morning, the temptation was too much for him. Instead of giving the alarm, he saw his chance to get hold of the crossword, and secure for himself the clue to the whereabouts of the gold. He slipped downstairs, and took possession of the dead man's pocket-book; in doing so, leaving fingerprints on the book itself, and on the handle of the door he had come out by, and so providing evidence that might very well have hanged him.'

'His finger-prints were on the handle of the knife used,' Major Markham pointed out.

'Why was that knife used at all?' Mitchell asked. 'It was used on an obviously dead man, remember. No one could have lived with his head battered in like that. My own theory is that Mrs Cooper in giving Ross, as he said she had done, a day or two before, one of the kitchen knives to handle, did so to get his finger-prints on it. Then it was thrust into the dead body of the victim to implicate Ross – great care, of course, being taken in handling it to leave no other finger-prints.'

'Yes, I know,' Markham said. 'If you hadn't put that possibility to me, I should have arrested Ross immediately.'

'It might have saved his life if we had done so,' Mitchell observed musingly. 'One can't tell. I think he would have kept quiet about the hidden gold though. Anyhow, it's too late to think of that now. But until Owen got hold of the copy of the crossword Miss Raby made, only Ross had any clue to the whereabouts of the gold, and the first thing that went wrong with Mrs Cooper's plans was when they dug up the summer-house floor and found the gold had gone. That must have been a nasty jar. I take it that then they began to suspect Ross had some idea where it was. They watched him and followed him. They found him in the garage, overcome by the gas, and I suppose we can guess the rest. Had Owen not worked out the crossword in the same way that Ross did, I suppose most likely they would have brought it all to what they would have called a satisfactory conclusion, and Mrs Cooper, with the power of the gold behind her, would gradually have emerged from housekeeper at the contemplated Fairview club to be a director of the whole concern on the lines drawn up and submitted to Shorton he was so much impressed by. For it is that she has been aiming at all the time, not merely a parcel of sovereigns, but to give herself place and opportunity.'

'Are you sure this plan or scheme of the development here, you told us about, was all her work?'

'There is no one else,' Mitchell answered. 'It all came out of her mind. It is her mind we have been struggling against all through.' He added, a little heavily, a little slowly: 'Now it is her mind that it is our duty to settle accounts with.'

One of the county constables came up and saluted.

'All ready now, sir,' he reported.

'Then we'll get along,' Major Markham said.

CHAPTER XXX

Conclusion

BOBBY's dash on his motor-cycle through the village at an hour so early had naturally not been unnoticed by the inhabitants, nor had the appearance of the two motor-cars a little later on gone unremarked. Three-fourths, indeed, of the villagers were watching as the police party came back on their way towards Fairview, and when they were quite near the village, just by the bridge that crossed the creek, Bobby leaned forward to speak to Mitchell.

'Beg pardon, sir,' he said, 'but there's a man running across the fields over there, towards the house, and he looks to me like Cooper.'

'Got word something was happening, came out to see, and now he's running back to warn his wife,' Mitchell commented. 'Too late for that to help them any.'

Major Markham halted the cars.

'Better stop him getting there, if we can,' he remarked. 'He may make trouble, one way or another.'

He directed Inspector Wake and one of the constables to try to cut off Cooper before he reached the house. Bobby asked, and received, permission to accompany them. Major Markham said:

'He seems to be making straight across country for the house. You ought to be able to cut him off easily enough.'

Bobby and his two companions had, in fact, a shorter distance to traverse than had Cooper to the point where their paths must cross if he kept straight on towards Fairview. They ran therefore, indeed, but not at their best speed, for they all three thought they had time in hand, till abruptly they became aware that Cooper was outpacing them.

For he was running, that pasty-faced, flat-footed butler, like a man possessed; racing over the roughest ground as over a smooth cinder track; taking the hedges in his stride like a practised hurdler; covering the distance with huge leaps and bounds; his coat-tails flapping grotesquely behind him; his rather long hair streaming out in the wind, for he had long since lost his hat.

'Gosh, look at that,' Wake exclaimed.

Cooper had cut straight across a field, not towards the gate, which would have brought him out nearer the course his pursuers were taking, but straight for a corner where the hedge was high, and strong, and laced with wire – it had been specially strengthened for the field it bounded as that held a bull, valuable and pure bred, but also of uncertain temper. The field he was in was wide and broad, but Cooper seemed to cross it in a stride or two, like Speed itself made incarnate in the form of a flat-footed, middle-aged butler, with such amazing ease and lightness did he flash by, straight for that high fence behind which the great bull grazed. One might have thought he did not see the hedge. The thing was a good six-foot high, close-growing, wire supported, and whether he jumped it clear, as Wake afterwards maintained, or whether somehow he crashed his way through it, as the others thought, at any rate in a moment he was over, and still upon his feet, and still running swift and straight. That was all they could be sure of, that, and that the great bull, indignant at this sudden irruption into its domain, had snorted its anger, and put its huge head down to charge.

Cooper paid the creature no attention. Still, with those great leaps and bounds of his, he ran straight on. The bull might not have been there, he ran at it, straight at it, and passed it like the wind; he reached the fence upon the field's further side, and was over it and away, while, behind, the bull bellowed disapproval, and tore up and down its domain in search of something whereon to vent its wrath and indignation.

At the gate, Wake paused and looked thoughtful. So did Bobby. So did their companion. The bull saw them, and, pawing at the ground, snorted a challenge to them to come on.

'I think,' decided Wake, 'we'll go round.'

It was certainly a wise decision. The bull, now thoroughly aroused, was making quite clear it would allow no further passage through its territory without offering very active protest. To have challenged that determination would plainly have occupied more time than would be lost in going round, and Wake added consolingly:

'Anyway, he's making straight for the house. The cars will get there first, and our people will be waiting for him. Whoever would have thought the blighter could run like that?' He added reproachfully to Bobby: 'You never told us he was that kind of champion athlete.'

'He isn't,' Bobby said. 'He's fat and forty, and can't go upstairs without wheezing.' He added, rather gravely: 'We have seen a miracle.'

Wake stared and shrugged his shoulders, but made no comment, and they went on together, leaving the big bull pawing at the ground in undisputed possession of its territory. Beyond the next field they came in sight of Fairview. At the entrance to the drive leading up to the house the cars had stopped. Their inmates had seen what had happened, had seen Cooper, still running, as straight and swift as before, straight for the gate to the drive where they were waiting. They alighted, and stood in a little group watching him as he raced towards them, taking no more heed that they were there than he had done before of the presence and resentment of the great bull. Seeing how fiercely he still ran, the constable driving one of the cars backed it across the road to make him stop. Still he took no heed, but made one leap to the bonnet of the car, and touched it lightly with his right foot, and took fresh impetus for another leap that landed him right into the midst of the little group waiting for him. Mitchell tried to tackle him, but failed, for he went by like a darting bird. Markham jumped in his way, and got a blow, or rather push, on the chest that sent him reeling to fall flat on his back in the ditch by the wayside, where the next moment Andrews joined him, flung aside as one might fling aside a straw that had drifted across one's path.

'Well, I'm blessed,' Mitchell said, and began to run.

'He's mad, mad,' Markham panted, as he and Andrews scrambled to their feet and followed.

The driver of the second car followed, too, and all four of them fled up the drive, with Cooper leading and gaining at every stride, so fast he ran – faster even than before.

So he gained the house the first, and they saw him vanish within and crash-to the door behind him.

'Round to the back,' Mitchell shouted.

He led the way, running at his best speed, and the others followed. The back door was open. They went in, and Major Markham called out:

'Take care, he may be armed.'

They heard his voice in the kitchen.

'Quick, quick, while there's time. I can hold them back. I can hold the lot of them back while you get away.'

They heard Mrs Cooper answer.

'Too late for that.'

They were in a narrow, stone-flagged passage. In front

of them were three or four steps leading to the dining-room, and on their right was a door. Someone pushed it open, and they entered. They were in the kitchen, a big, long, low, dark room, very badly lighted by two small windows. In the middle of the floor, on the nearer side of the table that ran across the room, stood Cooper. He was holding in one hand a short iron bar. He looked fierce and wild and formidable; he had the air of being about to hurl himself upon them, as in days gone by berserk warriors charged upon their enemies, careless of death, if only first they themselves could slay. His eyes were pin-points of fire, and on his lips a little white foam showed. But Mrs Cooper looked at the new-comers, and then at him, and shook her head slightly.

'Drop that,' she said. 'No use. Too late.'

And then they saw a strange thing happen, for at once it was as though all strength and energy drained from him. Almost visibly he shrank; almost visibly his vigour and the passion of his wrought-up will went from him; as they watched it seemed as though that which had sustained him vanished quite away and he grew small again. There was no more light in his eyes, the fierce alert determination of his pose changed, so that now he sagged and drooped. Very carefully he put down upon the table the iron bar he had been holding, and went, shuffling, dragging his steps, to sit down carefully in a corner by the nearest window. He had the air of having suddenly been emptied, so that one felt there was no more in him.'

'I'm not sorry,' Andrews muttered below his breath. 'If he had fought the way he ran, the four of us would have had our work cut out.'

And he took care to get possession of that short iron bar, and to put it safely out of the way.

They forgot Cooper now, and turned their attention to his wife. At the further end of the kitchen where she was standing was an enormous, old-fashioned, coal-using range. In it a great fire burned, making the air in the room on that warm summer day intolerably hot. On the fire stood a huge iron cauldron, and in one hand Mrs Cooper held a great ladle. That end of the room, even at high noon, was always dark, and perhaps it was the effect of the shadows clustering there, of the great fire that burned and crackled behind her, of the heat waves and currents of hot air that filled the room, that together combined to give them, as they looked at her, an impression of almost superhuman size. Gigantic she seemed as she stood there in the shadow against that background of fire, and smoke, and the steam from the huge iron cauldron. No one spoke, and slowly she lifted both arms with a gesture alike of defiance and despair, as of one who knew that all was lost yet repented nothing, regretted nothing, and even in the dust would yield and acknowledge nothing. Irresistibly, Bobby was reminded of a drawing by William Blake he had once seen somewhere, depicting Satan calling on the fallen angels to rise and resume their hopeless struggle against their God. Just such was Mrs Cooper's gesture of her lifted arms. She lowered them, and said aloud:

'Little men, little men, have you found me at last?'

Major Markham stepped forward, and cleared his throat. Somehow the usual formulæ seemed to him oddly banal now, and he hesitated to make use of them. Mrs Cooper turned back to her cauldron, picking up her huge iron ladle, and stirring gently with it the contents of the cauldron.

'Is she making soup?' Andrews muttered in a very puzzled tone.

'Odd soup, I think,' Mitchell answered in the same low tone.

As if she had heard them, she lifted her ladle, and let the contents stream back into the cauldron. It shone as it fell; it glittered, like the sunshine, in a great stream of light – of liquid, running light – against the mirk of that background of dark shadows and shifting smoke and steam. The flame that leaped upwards from a displaced coal was not brighter or more living than that downward stream she poured back again into the cauldron.

'My God, it's molten gold,' Markham whispered. Yet his whisper sounded almost loud, so clearly did they all hear it.

'Molten gold,' she repeated, looking at them over her shoulder. 'It wasn't much of a chance. We thought, if I melted the sovereigns down, they could not be identified.' Then suddenly she laughed, quite naturally, even pleasantly. ' "Double, double toil, and trouble",' she quoted, and looked at Bobby, who, with his two companions, had now joined the others. 'Was that what you meant,' she said to him, 'when you got talking about Shakespeare and *Macbeth?* But in the play the cauldron and the witches come at the beginning, and this is the end of it all. Or was it as Lady Macbeth that you saw me? I never thought of myself like that, you know.'

Bobby did not answer, and she went on slowly:

'No, I never thought of myself like that, and yet I suppose that like her I wanted to rule, to be a sort of queen, too, for to-day it is the rich who are kings and queens, and I meant to be rich, and I meant no old men to stand in the way – but they had no silver hair to lace with golden blood, because they were both bald. You know, I expect Lady Macbeth would have made a good queen. She knew her mind, and what she wanted, and if only you had left me alone' – she paused and drew a deep breath – 'I would have done great things,' she said. 'I would have made all this part the biggest pleasure resort in the world. I had every detail thought out. But that would only have been a beginning. It's the land that counts, always the land, and at my pleasure resort I would have used English fruit and English meat, and English birds, and fish straight from the sea, till no one would have dared to talk of good living till they had been here and seen what we could do, till every English farm was flourishing again with providing, not beetroot and corn and turnips anyone can grow anywhere, but the apples and cherries and strawberries, the cream and butter, and the beef and mutton, only our soft, rainy climate can give in perfection. Why, I would have made all England a garden once again, if only you little men had let me be.'

Major Markham stepped forward again.

'All that has nothing to do with us,' he began. 'We are police officers and——'

Involuntarily he shrank back. With a quick, fierce gesture, she had whirled the great iron ladle she held so that a portion of its molten contents splashed on table and floor, searing and burning where it fell.

'Take care, take care,' she said. 'Stand back a little time, for I am not ready yet.'

'The woman's mad,' Markham exclaimed, and Mitchell said:

'Not mad, I think, but there's a kind of greatness in her, a greatness that's turned sour now.'

She pointed with her ladle at the huddled figure of her husband.

'You'll hang him, I suppose,' she observed meditatively. 'It's not worth while, it's not even fair, for there's not a thing he did but I did it – all he did was my doing, and only mine.'

For the first time Cooper seemed aware of what was going on.

'No, it's not worth while hanging me,' he agreed; 'but they will – at least, not me, but the bit of me that was left alive after you said it was no use, too late.'

'Come, Mrs Cooper,' Markham began again, 'be reasonable——'

'Why, you fool,' she interrupted, 'only the dead are reasonable, and so will I be soon, but not yet, so keep your distance for a time,' and again, with a twirl of her great ladle, she sent a sprinkle of molten, burning, golden death to fall like a barrier between them, and to smoke and burn and sear where it fell. 'But I suppose that boy who trapped me with his innocent face, and his talk about toothache, and lost watches, and all the rest of it, that I never saw through till just the other day when it dawned on me, too late, he was the detective old George Winterton had babbled about – I daresay he is right enough. Very likely, if I had been in Lady Macbeth's place, I should have done what she did, and in my place she would have done as I did. She wanted rule, power, to make things go the way she wanted them to go. Why shouldn't I,' she demanded suddenly, 'when I felt I could? Who had the right to stop my doing what I knew I could do? Was I to let two doddering old men stand in the way? Hadn't I the right to remove them? I knew what I could do; I felt it burn inside me; it would have killed me instead of them if I had held it back – rather them than me, I said, that's all. As for young Ross – well, I won, and he lost, that's all there's to it. Now I've lost myself, but better try and lose, than sit and dodder all day long, like those two old men. Why, there were things I meant to do, plans, schemes, all thought out, all ready, all – but that wasn't what I wanted really; at the bottom of it all, what I wanted was just to be myself, to use myself – power. And to-day that means gold – it wasn't the gold I wanted, it was power to do things – power that's gold, gold that's power – that's what I tried to get; that's what I lived for; that's what I'll die by,' and before they knew her dreadful purpose, or could prevent it, she had lifted a great ladle full of the molten gold of the sovereigns she had melted down, and had emptied it, pouring it on herself, on her upturned face, into her open mouth, down her throat, and so fell writhing and choked, a dreadful, disfigured thing no longer human; nor was there one of them that could move a muscle, or utter so much as a cry, so held in utter stillness were they by the horror and the greatness of the deed.

THE END